D0871941

The Wilt
Alternative

By the same author

RIOTOUS ASSEMBLY
INDECENT EXPOSURE
PORTERHOUSE BLUE
BLOTT ON THE LANDSCAPE
WILT
THE GREAT PURSUIT
THE THROWBACK
ANCESTRAL VICES
VINTAGE STUFF

The Wilt Alternative

Tom Sharpe

SECKER & WARBURG
LONDON

First published in England 1979 by
Martin Secker & Warburg Limited
54 Poland Street, London W1V 3DF

Copyright © Tom Sharpe 1979

Reprinted 1979, 1984

ISBN: 0-436-45808-X

Printed and bound in Great Britain by
Biddles Ltd, Guildford and King's Lynn

To Bill and Tina Baker

Chapter 1

It was Enrolment Week at the Tech. Henry Wilt sat at a table in Room 467 and stared into the face of the earnest woman opposite him and tried to look interested.

'Well, there is a vacancy in Rapid Reading on Monday evenings,' he said. 'If you'll just fill in the form over there . . .' He waved vaguely in the direction of the window but the woman was not to be fobbed off.

'I would like to know a little more about it. I mean it does help, doesn't it?'

'Help?' said Wilt refusing to be drawn into sharing her enthusiasm for self-improvement. 'It depends what you mean by help.'

'My problem has always been that I'm such a slow reader I can't remember what the beginning of a book was about by the time I've finished it,' said the woman. 'My husband says I'm practically illiterate.'

She smiled forlornly and implied a breaking marriage which Wilt could save by encouraging her to spend her Monday evenings away from home and the rest of the week reading books rapidly. Wilt doubted the therapy and tried to shift the burden of counselling somewhere else.

'Perhaps you would be better off taking Literary Appreciation,' he suggested.

'I did that last year and Mr Fogerty was wonderful. He said I had potential.'

Stifling the impulse to tell her that Mr Fogerty's notion of potential had nothing to do with literature and was more physical in its emphasis—though what the hell he could see in this earnest creature was a mystery—Wilt surrendered.

'The purpose of Rapid Reading,' he said going into the patter, 'is to improve your reading skills both in speed and retention of what you have read. You will find that you concentrate more the faster you go and that . . .'

1

He went on for five minutes delivering the set speech he had learnt by heart over four years of enrolling potential Rapid Readers. In front of him the woman changed visibly. This was what she had come to hear, the gospel of evening-class improvement. By the time Wilt had finished and she had filled in the form there was a new buoyancy about her.

There was less about Wilt. He sat on for the rest of the two hours listening to other similar conversations at other tables and wondering how the devil Bill Paschendaele managed to maintain his proselytizing fervour for An Introduction To Fenland Sub-Culture after twenty years. The fellow positively glowed with enthusiasm. Wilt shuddered and enrolled six more Rapid Readers with a lack of interest that was calculated to dishearten all but the most fanatical. In the intervals he thanked God he didn't have to teach the subject any longer and was simply there to lead the sheep into the fold. As Head of Liberal Studies Wilt had passed beyond Evening Classes into the realm of timetables, committees, memoranda, wondering which of his staff was going to have a nervous breakdown next, and the occasional lecture to Foreign Students. He had Mayfield to thank for the latter. While the rest of the Tech. had been badly affected by financial cuts the Foreign Students paid for themselves and Dr Mayfield, now Head of Academic Development, had created an empire of Arabs, Swedes, Germans, South Americans and even several Japanese who marched from one lecture room to another pursuing an understanding of the English language and more impossibly English Culture and Customs, a hodge-podge of lectures which came under the heading of Advanced English For Foreigners. Wilt's contribution was a weekly discourse on British Family Life which afforded him the opportunity to discuss his own family life with a freedom and frankness which would have infuriated Eva and embarrassed Wilt himself had he not known that his students lacked the insight to understand what he was telling them. The discrepancy between Wilt's appearance and the facts had baffled even his closest friends. In front of eighty foreigners he was assured of anonymity. He was assured of anonymity, period. Sitting in Room 467 Wilt could while away the time speculating on the ironies of life.

In room after room, on floor above floor, in departments all over the Tech., lecturers sat at tables, people asked questions, received concerned answers and finally filled in the forms that ensured that lecturers would keep their jobs for at least another year. Wilt would keep his for ever. Liberal Studies couldn't fail for lack of students. The Education Act saw to that. Day Release Apprentices had to have their weekly hour of progressive opinions whether they liked it or not. Wilt was safe, and if it hadn't been for the boredom he would have been a happy man. The boredom and Eva.

Not that Eva was boring. Now that she had the quads to look after Eva Wilt's enthusiasms had widened to include every 'Alternative' under the sun. Alternative Medicine alternated with Alternative Gardening and Alternative Nutrition and even various Alternative Religions so that Wilt, coming home from each day's lack of choice at the Tech., could never be sure what was in store for him except that it was not what it had been the night before. About the only constant was the din made by the quads. Wilt's four daughters had taken after their mother. Where Eva was enthusiastic and energetic they were inexhaustible and quadrupled her multiple enthusiasms. To avoid arriving home before they were in bed Wilt had taken to walking to and from the Tech. and was resolutely unselfish about using the car. To add to his problems, Eva had inherited a legacy from an aunt and since Wilt's salary had doubled they had moved from Parkview Avenue to Willington Road and a large house in a large garden. The Wilts had moved up the social scale. It was not an improve-ment, in Wilt's opinion, and there were days when he hankered for the old times when Eva's enthusiasms had been slightly muted by what the neighbours might think. Now, as the mother of four and the matron of a mansion, she no longer cared. A dreadful self-confidence had been born.

And so at the end of his two hours Wilt took his register of new students to the office and wandered along the corridor of the Administration Block towards the stairs. He was going down when Peter Braintree joined him.

'I've just enrolled fifteen landlubbers for Nautical Navigation. What about that to start the year off with a bang?'

'The bang starts tomorrow with Mayfield's bloody course

board meeting,' said Wilt. 'Tonight was as nothing. I tried to dissuade several insistent women and four pimply youths from taking Rapid Reading and failed. I wonder we don't run a course on how to solve *The Times* crossword puzzle in fifteen minutes flat. It would probably boost their confidence more than beating the track record for *Paradise Lost*.'

They went downstairs and crossed the hall where Miss Pansak was still recruiting for Beginners' Badminton.

'Makes me feel like a beer,' said Braintree. Wilt nodded. Anything to delay going home. Outside, stragglers were still coming in and cars were parked densely along Post Road.

'What sort of time did you have in France?' asked Braintree.

'The sort of time you would expect with Eva and the brood in a tent. We were asked to leave the first camp-site after Samantha had let down the guy ropes on two tents. It wouldn't have been so bad if the woman inside one hadn't had asthma. That was on the Loire. In La Vendée we were stuck next to a German who had fought on the Russian front and was suffering from shell-shock. I don't know if you've ever been woken in the night by a man screaming about *Flammenwerfern* but I can tell you it's unnerving. That time we moved on without being asked.'

'I thought you were going down to the Dordogne. Eva told Betty she'd been reading a book about three rivers and it was simply enthralling.'

'The reading may have been but the rivers weren't,' said Wilt, 'not the one we were next to. It rained and of course Eva had to have the tent in what amounted to a tributary. It was bad enough putting the thing up dry. Weighed a ton then, but moving it out of a flashflood up a hundred yards of bramble banks at twelve o'clock at night when the damned thing was sodden . . .' Wilt stopped. The memory was too much for him.

'And I suppose it went on raining,' said Braintree sympathetically. 'That's been our experience, anyway.'

'It did,' said Wilt. 'For five whole days. After that we moved into a hotel.'

'Best thing to do. You can eat decent meals and sleep in comfort.'

'You can perhaps. We couldn't. Not after Samantha shat in

the bidet. I wondered what the stench was sometime around 2 a.m. Anyway let's talk about something civilized.'

They went into The Pig In A Poke and ordered pints.

'Of course all men are selfish,' said Mavis Mottram as she and Eva sat in the kitchen at Willington Road. 'Patrick hardly ever gets home until after eight and he always has an excuse about the Open University. It's nothing of the sort, or if it is it's some divorcee student who wants extra coition. Not that I mind any longer. I said to him the other night, "If you want to make a fool of yourself running after other women that's your affair but don't think I'm going to take it lying down. You can go your way and I'll go mine." '

'What did he say to that?' Eva asked, testing the steam iron and starting on the quads' dresses.

'Oh just something stupid about not wanting it standing up anyway. Men are so coarse. I can't think why we bother with them.'

'I sometimes wish Henry was a bit coarser,' said Eva pensively. 'He always was lethargic but now he claims he's too tired because he walks to the Tech. every day. It's six miles so I suppose he could be.'

'I can think of another reason,' said Mavis bitterly. 'Still waters etcetera . . .'

'Not with Henry. I'd know. Besides, ever since the quads were born he's been very thoughtful.'

'Yes, but what's he been thoughtful about? That's what you have to ask yourself, Eva.'

'I meant he's been considerate to me. He gets up at seven and brings me tea in bed and at night he always makes me Horlicks.'

'If Patrick started acting like that I'd be very suspicious,' said Mavis. 'It doesn't sound natural.'

'It doesn't, does it, but that's Henry all over. He's really kind. The only thing is he isn't very masterful. He says it's because he's surrounded by five women and he knows when he's beaten.'

'If you go ahead with this au pair girl plan that will make six,' said Mavis.

'Irmgard isn't a proper au pair girl. She's renting the top-floor

5

flat and says she'll help around the house whenever she can.'

'Which, if the Everards' experience with their Finn is anything to go by, will be never. She stayed in bed till twelve and practically ate them out of house and home.'

'Finns are different,' said Eva. 'Irmgard is German. I met her at the Van Donkens' World Cup Protest Party. You know they raised nearly a hundred and twenty pounds for the Tortured Tupamaros.'

'I didn't think there were any Tupamaros in Argentina any more. I thought they had all been killed off by the army.'

'These are the ones who escaped,' said Eva. 'Anyway I met Miss Mueller and mentioned that we had this top flat and she was ever so eager to have it. She'll do all her own cooking and things.'

'Things? Did you ask her what things she had in mind?'

'Well, not exactly, but she says she wants to study a lot and she's very keen on physical fitness.'

'And what does Henry have to say about her?' asked Mavis moving closer to her real concern.

'I haven't told him yet. You know what he's like about having other people in the house, but I thought if she stays in the flat in the evenings and keeps out of his way . . .'

'Eva dear,' said Mavis with advanced sincerity, 'I know this is none of my business but aren't you tempting fate just a little?'

'I can't see how. I mean it's such a good arrangement. She can baby-sit when we want to go out, and the house is far too big for us and nobody ever goes up to the flat.'

'They will with her up there. You'll have all sorts of people coming through the house and she's bound to have a record player. They all do.'

'Even if she does we won't hear it. I've ordered rush matting from Soales and I went up the other day with the transistor and you can hardly hear a thing.'

'Well, it's your affair, dear, but if I had an au pair girl in the house with Patrick around I'd want to be able to hear some things.'

'I thought you said you'd told Patrick he could do what he liked?'

'I didn't say in my house,' said Mavis. 'He can do what he

6

likes elsewhere but if I ever caught him playing Casanova at home he'd live to regret it.'

'Well, Henry is different. I don't suppose he will even notice her,' said Eva complacently. 'I've told her he's very quiet and home-loving and she says all she wants is peace and quiet herself.'

With the private thought that Miss Irmgard Mueller was going to find living in the same house as Eva and the quads neither peaceful nor quiet, Mavis finished her coffee and got up to go. 'All the same I would keep an eye on Henry,' she said. 'He may be different but I wouldn't trust a man further than I could throw him. And my experience of foreign students is that they come over here to do a lot more than learn the English language.'

She went out to her car and drove home wondering what there was about Eva's simplicity that was so sinister. The Wilts were an odd couple, but since their move to Willington Road Mavis Mottram's dominance had diminished. The days when Eva had been her protégée in flower-arranging were over and Mavis was frankly jealous. On the other hand Willington Road was definitely in one of the best neighbourhoods in Ipford and there were social advantages to be gained from knowing the Wilts.

At the corner of Regal Gardens her headlights picked Wilt out as he walked slowly home and she called out to him. But he was deep in thought and didn't hear her.

As usual Wilt's thoughts were dark and mysterious and made the more so by the fact that he didn't understand why he had them. They had to do with strange violent fantasies that welled up inside him, with dissatisfactions which could only be partly explained by his job, his marriage to a human dynamo, the dislike he felt for the atmosphere of Willington Road where everyone else was something important in high-energy physics or low-temperature conductivity and made more money than he did. And after all these explicable grounds for grumbling there was the feeling that his life was largely meaningless and that beyond the personal there was a universe which was random, chaotic and yet had some weird coherence about it which he would never fathom. Wilt specu-

lated on the paradox of material progress and spiritual deca-
dence and as usual came to no conclusion except that beer on
an empty stomach didn't agree with him. One consolation was
that now Eva was into Alternative Gardening he was likely
to get a good supper and the quads would be fast asleep. If
only the little buggers didn't wake in the night. Wilt had had
his fill of broken sleep in the early years of breast-feeding
and bottle-warming. Those days were largely over now and,
apart from Samantha's occasional bout of sleepwalking and
Penelope's bladder problem, his nights were undisturbed. And
so he made his way along under the trees that lined Willington
Road and was greeted by the smell of casserole from the
kitchen. Wilt felt relatively cheerful.

Chapter 2

He left the house next morning in a far more despondent mood. 'I should have been warned by that casserole that she had some bloody ominous message to impart,' he muttered as he set off for the Tech. And Eva's announcement that she had found a lodger for the top flat had been ominous indeed. Wilt had been alert to the possibility ever since they had bought the house but Eva's immediate enthusiasms—gardening, herbalism, progressive playgrouping for the quads, redecorating the house and designing the ultimate kitchen—had postponed any decision about the top flat. Wilt had hoped that the matter would be forgotten. Now she had let the rooms without even bothering to tell him Wilt felt distinctly aggrieved. Worse still, he had been outwitted by the decoy of that splendid stew. When Eva wanted to cook she could, and Wilt had finished his second helping and a bottle of his better Spanish burgundy before she had announced this latest disaster. It had taken Wilt several seconds before he could focus on the problem.

'You've done what?' he said.

'Let it to a very nice young German girl,' said Eva. 'She's paying fifteen pounds a week and promises to be very quiet. You won't even know she's there.'

'I bloody well will. She'll have lovers fumbling their lascivious way up and down stairs all night and the house will reek of sauerkraut.'

'It won't. There's an extractor fan in the kitchenette up there and she's entitled to have boyfriends so long as they behave themselves nicely.'

'Nicely! Show me some loutish lover behaving nicely and I'll show you a camel with four humps. . . .'

'They're called dromedaries,' said Eva using the tactic of muddled information that usually distracted Wilt and lured him into correcting her. But Wilt was too distracted already to bother.

'They're not. They're called fucking foreigners and I'm using fucking properly for once and if you think I want to lie in bed every night listening to some ruddy Latin prove his virility by imitating Popocatepetl in eruption on an inner sprung mattress eight feet above my head—'

'Dunlopillo,' said Eva. 'You never get things right.'

'Oh yes I do,' snarled Wilt. 'I knew this was in the wind ever since your bloody aunt had to die and leave you a legacy and you had to buy this miniature hotel. I knew then that you would turn it into some foul commune.'

'It's not a commune and anyway Mavis says the extended family was one of the good things about the old days.'

'She'd know all about extended families, Mavis would. Patrick has been extending his family for as long as I can remember, and into other people's.'

'Mavis has given him an ultimatum,' said Eva. 'She's not putting up with his carryings on any longer.'

'And I'm giving you an ultimatum,' said Wilt. 'One squeak out of those bedsprings up there, one whiff of pot, one twang of a guitar, one giggle on the stairs and I'll extend this family by finding digs in town until Miss Schickelgruber has moved out.'

'Her name isn't Schickelwhatchamacallit. It's Mueller. Irmgard Mueller.'

'So was one of Hitler's nastier Obergruppenführers and all I'm saying is—'

'You're just jealous,' said Eva. 'If you were a proper man and hadn't got hang-ups about sex from your parents you wouldn't get so hot under the collar about what other people do.'

Wilt regarded her balefully. Whenever Eva wanted to subdue him she launched a sexual offensive. Wilt retired to bed defeated. Discussions of his sexual inadequacies tended to result in his having to prove Eva wrong practically and after that stew he didn't feel up to it.

He didn't feel up to much by the time he reached the Tech. next morning. The quads had fought their usual intersororial war about who was going to wear what dress before being dragged off to playgroup and there had been another letter in *The Times* from Lord Longford demanding the release of Myra Hindley, the Moors murderess, from prison on the grounds that she was now thoroughly reformed, a convinced Christian and a socially valuable citizen. 'In which case she can prove her social value and Christian charity by staying in prison and helping her fellow-convicts,' had been Wilt's infuriated reaction. The other news was just as depressing. Inflation was up again. Sterling down. North Sea gas would run out in five years and the Rhodesians had just massacred fifty more blacks while the blacks had butchered more missionaries. All in all the world was in its usual filthy mess and now he had to listen to Dr Mayfield extol the virtues of the Advanced Course in English For Foreigners for several intolerably boring hours before dealing with complaints from his Liberal Studies lecturers about the way he had done the timetable.

One of the worst things about being Head of Liberal Studies was that he had to spend a large part of his summer vacation fitting classes into rooms and lecturers into classes, and when he had finished and had defeated the Head of Art who wanted Room 607 for Life Studies while Wilt needed it for Meat Three, he was still faced with a hassle at the beginning of the year and had to readjust the timetable because Mrs Fyfe couldn't make Tuesday at 2 with DMT One because her husband . . . It was on such occasions that Wilt wished he was back teaching *The Lord of the Flies* to Gasfitters instead of running the department. But his salary was good, the rates on Willington Road were exorbitant, and for the rest of the year he could spend much of his time sitting in his office dreaming.

He could sit through most committee meetings in a coma too but Dr Mayfield's course board was the one exception. Wilt had to stay awake to prevent Mayfield lumbering him with several more lectures in his relative absence. Besides, Dr Board would start the term off with a row.

He did. Mayfield had only just begun to stress the need for a more student-oriented curriculum with special emphasis on socio-economic awareness when Dr Board intervened.

'Codswallop,' he said. 'The business of my department is to teach English students how to speak German, French, Spanish and Italian, not to explain the origins of their own languages to a whole lot of aliens, and as for socio-economic awareness, I suggest that Dr Mayfield has his priorities wrong. If the Arabs I had last year were anything to go by they were economically aware to the nth degree about the purchasing power of oil and so socially backward that it will take more than a three-year course to persuade the sods that stoning women to death for being unfaithful isn't cricket. Perhaps if we had three hundred years . . .'

'Dr Board, this meeting may well last as long if you keep interrupting,' said the Vice-Principal. 'Now if Dr Mayfield will just continue . . .'

The Head of Academic Development continued for another hour, and was all set for the entire morning when the Head of Engineering objected.

'I see that several of my staff are scheduled to deliver lectures on British Engineering Achievements in the Nineteenth Century. Now I would like to inform Dr Mayfield and this board that my department consists of engineers, not historians, and quite frankly they see no reason why they should be asked to lecture on topics outside their field.'

'Hear, hear,' said Dr Board.

'What is more, I would like to be informed why so much emphasis is being placed on a course for foreigners at the expense of our own British students.'

'I think I can answer that,' said the Vice-Principal. 'Thanks to the cuts that have been imposed on us by the local authority we have been forced to subsidize our existing non-paying courses and staff numbers by expanding the foreign sector where students pay substantial fees. If you want the figures of the profit we made last year . . .'

But no one took up the invitation. Even Dr Board was momentarily silenced.

'Until such time as the economy improves,' continued the Vice-Principal, 'a great many lecturers are only going to keep their jobs because we are running this course. What is more, it may well be possible to expand Advanced English for Foreigners into a degree course approved by the CNAA. I think you will all agree that anything which increases our chances of becoming a Polytechnic is to everyone's advantage.'

The Vice-Principal stopped and looked round the room but nobody demurred. 'In which case all that remains is for Dr Mayfield to allocate the new lectures to the various departmental heads.'

Dr Mayfield distributed xeroxed lists. Wilt studied his new burden and found that it included The Development of Liberal and Progressive Social Attitudes in English Society, 1688 to 1978, and was just about to protest when the Head of Zoology got in first.

'I see here that I am down for Animal Husbandry and Agriculture with special reference to Intensive Farming of Pigs, Hens, and Stock-Rearing.'

'The subject has ecological significance—'

'And is student-oriented,' said Dr Board. 'Battery Education or possibly Hog Raising by Continuous Assessment. Perhaps we could even run a course on Composting.'

'Don't,' said Wilt with a shudder. Dr Board looked at him with interest.

'Your magnificent wife?' he enquired.

Wilt nodded dolefully. 'Yes, she has taken up—'

'If I may just get back to my original objection instead of hearing about Mr Wilt's matrimonial problems,' said the Head of Zoology. 'I want to make it absolutely clear now that I am not qualified to lecture on Animal Husbandry. I am a zoologist not a farmer and what I know about Stock-Rearing is zero.'

'We must all extend ourselves,' said Dr Board. 'After all if we are to acquire the doubtful privilege of calling ourselves a Polytechnic we must put the College before personal interest.'

'Perhaps you haven't seen what you're down to teach, Board,' Zoology continued, 'Sementic Influences . . . shouldn't that be Semantic, Mayfield?'

'Must be the typist's error,' said Mayfield. 'Yes it should read Semantic Influences on Current Sociological Theories. The bibliography includes Wittgenstein, Chomsky and Wilkes . . .'

'It doesn't include me,' said Board. 'You can count me out. I don't care if we descend to the level of a primary school but I am not going to mug up Wittgenstein or Chomsky for the benefit of anyone.'

'Well then, don't talk about my having to extend myself,' said

13

the Head of Zoology. 'I am not going into a lecture room filled with Moslems to explain, even with my limited knowledge of the subject, the advantages of raising pigs in the Persian Gulf.'

'Gentlemen, while recognizing that there are one or two minor amendments necessary to the lecture titles I think they can be ironed out—'

'Wiped out more likely,' said Dr Board. The Vice-Principal ignored his interruption. '—and the main thing is to keep the lectures in their present format while presenting them at a level suitable for the individual students.'

'I'm still not mentioning pigs,' said Zoology.

'You don't have to. You can do an elementary series of talks on plants,' said the Vice-Principal wearily.

'Great. And will someone tell me how in God's name I can even begin to talk in an elementary way about Wittgenstein? I had an Iraqi last year who couldn't even spell his own name, so what's the poor bugger going to do with Wittgenstein?' said Dr Board.

'And if I may just bring another subject up,' said a lecturer from the English department rather diffidently, 'I think we are going to have something of a communications problem with the eighteen Japanese and the young man from Tibet.'

'Oh really,' said Dr Mayfield. 'A communications problem. You know, it might be as well to add a lecture or two on Intercommunicational Discourse. It's the sort of subject which is likely to appeal to the Council for National Academic Awards.'

'It may appeal to them but it certainly doesn't to me,' said Board, 'I've always said they were the scourings of the Academic world.'

'Yes, and we've already heard you on the subject,' said the Vice-Principal. 'And now to get back to the Japanese and the young man from Tibet. You did say Tibet, didn't you?'

'Well, I said it, but I can't be too sure,' answered the English lecturer. 'That's what I meant about a communications problem. He doesn't speak a word of English and my Tibetanese isn't exactly fluent. It's the same with the Japanese.'

The Vice-Principal looked round the room. 'I suppose it is too much to expect anyone here to have a smattering of Japanese?'

14

'I've got a bit,' said the Head of Art, 'but I'm damned if I'm going to use it. When you've spent four years in a Nip prisoner-of-war camp the last thing you want is to have to talk to the bastards in later life. My digestive system is still in a hell of a mess.'

'Perhaps you could tutor our Chinese student instead. Tibet is part of China now and if we include him with the four girls from Hong Kong . . .'

'We'll be able to advertise Take-Away Degrees,' said Dr Board and provoked another acrimonious exchange which lasted until lunchtime.

Wilt returned to his office to find that Mrs Fyfe couldn't take Mechanical Technicians at 2 on Tuesday because her husband had . . . It was exactly as he had anticipated. The Tech.'s year had begun as it always did. It continued in the same trying vein for the next four days. Wilt attended meetings on Interdepartmental Course Collaboration, gave a seminar to student teachers from the local training college on The Meaning of Liberal Studies, which was a contradiction in terms as far as he was concerned, was lectured by a Sergeant from the Drug Squad on Pot Plant Recognition and Heroin Addiction and finally managed to fit Mrs Fyfe into Room 29 with Bread Two on Monday at 10 a.m. And all the time he brooded over Eva and her wretched lodger.

While Wilt busied himself lethargically at the Tech., Eva put her own plans implacably into operation. Miss Mueller arrived two mornings later and installed herself inconspicuously in the flat; so inconspicuously that it took Wilt two more days to realize she was there, and then only the delivery of nine milk bottles where there were usually eight gave him the clue. Wilt said nothing but waited for the first hint of gaiety upstairs before launching his counter-offensive of complaints.

But Miss Mueller lived up to Eva's promise. She was exceedingly quiet, came in unobtrusively when Wilt was still at the Tech. and left in the morning after he had begun his daily walk. By the end of a fortnight he was beginning to think his worst fears were unjustified. In any case, he had his lectures to foreign students to prepare and the teaching term had finally started. The question of the lodger receded into the background as he

tried to think what the hell to tell Mayfield's Empire, as Dr
Board called it, about Progressive Social Attitudes in English
Society since 1688. If Gasfitters were any indication there had
been a regression, not a progressive development. The bastards
had graduated to queer-bashing.

Chapter 3

But if Wilt's fears were premature they were not long being realized. He was sitting one Saturday evening in the Piagetory, the purpose-built summerhouse at the bottom of the garden in which Eva had originally tried to play conceptual games with the 'wee ones', a phrase Wilt particularly detested, when the first blow fell.

It was less a blow than a revelation. The summerhouse was nicely secluded, set back among old apple trees with an arbour of clematis and climbing roses to hide it from the world and Wilt's consumption of homemade beer from Eva. Inside, it was hung with dried herbs. Wilt didn't approve of the herbs but he preferred them in their hung form rather than in the frightful infusions Eva sometimes tried to inflict on him, and they seemed to have the added advantage of keeping the flies from the compost heap at bay. He could sit there with the sun dappling the grass around and feel at relative peace with the world, and the more beer he drank the greater that peace became. Wilt prided himself on the effect of his beer. He brewed it in a plastic dustbin and occasionally fortified it with vodka before bottling it in the garage. After three bottles even the quads' din somehow receded and became almost natural, a chorus of whines, squeals and laughter, usually malicious when someone fell off the swing, but at least distant. And even that distraction was absent this evening. Eva had taken them to the ballet in the hope that early exposure to Stravinsky would turn Samantha into a second Margot Fonteyn. Wilt had his doubts about Samantha and Stravinsky. As far as he was concerned his daughter's talents were more suitable for an all-in wrestler, and Stravinsky's genius was overrated. It had to be if Eva approved it. Wilt's own taste ran to Mozart and Mugsy Spanier, an eclecticism Eva couldn't understand but which allowed him to annoy her by switching from a piano sonata she was enjoying to twenties jazz which she didn't.

Anyway, this evening there was no need to play his tape-

17

recorder. It was sufficient to sit in the summerhouse and know that even if the quads woke him at five next morning he could still stay in bed until ten, and he was just uncorking his fourth bottle of fortified lager when his eye caught sight of a figure on the wooden balcony outside the dormer window of the top-floor flat. Wilt's hand on the bottle loosened and a moment later he was groping for the binoculars Eva had bought for bird-watching. He focused on the figure through a gap in the roses and forgot about beer. All his attentions was riveted on Miss Irmgard Mueller.

She was standing looking out over the trees to the open country beyond, and from where Wilt sat and focused he had a particularly interesting view of her legs. There was no denying that they were shapely legs. In fact they were startlingly shapely legs and her thighs . . . Wilt moved up, found her breasts beneath a cream blouse entrancing, and finally reached her face. He stayed there. It wasn't that Irmgard—Miss Mueller and that bloody lodger were instantaneously words of the past—was an attractive young woman. Wilt had been faced by attractive young women at the Tech. for too many years, young women who ogled him and sat with their legs distractingly apart, not to have built up sufficient sexual antibodies to deflect their juvenile charms. But Irmgard was not a juvenile. She was a woman, a woman of around twenty-eight, a beautiful woman with glorious legs, discreet and tight breasts, 'unsullied by suckling' was the phrase that sprang to Wilt's mind, with firm neat hips, even her hands grasping the balcony rail were some-how delicately strong with tapering fingers, lightly tanned as by some midnight sun. Wilt's mind spun into meaningless metaphors far removed from Eva's washing-up mitts, the canyon wrinkles of her birth-pocked belly, the dugs that haunched her flaccid hips and all the physical erosion of twenty years of married life. He was swept into fancy by this splendid creature, but above all by her face.

Irmgard's face was not simply beautiful. In spite of the beer Wilt might have withstood the magnetism of mere beauty. He was defeated by the intelligence of her face. In fact there were imperfections in that face from a purely physical point of view. It was too strong for one thing, the nose was a shade retroussé to be commercially perfect, and the mouth too generous but it was individual, individual and intelligent and sensitive and mature and thoughtful and . . . Wilt gave up the addition in despair and as he did so it seemed to him that Irmgard was gazing down into his two adoring eyes, or anyway into the binoculars, and that a subtle smile played about her gorgeous lips. Then she turned away and went back into the flat. Wilt dropped the binoculars and reached trancelike for the beer bottle. What he had just seen had changed his view of life.

He was no longer Head of Liberal Studies, married to Eva, the father of four quarrelsome repulsive daughters, and thirty-eight. He was twenty-one again, a bright, lithe young man who wrote poetry and swam on summer mornings in the river and whose future was alight with achieved promise. He was already a great writer. The fact that being a writer involved writing was wholly irrelevant. It was being a writer that mattered and Wilt at twenty-one had long since settled his future in advance by reading Proust and Gide, and then books on Proust and Gide and books about books on Proust and Gide, until he could visualize himself at thirty-eight with a delightful anguish of anticipation. Looking back on those moments he could only compare them to the feeling he now had when he came out of the dentist's surgery without the need for any fillings. On an intellectual plane, of course. Spiritual, with smoke-filled, cork-lined rooms and pages of illegible but beautiful prose littering, almost fluttering from, his desk in some deliciously nondescript street in Paris. Or in a white-walled bedroom on white sheets entwined with a tanned woman with the sun shining through the shutters and shimmering on the ceiling from the azure sea somewhere near Hyères. Wilt had tasted all these pleasures in advance at twenty-one. Fame, fortune, the modesty of greatness, bons mots drifting effortlessly from his tongue over absinthe, allusions tossed and caught, tossed back again like intellectual shuttlecocks, and the intense walk home through dawn-deserted streets in Montparnasse.

About the only thing Wilt had eschewed from his borrowings off Proust and Gide had been small boys. Small boys and plastic dustbins. Not that he could see Gide buggering about brewing beer anyway, let alone in plastic dustbins. The sod was probably a teetotaller. There had to be some deficit to make up for the small boys. So Wilt had lifted Frieda from Lawrence while

19

hoping to hell he didn't get TB, and had endowed her with a milder temperament. Together they had lain on the sand making love while the ripples of the azure sea broke over them on an empty beach. Come to think of it, that must have been about the time he saw *From Here to Eternity* and Frieda had looked like Deborah Kerr. The main thing was she had been strong and firm and in tune, if not with the infinite as such, with the infinite variations of Wilt's particular lusts. Only they hadn't been lusts. Lust was too insensitive a word for the sublime contortions Wilt had had in mind. Anyway, she had been a sort of sexual muse, more sex than muse, but someone to whom he could confide his deepest perceptions without being asked who Rochefou . . . what's-his-name was which was about as near being a blasted muse as Eva ever got. And now look at him, lurking in a bleeding Spockery drinking himself into a beer belly and temporary oblivion on something pretending to be lager that he'd brewed in a plastic dustbin. It was the plastic that got Wilt. At least a dustbin was appropriate for the muck but it could have had the dignity of being a metal one. But no, even that slight consolation had been denied him. He'd tried one and had damned near poisoned himself. Never mind that. Dustbins weren't important and what he had just seen had been his Muse. Wilt endowed the word with a capital M for the first time in seventeen disillusioning years and then promptly blamed the bloody lager for this lapse. Irmgard wasn't a muse. She was probably some dumb, handsome bitch whose Vater was Lagermeister of Cologne and owned five Mercedes. He got up and went into the house.

When Eva and the quads returned from the theatre he was sitting morosely in front of the television ostensibly watching football but inwardly seething with indignation at the dirty tricks life played on him.

'Now then you show Daddy how the lady danced,' said Eva, 'and I'll put the supper on.'

'She was ever so beautiful, Daddy,' Penelope told him. 'She went like this and there was this man and he . . .' Wilt had to sit through a replay of *The Rite of Spring* by four small lumpish girls who hadn't been able to follow the story anyway and who took turns to try to do a pas de deux off the arm of his chair.

'Yes, well, I can see she must have been brilliant from your performance,' said Wilt. 'Now if you don't mind I want to see who wins . . .'

But the quads took no notice and continued to hurl themselves about the room until Wilt was driven to take refuge in the kitchen.

'They'll never get anywhere if you don't take an interest in their dancing,' said Eva.

'They won't get anywhere anyway if you ask me and if you call that dancing I don't. It's like watching hippos trying to fly. They'll bring the bloody ceiling down if you don't look out.'

Instead Emmeline banged her head on the fireguard and Wilt had to put a blob of Savlon on the scratch. To complete the evening's miseries Eva announced that she had asked the Nyes round after supper.

'I want to talk to him about the Organic Toilet. It's not working properly.'

'I don't suppose it's meant to,' said Wilt. 'The bloody thing is a glorified earth closet and all earth closets stink.'

'It doesn't stink. It has a composty smell, that's all, but it doesn't give off enough gas to cook with and John said it would.'

'It gives off enough gas to turn the downstairs loo into a death-chamber if you ask me. One of these days some poor bugger is going to light a cigarette in there and blow us all to Kingdom Come.'

'You're just biased against the Alternative Society in general,' said Eva. 'And who was it who was always complaining about my using chemical toilet cleaner? You were. And don't say you didn't.'

'I have enough trouble with society as it is without being bunged into an alternative one, and, while we are on the subject, there must be an alternative to poisoning the atmosphere with methane and sterilizing it with Harpic. Frankly I'd say Harpic had something to recommend it. At least you could flush the bloody stuff down the drain. I defy anyone to flush Nye's filthy crap-digester with anything short of dynamite. It's a turd-encrusted drainpipe with a barrel at the bottom.'

'It has to be like that if you're going to put natural goodness back into the earth.'

'And get food poisoning,' said Wilt.

'Not if you compost it properly. The heat kills all the germs before you empty it.'

'I don't intend to empty it. You had the beastly thing installed and you can risk your life in the cellar disgorging it when it's good and ready. And don't blame me if the neighbours complain to the Health Department again.'

They argued on until supper and Wilt took the quads up to bed and read them *Mr Gumpy* for the umpteenth time. By the time he came down the Nyes had arrived and were opening a bottle of stinging-nettle wine with an alternative corkscrew John Nye had fashioned from an old bedspring.

'Ah, hullo Henry,' he said with that bright, almost religious goodwill which all Eva's friends in the Self-Sufficiency world seemed to affect. 'Not a bad vintage, 1976, though I say it myself.'

'Wasn't that the year of the drought?' asked Wilt.

'Yes, but it takes more than a drought to kill stinging-nettles. Hardy little fellows.'

'Grow them yourself?'

'No need to. They grow wild everywhere. We just gathered them from the wayside.'

Wilt looked doubtful. 'Mind telling which side of the way you harvested this particular *cru*?'

'As far as I remember it was between Ballingbourne and Umpston. In fact, I'm sure of it.' He poured a glass and handed it to Wilt.

'In that case I wouldn't touch the stuff myself,' said Wilt handing it back. 'I saw them cropspraying there in 1976. These nettles weren't grown organically. They've been contaminated.'

'But we've drunk gallons of the wine,' said Nye. 'It hasn't done us any harm.'

'Probably won't feel the effects until you're sixty,' said Wilt, 'and then it will be too late. It's the same with fluoride, you know.'

And having delivered himself of this dire warning he went through to the lounge, now rechristened by Eva the 'Being Room', and found her deep in conversation with Bertha Nye about the joys and deep responsibilities of motherhood. Since the Nyes were childless and lavished their affection on humus, two pigs, a dozen chickens and a goat, Bertha was receiving

Eva's glowing account with a stoical smile. Wilt smiled stoically back and wandered out through the french windows to the summerhouse and stood in the darkness looking hopefully up at the dormer window. But the curtains were drawn. Wilt sighed, thought about what might have been and went back to hear what John Nye had to say about his Organic Toilet.

'To make the methane you have to maintain a steady temperature, and of course it would help if you had a cow.'

'Oh, I don't think we could keep a cow here,' said Eva. 'I mean we haven't the ground and . . .'

'I can't see you getting up at five every morning to milk it,' said Wilt, determined to put a stop to the awful possibility that 9 Willington Road might be turned into a smallholding. But Eva was back on the problem of the methane conversion.

'How do you go about heating it?' she asked.

'You could always install solar panels,' said Nye. 'All you need are several old radiators painted black and surrounded with straw and you pump water through them . . .'

'Wouldn't want to do that,' said Wilt. 'We'd need an electric pump and with the energy crisis what it is I have moral scruples about using electricity.'

'You don't need to use a significant amount,' said Bertha. 'And you could always work a pump off a Savonius rotor. All you require are two large drums . . .'

Wilt drifted off into his private reverie, awakening from it only to ask if there was some way of getting rid of the filthy smell from the downstairs loo, a question calculated to divert Eva's attention away from Savonius rotors, whatever they were.

'You can't have it every way, Henry,' said Nye. 'Waste not want not is an old motto, but it still applies.'

'I don't want that smell,' said Wilt. 'And if we can't produce enough methane to burn the pilot light on the gas stove without turning the garden into a stockyard, I don't see much point in wasting time stinking the house out.'

The problem was still unresolved when the Nyes left.

'Well, I must say you weren't very constructive,' said Eva as Wilt began undressing. 'I think those solar radiators sound very sensible. We could save all our hot water bills in the summer and if all you need are some old radiators and paint . . .'

'And some damned fool on the roof fixing them there. You

can forget it. Knowing Nye, if he stuck them up there they'd fall off in the first gale and flatten someone underneath, and anyway with the summers we've had lately we'd be lucky to get away without having to run hot water up to them to stop them freezing and bursting and flooding the top flat.'

'You're just a pessimist,' said Eva, 'you always look on the worst side of things. Why can't you be positive for once in your life.'

'I'm a ruddy realist,' said Wilt, 'I've come to expect the worst from experience. And when the best happens I'm delighted.'

He climbed into bed and turned out the bedside lamp. By the time Eva bounced in beside him he was pretending to be asleep. Saturday nights tended to be what Eva called Nights of Togetherness, but Wilt was in love and his thoughts were all about Irmgard. Eva read another chapter on Composting and then turned her light out with a sigh. Why couldn't Henry be adventurous and enterprising like John Nye? Oh well, they could always make love in the morning.

But when she woke it was to find the bed beside her empty. For the first time since she could remember Henry had got up at seven on a Sunday morning without being driven out of bed by the quads. He was probably downstairs making her a pot of tea. Eva turned over and went back to sleep.

Wilt was not in the kitchen. He was walking along the path by the river. The morning was bright with autumn sunlight and the river sparkled. A light wind ruffled the willows and Wilt was alone with his thoughts and his feelings. As usual his thoughts were dark while his feelings were expressing themselves in verse. Unlike most modern poets Wilt's verse was not free. It scanned and rhymed. Or would have done if he could think of something that rhymed with Irmgard. About the only word that sprang to mind was Lifeguard. After that there was yard, sparred, barred and lard. None of them seemed to match the sensitivity of his feelings. After three fruitless miles he turned back and trudged towards his responsibilities as a married man. Wilt didn't want them.

Chapter 4

He didn't much want what he found on his desk on Monday morning. It was a note from the Vice-Principal asking Wilt to come and see him at, rather sinisterly, 'your earliest, repeat earliest, convenience'.

'Bugger my convenience,' muttered Wilt. 'Why can't he say "immediately" and be done with it?'

With the thought that something was amiss and that he might as well get the bad news over and done with as quickly as possible, he went down two floors and along the corridor to the Vice-Principal's office.

'Ah Henry, I'm sorry to bother you like this,' said the Vice-Principal, 'but I'm afraid we've had some rather disturbing news about your department.'

'Disturbing?' said Wilt suspiciously.

'Distinctly disturbing. In fact all hell has been let loose up at County Hall.'

'What are they poking their noses into this time? If they think they can send any more advisers like the last one we had who wanted to know why we didn't have combined classes of bricklayers and nursery nurses so that there was sexual equality you can tell them from me . . .'

The Vice-Principal held up a protesting hand. 'That has nothing to do with what they want this time. It's what they don't want. And, quite frankly, if you had listened to their advice about multi-sexed classes this wouldn't have happened.'

'I know what would have,' said Wilt. 'We'd have been landed with a lot of pregnant nannies and—'

'If you would just listen a moment. Never mind nursery nurses. What do you know about buggering crocodiles?'

'What do I know about . . . did I hear you right?'

The Vice-Principal nodded. 'I'm afraid so.'

'Well if you want a frank answer I shouldn't have thought it was possible. And if you're suggesting . . .'

'What I am telling you, Henry, is that someone in your

25

department has been doing it. They've even made a film of it.'

'Film of it?' said Wilt, still grappling with the appalling zoological implications of even approaching a crocodile, let alone buggering the brute.

'With some apprentice class,' continued the Vice-Principal, 'and the Education Committee have heard about it and want to know why.'

'I can't say I blame them,' said Wilt, 'I mean you'd have to be a suicidal candidate for Krafft-Ebing to proposition a fucking crocodile and while I know I've got some demented sods as part-timers I'd have noticed if any of them had been eaten. Where the hell did he get the crocodile from?'

'No use asking me,' said the Vice-Principal. 'All I know is that the Committee insist on seeing the film before passing judgment.'

'Well they can pass what judgments they like,' said Wilt, 'just so long as they leave me out of it. I accept no responsibility for any filming that's done in my department and if some maniac chooses to screw a crocodile, that's his business, not mine. I never wanted all those TV cameras and cines they foisted onto us. They cost a fortune to run and some damned fool is always breaking the things.'

'Whoever made this film should have been broken first if you ask me,' said the Vice-Principal. 'Anyway, the Committee want to see you in Room 80 at six and I'd advise you to find out what the hell has been going on before they start asking you questions.'

Wilt went wearily back to his office desperately trying to think which of the lecturers in his department was a reptile-lover, a follower of *nouvelle vague* brutalism in films and clean off his rocker. Pasco was undoubtedly insane, the result, in Wilt's opinion, of fourteen years continuous effort to get Gasfitters to appreciate the linguistic subtleties of *Finnegans Wake*, but although he had twice spent a year's medical sabbatical in the local mental hospital he was relatively amiable and too hamfisted to use a cine-camera, and as for crocodiles . . . Wilt gave up and went along to the Audio-Visual Aid room to consult the register.

'I'm looking for some blithering idiot who's made a film about crocodiles,' he told Mr Dobble, the A.V.A. caretaker. Mr Dobble snorted.

26

'You're a bit late. The Principal's got that film and he's carrying on something horrible. Mind you, I don't blame him. I said to Mr Macaulay when it came back from processing, "Blooming pornography and they pass that through the labs. Well I'm not letting that film out of here until it's been vetted." That's what I said and I meant it.'

'Vetted being the operative word,' said Wilt caustically. 'And I don't suppose it occurred to you to let me see it first before it went to the Principal?'

'Well, you don't have no control over the buggers in your department, do you Mr Wilt?'

'And which particular bugger made this film?'

'I'm not one for naming names but I will say this, Mr Bilger knows more about it than meets the eye.'

'Bilger? That bastard. I knew he was punch-drunk politically but what the hell's he want to make a film like this for?'

'No names, no packdrill,' said Mr Dobble, 'I don't want any trouble.'

'I do,' said Wilt and went out in pursuit of Bill Bilger. He found him in the staff-room drinking coffee and deep in dialectics with his acolyte, Joe Stoley, from the History Department. Bilger was arguing that a truly proletarian consciousness could only be achieved by destabilizing the fucking linguistic infrastructure of a fucking fascist state fucking hegemony.

'That's fucking Marcuse,' said Stoley rather hesitantly following Bilger into the semantic sewer of destabilization.

'And this is Wilt,' said Wilt. 'If you've got a moment to spare from discussing the millennium I'd like a word with you.'

'I'm buggered if I'm taking anyone else's class,' said Bilger adopting a sound trade-union stance. 'It's not my stand-in period you know.'

'I'm not asking you to do any extra work. I am simply asking you to have a private word with me. I realize this is infringing your inalienable right as a free individual in a fascist state to pursue happiness by stating your opinions but I'm afraid duty calls.'

'Not my bloody duty, mate,' said Bilger.

'No. Mine,' said Wilt. 'I'll be in my office in five minutes.'

'More than I will,' Wilt heard Bilger say as he headed towards the door but Wilt knew better. The man might swagger and pose to impress Stoley but Wilt still had the sanction of altering the timetable so that Bilger started the week at nine on Monday morning with Printers Three and ended it at eight on Friday evening with part-time Cooks Four. It was about the only sanction he possessed, but it was remarkably effective. While he waited he considered tactics and the composition of the Education Committee. Mrs Chatterway was bound to be there defending to the last her progressive opinion that teenage muggers were warm human beings who only needed a few sympathetic words to stop them from beating old ladies over the head. On her right there was Councillor Blighte-Smythe who would, given half a chance, have brought back hanging for poaching and probably the cat o' nine tails for the unemployed. In between these two extremes there were the Principal who hated anything or anyone who upset his leisurely schedule, the Chief Education Officer, who hated the Principal, and finally Mr Squidley, a local builder, for whom Liberal Studies was an anathema and a bloody waste of time when the little blighters ought to have been putting in a good day's work carrying hods of bricks up blooming ladders. All in all the prospect of coping with the Education Committee was a grim one. He would have to handle them tactfully.

But first there was Bilger. He arrived after ten minutes and entered without knocking. 'Well?' he asked sitting down and staring at Wilt angrily.

'I thought we had better have this chat in private,' said Wilt. 'I just wanted to enquire about the film you made with a crocodile. I must say it sounds most enterprising. If only all Liberal Studies lecturers would use the facilities provided by the local authority to such effect . . .' He left the sentence with a tag end of unspoken approval. Bilger's hostility softened.

'The only way the working classes are going to understand how they're being manipulated by the media is to get them to make films themselves. That's all I do.'

'Quite so,' said Wilt, 'and by getting them to film someone buggering a crocodile helps them to develop a proletarian consciousness transcending the false values they've been inculcated with by a capitalist hierarchy?'

'Right, mate,' said Bilger enthusiastically. 'Those fucking things are symbols of exploitation.'

28

'The bourgeoisie biting its conscience off, so to speak.'

'You've said it,' said Bilger, snapping at the bait.

Wilt looked at him in bewilderment. 'And what classes have you done this . . . er . . . fieldwork with?'

'Fitters and Turners Two. We got this croc thing in Nott Road and . . .'

'In Nott Road?' said Wilt, trying to square his knowledge of the street with docile and presumably homosexual crocodiles.

'Well, it's street theatre as well,' said Bilger, warming to his task. 'Half the people who live there need liberating too.'

'I daresay they do, but I wouldn't have thought encouraging them to screw crocodiles was exactly a liberating experience. I suppose as an example of the class struggle . . .'

'Here,' said Bilger, 'I thought you said you'd seen the film?'

'Not exactly. But news of its controversial content has reached me. Someone said it was almost sub-Buñuel.'

'Really? Well, what we did is we got this toy crocodile, you know, the ones kiddies put pennies in and they get the privilege of a ride on them . . .'

'A *toy* crocodile? You mean you didn't actually use a real live one?'

'Of course we bloody didn't. I mean who'd be loony enough to rivet a real fucking crocodile? He might have been bitten.'

'Might?' said Wilt. 'I'd have said the odds on any self-respecting crocodile . . . Anyway, do go on.'

'So one of the lads gets on this plastic toy thing and we film him doing it.'

'Doing it? Let's get this quite straight. Don't you mean buggering it?'

'Sort of,' said Bilger. 'He didn't have his prick out or anything like that. There was nowhere he could have put it. No, all he did was simulate buggering the thing. That way he was symbolically screwing the whole reformist welfare statism of the capitalist system.'

'In the shape of a rocking crocodile?' said Wilt. He leant back in his chair and wondered yet again how it was that a supposedly intelligent man like Bilger, who had after all been to university and was a graduate, could still believe the world would be a better place once all the middle classes had been put up against a wall and shot. Nobody ever seemed to learn anything from the past. Well, Mr Bloody Bilger was going to learn something from the present. Wilt put his elbows on the desk.

'Let's get the record clear once and for all,' he said. 'You definitely consider it part of your duties as a Liberal Studies lecturer to teach apprentices Marxist-Leninist-Maoist-crocodile-buggerism and any other -Ism you care to mention?'

Bilger's hostility returned. 'It's a free country and I've a right to express my own personal opinions. You can't stop me.'

Wilt smiled at these splendid contradictions. 'Am I trying to?' he asked innocently. 'In fact you may not believe this, but I am willing to provide you with a platform on which to state them fully and clearly.'

'That'll be the day,' said Bilger.

'It is, Comrade Bilger, believe me it is. The Education Committee is meeting at six. The Chief Education Officer, the Principal, Councillor Blighte-Smythe—'

'That militaristic shit. What's he know about education? Just because they gave him the M.C. in the war he thinks he can go about trampling on the faces of the working classes.'

'Which, considering he has a wooden leg, doesn't say much for your opinion of the proletariat, does it?' said Wilt warming to his task. 'First you praise the working class for their intelligence and solidarity, then you reckon they are so dumb they can't tell their own interests from a soap advert on TV and have to be forcibly politicized, and now you tell me that a man who lost his leg can trample all over them. The way you talk they sound like morons.'

'I didn't say that,' said Bilger.

'No, but that seems to be your attitude and if you want to express yourself on the subject more lucidly you may do so to the Committee at six. I am sure they will be most interested.'

'I'm not going before any fucking Committee. I know my rights and—'

'This is a free country, as you keep telling me. Another splendid contradiction, and considering the country allows you to go around getting teenage apprentices to simulate fucking toy crocodiles I'd say a free fucking society just about sums it up. I just wish sometimes we were living in Russia.'

'They'd know what to do with blokes like you, Wilt,' said Bilger. 'You're just a deviationist reformist swine.'

'Deviationist, coming from you, is great,' shouted Wilt, 'and with their draconian laws anyone who went about filming Russian fitters buggering crocodiles would end up smartly in the Lubianka and wouldn't come out until they had put a bullet in the back of his mindless head. Either that or they would lock you up in some nuthouse and you'd probably be the only inmate who wasn't sane.'

'Right, Wilt,' Bilger shouted back, leaping from his chair, 'that does it. You may be Head of Department but if you think you can insult lecturers I know what I'm going to do. Lodge a complaint with the union.' He headed for the door.

'That's right,' yelled Wilt, 'run for your collective mummy and while you're about it tell the secretary you called me a deviationist swine. They'll appreciate the term.'

But Bilger was already out of the office and Wilt was left with the problem of finding some plausible excuse to offer the Committee. Not that he would have minded getting rid of Bilger but the idiot had a wife and three children and certainly couldn't expect help from his father, Rear-Admiral Bilger. It was typical of that kind of intellectual radical buffoon that he came from what was known as 'a good family'.

In the meantime he had to finish preparing his lecture to the Advanced Foreigners. Liberal and Progressive attitudes be damned. From 1688 to 1978, almost three hundred years of English history compressed into eight lectures, and all with Dr Mayfield's bland assumption that progress was continuous and that liberal attitudes were somehow independent of time and place. What about Ulster? A fat lot of liberal attitudes applied there in 1978. And the Empire hadn't exactly been a model of liberalism. The most you could say about it was that it hadn't been as bloody awful as the Belgian Congo or Angola. But then Mayfield was a sociologist and what he knew about history was dangerous. Not that Wilt knew much himself. And why English Liberalism? Mayfield seemed to think that the Welsh and Scots and Irish didn't exist, or if they did that they weren't progressive and liberal too.

Wilt got out a ballpoint and jotted down notes. They had nothing at all to do with Mayfield's proposed course. He was still rambling speculatively on when lunchtime came. He went

31

down to the canteen and ate what was called curry and rice at a table by himself and returned to his office with fresh ideas. This time they concerned the influence of the Empire on England. Curry, baksheesh, pukka, posh, polo, thug—words that had infiltrated the English language from farflung outposts where the Wilts of a previous age had lorded it with an arrogance and authority he found it hard to imagine. He was interrupted in these pleasantly nostalgic speculations by Mrs Rosery, the Department secretary, who came to say that Mr Germiston was sick and couldn't take Electronic Technicians Three and that Mr Laxton, his stand-in, had done a swop with Mrs Vaugard without telling anyone and she wasn't available because she had previously made an appointment at the dentist and . . .

Wilt went downstairs and crossed to the hut where Electronic Technicians were sitting in a stupor of pub-lunch beer. 'Right,' he said sitting down behind the table, 'Now what have you been doing with Mr Germiston?'

'Haven't done a bloody thing with him,' said a red-headed youth in the front. 'He isn't worth it. One punch up the snout and . . .'

'What I meant,' said Wilt before redhead could go into the details of what would happen to Germiston in a fight, 'was what has he been talking to you about so far this term?'

'Fucking darkies,' said another technician.

'Not literally, I trust,' said Wilt hoping that his irony would not lead to a discussion of interracial sex. 'You mean race relations?'

'I mean spades. That's what I mean. Nignogs, wogs, foreigners, all them buggers what come in here and take jobs away from decent white blokes. What I say is . . .'

But he was interrupted by another ET 3. 'You don't want to listen to what he says. Joe's a member of the National Front—'

'What's so wrong with that?' demanded Joe. 'Our policy is to keep—'

'Out of politics,' said Wilt. 'That's my policy and I mean to stick with it. What you say outside is your affair but in the classroom we'll discuss something else.'

'Yeah, well you ought to tell old Germ-Piston that. He spends his bloody life telling us we got to be christians and love our neighbours like ourselves. Well if he lived in our street he'd know different. We got a load of Jamrags two doors off and they play bongo drums and dustbins till four in the ruddy morning. If old Germy knows a way of loving that din all fucking night he must be blooming deaf.'

'You could always ask them to quieten down a bit or stop at eleven,' said Wilt.

'What, and get a knife in the guts for the privilege? You must be joking.'

'Then the police . . .'

Joe looked at him incredulously. 'A bloke four doors down went to the fuzz and you know what happened to him?'

'No,' said Wilt.

'Had his car tyres slashed two days later. That's what. And did the cops want to know? Did they fuck.'

'Well I can see you've got a problem,' Wilt had to admit.

'Yeah, and we know how to solve it too,' said Joe.

'You're not going to solve it by sending them back to Jamaica,' said the Technician who was anti the National Front. 'The ones in your street didn't come from there anyway. They was born in Brixton.'

'Brixton Nick if you ask me.'

'You're just prejudiced.'

'So would you be if you didn't get a night's kip in a month.' The battle raged on while Wilt sat contemplating the class. It was just as he had remembered it from his old days. You got the apprentices going and then left them to it, only prodding them into further controversy with a provocative comment when the argument flagged. And these were the selfsame apprentices the Bilgers of this world wanted to instil with political consciousness as if they were proletarian geese to be force-fed to produce a totalitarian pâté de foie gras.

But already Electronic Technicians Three had veered away from race and were arguing about last year's Cup Final. They seemed to have stronger feelings about football than politics. At the end of the hour Wilt left them and made his way across to the auditorium to deliver his lecture to Advanced Foreigners. To his horror he found the place packed. Dr Mayfield had been right in saying that the course was popular ard immensely profitable. Looking up the rows, Wilt made a mental note that

33

he was probably about to address several million poundsworth of oil wells, steelworks, shipyards and chemical industries scattered from Stockholm to Tokyo via Saudi Arabia and the Persian Gulf. Well, the blighters had come to learn about England and the English attitudes and he might as well give them their money's worth.

Wilt stepped up to the rostrum, arranged his few notes, tapped the microphone so that several loud booms issued from the loudspeakers at the back of the auditorium and began his lecture.

'It may come as something of a surprise to those of you who come from more authoritarian societies that I intend to ignore the title of the course of lectures I am supposed to be giving, namely The Development of Liberal and Progressive Social Attitudes in English Society from 1688 to the present day, and to concentrate on the more essential problem, not to say the enigma, of what constitutes the nature of being English. It is a problem that has baffled the finest foreign minds for centuries and I have no doubt that it will baffle you. I have to admit that I myself, although English, remain bewildered by the subject and I have no reason to suppose that I will be any clearer in my mind at the end of these lectures than I am now.'

Wilt paused and looked at his audience. Their heads were bent over notebooks and their ballpoints scribbled away. It was what he had come to expect. They would dutifully write down everything he had to tell them as unthinkingly as previous groups he had lectured, but somewhere among them there might be one person who would puzzle over what he had to say. He would give them all something to puzzle over this time.

'I will start with a list of books which are essential reading, but before I do so I will draw your attention to an example of the Englishness I hope to explore. It is that I have chosen to ignore the subject I am supposed to be teaching and have taken a topic of my own choice. I am also confining myself to England and ignoring Wales, Scotland, and what is popularly known as Great Britain. I know less about Glasgow than I do about New Delhi, and the inhabitants of those parts would feel insulted were I to include them among the English. In particular I shall avoid discussing the Irish. They are wholly beyond my comprehension as an Englishman and their methods of settling

34

disputes are not ones that appeal to me. I will only repeat what Metternich, I believe, had to say about Ireland, that it is England's Poland.' Wilt paused again and allowed the class to make another wholly inconsequential note. If the Saudis had ever heard of Metternich he would be very surprised.

'And now the book list. The first is *The Wind in the Willows* by Kenneth Grahame. This gives the finest description of English middle-class aspirations and attitudes to be found in English literature. You will find that it deals entirely with animals, and that these animals are all male. The only women in the book are minor characters, one a bargewoman and the others a jailer's daughter and her aunt, and strictly speaking they are irrelevant. The main characters are a Water Rat, a Mole, a Badger and a Toad, none of whom is married or evinces the slightest interest in the opposite sex. Those of you who come from more torrid climates, or who have sauntered through Soho, may find this lack of sexual motif surprising. I can only say that its absence is entirely in keeping with the values of middle-class family life in England. For those students who are not content with aspirations and attitudes but wish to study the subject in greater, if prurient, depth I can recommend certain of the daily newspapers, and in particular the Sunday ones. The number of choirboys indecently assaulted annually by vicars and church-wardens may lead you to suppose that England is a deeply religious country. I incline to the view held by some that . . .'

But whatever view Wilt was about to incline to, the class never learnt. He stopped in mid-sentence and stared down at a face in the third row. Irmgard Mueller was one of his students. Worse still, she was looking at him with a curious intensity and had not bothered to take any notes. Wilt gazed back and then looked down at his own notes and tried to think what to say next. But all the ideas he had so ironically rehearsed had disintegrated. For the first time in a long career of improvisation, Wilt dried up. He stood at the rostrum with sweating hands and looked at the clock. He had to say something for the next forty minutes, something intense and serious and . . . yes, even significant. That dread word of his sensitive youth burped to the surface. Wilt steeled himself.

'As I was saying,' he stammered just as his audience began to whisper among themselves, 'none of the books I have recommended will do more than scratch the surface of the problem of being English . . . or rather of knowing the nature of the English.' For the next half an hour he strung disjointed sentences together and finally muttering something about pragmaticism gathered his notes together and ended the lecture. He was just climbing down from the stage when Irmgard left her seat and approached him.

'Mr Wilt,' she said, 'I want to say how interesting I found your lecture.'

'Very good of you to say so,' said Wilt dissembling his passion.

'I was particularly interested in what you said about the parliamentary system only seeming to be democratic. You are the first lecturer we have had who has put the problem of England in the context of social reality and popular culture. You were very illuminating.'

It was an illuminated Wilt who floated out of the auditorium and up the steps to his office. There could be no doubt about it now. Irmgard was not simply beautiful. She was also radiantly intelligent. And Wilt had met the perfect woman twenty years too late.

Chapter 5

He was so preoccupied with this new and exhilarating problem that he was twenty minutes late for the meeting of the Education Committee and arrived as Mr Dobble was leaving with the film projector and the air of a man who has done his duty by putting the cat among the pigeons.

'Don't blame me, Mr Wilt,' he said as Wilt scowled, 'I'm only here to . . .'

Wilt ignored him and entered the room to find the Committee arranging themselves around a long table. A solitary chair was placed conspicuously at the far end and, as Wilt had foreseen, they were all there, the Principal, the Vice-Principal, Councillor Blighte-Smythe, Mrs Chatterway, Mr Squidley and the Chief Education Officer.

'Ah, Wilt,' said the Principal by way of unenthusiastic greeting. 'Take a seat.'

Wilt steeled himself to avoid the solitary chair and sat down beside the Education Officer. 'I gather you want to see me about the anti-pornographic film made by a member of the Liberal Studies Department,' he said, trying to take the initiative.

The Committee glared at him.

'You can cut the anti for a start,' said Councillor Blighte-Smythe, 'what we have just seen buggers . . . er . . . beggars belief. The thing is downright pornography.'

'I suppose it might be to someone with a fetish about crocodiles,' said Wilt. 'Personally, since I haven't had the chance to see the film, I can't say how it would affect me.'

'But you did say it was anti-pornographic,' said Mrs Chatterway whose progressive opinions invariably put her at odds with the Councillor and Mr Squidley, 'and as Head of Liberal Studies you must have sanctioned it. I'm sure the Committee would like to hear your reasons.'

Wilt smiled wryly. 'I think the title of Head of Department

37

needs some explaining, Mrs Chatterway,' he began, only to be interrupted by Blighte-Smythe.

'So does this fuc . . . filthy film we've just had to see. Let's stick to the issue,' he snapped.

'It happens to be the issue,' said Wilt. 'The mere fact that I am called Head of Liberal Studies doesn't mean I am in a position to control what the members of my so-called staff do.'

'We know what they ruddy well do,' said Mr Squidley, 'and if any man on my workforce started doing what we've watched I'd soon give him the boot.'

'Well, it's rather different in education,' said Wilt. 'I can lay down guidelines in regard to teaching policy, but I think the Principal will agree that no Head of Department can sack a lecturer for failing to follow them.' Wilt looked at the Principal for confirmation. It came regretfully. The Principal would happily have sacked Wilt years ago. 'True,' he muttered.

'You mean to tell us you can't get rid of the pervert who made this film?' demanded Blighte-Smythe.

'Not unless he continually fails to turn up for his teaching periods, is habitually drunk, or openly cohabits with students, no,' said Wilt.

'Is that true?' Mr Squidley asked the Education Officer.

'I'm afraid so. Unless we can prove blatant incompetence or sexual immorality involving a student, there's no way of removing a full-time lecturer.'

'If getting a student to bugger a crocodile isn't sexual immorality I'd like to know what is,' said Councillor Blighte-Smythe.

'As I understand it the object in question was not a proper crocodile and there was no actual intercourse,' said Wilt, 'and in any case the lecturer merely recorded the event on film. He didn't participate himself.'

'He'd have been arrested if he had,' said Mr Squidley. 'It's a wonder the sod wasn't lynched.'

'Aren't we in danger of losing the central theme of this meeting?' asked the Principal. 'I believe Mr Ranlon has some other questions to raise.'

The Education Officer shuffled his notes. 'I would like to ask Mr Wilt what his policy guidelines are in regard to Liberal Studies. They may have some bearing on a number of complaints

38

we have received from members of the public.' He glared at Wilt and waited.

'It might help if I knew what those complaints were,' said Wilt stalling for time but Mrs Chatterway intervened.

'Surely the purpose of Liberal Studies has always been to inculcate a sense of social responsibility and concern for others in the young people in our care, many of whom have themselves been deprived of a progressive education.'

'Depraved would be a better word if you ask me,' said Councillor Blighte-Smythe.

'Nobody did,' barked Mrs Chatterway. 'We all know very well what your views are.'

'Perhaps if we heard what Mr Wilt's views are . . .' suggested the Education Officer.

'Well, in the past Liberal Studies consisted largely of keeping day-release apprentices quiet for an hour by getting them to read books,' said Wilt. 'In my opinion they didn't learn anything and the system was a waste of time.' He halted in the hope that the Councillor would say something to infuriate Mrs Chatterway. Mr Squidley squashed the hope by agreeing with him.

'Always was and always will be. I've said it before and I'll say it again. They'd be better employed doing a proper day's work instead of wasting ratepayers' money loafing in classrooms.'

'Well at least we have some measure of agreement,' said the Principal pacifically. 'As I understand it Mr Wilt's guideline has been a more practical one. Am I right, Wilt?'

'The policy of the department has been to teach apprentices how to do things. I believe in interesting them in . . .'

'Crocodiles?' enquired Councillor Blighte-Smythe.

'No,' said Wilt.

The Education Officer looked down the list in front of him. 'I see here that your notion of practical education includes home brewing.'

Wilt nodded.

'May one ask why? I shouldn't have thought encouraging adolescents to become alcoholics served any educational purpose.'

'It serves to keep them out of pubs for a start,' said Wilt. 'And in any case Gas Engineers Four are not adolescents. Half of them are married men with children.'

39

'And does the course in home brewing extend to the manu-
facture of illicit stills?'

'Stills?' said Wilt.

'For making spirit.'

'I don't think anyone in my department would have the
expertise. As it is the stuff they brew is . . .'

'According to Customs and Excise almost pure alcohol,' said
the Education Officer. 'Certainly the forty-gallon drum they
unearthed from the basement of the Engineering block had to
be burnt. In the words of one Excise officer, you could run a
car on the muck.'

'Perhaps that's what they intended it for,' said Wilt.

'In which case,' continued the Education Officer, 'it hardly
seemed appropriate to have labelled several bottles Chateau
Tech. V.S.O.P.'

The Principal looked at the ceiling and prayed but the
Education Officer hadn't finished.

'Would you mind telling us about the class you have organized for Caterers on Self Sufficiency?'

'Well, actually it's called Living Off The Land,' said Wilt.

'Quite so. The land in question being Lord Podnorton's.'

'Never heard of him.'

'He has heard of this institution. His head gamekeeper caught
two apprentice cooks in the act of decapitating a pheasant with
the aid of a ten-foot length of plastic tubing through which had
been looped a strand of piano wire stolen from the Music
Department, which probably accounts for the fact that fourteen
pianos have had to be restrung in the past two terms.'

'Good Lord, I thought they had been vandalized,' muttered
the Principal.

'Lord Podnorton was under the same misapprehension about
his greenhouses, four cold frames, a currant cage . . .'

'Well, all I can say,' interrupted Wilt, 'is that breaking into
greenhouses wasn't part of the syllabus for Living Off The Land.
I can assure you of that. I got the idea from my wife who is very
keen on composting . . .'

'No doubt you got the next course from her too. I have here
a letter from Mrs Tothingford complaining that we conduct
classes in karate for nannies. Perhaps you would like to explain
that.'

40

'We do have a course called Rape Retaliation for Nursery Nurses. We thought it wise in the light of the rising tide of violence.'

'Very sensible too,' said Mrs Chatterway, 'I heartily approve.'

'Perhaps you do,' said the Education Officer looking at her critically over his glasses, 'Mrs Tothingford doesn't. Her letter is addressed from the hospital where she is being treated for a broken collar-bone, a dislocated Adam's apple, and internal injuries inflicted on her by her nanny last Saturday night. You're not going to tell me that Mrs Tothingford is a rapist?'

'She might be,' said Wilt. 'Have you asked her if she is a lesbian? It's been known for—'

'Mrs Tothingford happens to be the mother of five and wife of . . .' He consulted the letter.

'Three?' asked Wilt.

'Judge Tothingford, Wilt,' snarled the Education Officer. 'And if you're suggesting that a judge's wife is a lesbian I would remind you that there is such a thing as slander.'

'There's such a thing as a married lesbian too,' said Wilt. 'I knew one once. She lived down our . . .'

'We are not here to discuss your deplorable acquaintances.'

'I thought you were. After all you asked me here to talk about a film made by a lecturer in my department and while I would not call him a friend I am vaguely acquainted . . .'

He was silenced by a kick under the table from the V.-P.

'Is that the end of the casualty list?' asked the Principal hopefully.

'I could go on almost indefinitely, but I won't,' said the Education Officer. 'What it all adds up to is that the Liberal Studies Department is not only failing in its supposed function of instilling a sense of social responsibility in day-release apprentices but is actively fostering anti-social behaviour . . .'

'That's not my fault,' said Wilt angrily.

'You are responsible for the way your department is run, and as such answerable to the Local Authority.'

Wilt snorted. 'Local Authority, my foot. If I had any authority at all this film would never have been made. Instead of that I am lumbered with lecturers I didn't appoint and can't fire, half of whom are raving revolutionaries or anarchists, and the other half couldn't keep order if the students were in straitjackets and

41

you expect me to be answerable for everything that happens.'

Wilt looked at the members of the Committee and shook his head. Even the Education Officer was looking somewhat abashed.

'The problem is clearly a very complex one,' said Mrs Chatterway, who had swung round to Wilt's defence since hearing about the Rape Retaliation Course for Nursery Nurses. 'I think I can speak for the entire Committee when I say we appreciate the difficulties Mr Wilt faces.'

'Never mind what Mr Wilt faces,' intervened Blighte-Smythe. 'We are going to face a few difficulties ourselves if this thing ever gets out. If the press got wind of the story . . .'

Mrs Chatterway blanched at the prospect while the Principal covered his eyes. Wilt noted their reactions with interest.

'I don't know,' he said cheerfully. 'I'm all in favour of public debates on issues of educational importance. Parents ought to know the way their children are being taught. I've got four daughters and . . .'

'Wilt,' said the Principal violently, 'the Committee has generously agreed that you cannot be held wholly responsible for these deplorable incidents. I don't think we need detain you further.'

But Wilt remained seated and pursued his advantage. 'I take it then that you're not willing to bring this regrettable affair to the attention of the media. Well, if that is your decision . . .'

'Listen, Wilt,' snarled the Education Officer, 'if one word of this is leaked to the press or is discussed in any public form I'll see . . . Well, I wouldn't like to be in your shoes.'

Wilt stood up. 'I don't like being in them at the moment,' he said. 'You call me in here and cross-examine me about something I can't prevent because you refuse to give me any real authority and then when I propose making this disgraceful state of affairs a public issue you start threatening me. I've half a mind to complain to the union.' And having delivered this terrible threat he headed for the door.

'Wilt,' shouted the Principal, 'we haven't finished yet.'

'Nor have I,' said Wilt and opened the door. 'I find this whole attempt to cover up a matter of serious public concern most reprehensible. I do indeed.'

'Christ,' said Mrs Chatterway uncharacteristically calling for Divine guidance. 'You don't think he means it, do you?'

'I have long since given up trying to think what Wilt means,' said the Principal miserably. 'All I can be certain about is that I wish to God we'd never employed him.'

Chapter 6

and the Principal and...

'You'd be committing promotional suicide,' Peter Braintree told
Wilt as they sat over pints in The Glassblower's Arms later that
evening.

'I feel like committing real suicide,' said Wilt, ignoring the
pork pie Braintree had just bought him. 'And it's no use trying
to tempt me with pork pies.'

'You've got to have some supper. In your condition it's vital.'

'In my condition, nothing is vital. On the one hand I am
forced to fight battles with the Principal, the Chief Education
Officer and his foul Committee on behalf of lunatics like Bilger
who want a bloody revolution, and on the other, after I have
spent years thrusting down predatory lusts for Senior Secretaries,
Miss Trott and the occasional Nursery Nurse, Eva has to
introduce into the house the most splendid, the most ravishing
woman she can find. You may not believe me . . . remember that
summer and the Swedes?'

'The ones you had to teach *Sons and Lovers* to?'

'Yes,' said Wilt, 'four weeks of D. H. Lawrence and thirty
delectable Swedish girls. Well, if that wasn't a baptism of lust
I don't know what is. And I came through unscathed. I went
home to Eva every evening unblemished. If the sex war was
openly declared I'd have won the Marital Medal for chastity
beyond the call of duty.'

'Well we've all had to go through that phase,' said Braintree.

'And what exactly do you mean by "that phase"?' asked Wilt
stiffly.

'The body beautiful, boobs, bottoms, the occasional glimpse
of thigh. I remember once . . .'

'I prefer not to hear your loathsome fantasies,' said Wilt.
'Some other time perhaps. With Irmgard it's different. I am not
talking about the merely physical. We relate.'

'Good God, Henry . . .' said Braintree, flabbergasted.

'Exactly. When did you hear me use that dreaded word
before?'

'Never.'

'You're hearing it now. And if that doesn't indicate the fearful predicament I'm in, nothing will.'

'It does,' said Braintree. 'You're . . .'

'In love,' said Wilt.

'I was going to say out of your mind.'

'It amounts to the same thing. I am caught in the horns of a dilemma. I use that cliché advisedly, though to be perfectly frank horns don't come into it. I am married to a formidable, frenetic and basically insensitive wife . . .'

'Who doesn't understand you. We've heard all this before.'

'Who does understand me. And you haven't,' said Wilt and drank some more beer bitterly.

'Henry, someone has been putting stuff in your tea,' said Braintree.

'Yes, and we all know who that is. Mrs Crippen.'

'Mrs Crippen? What the hell are you talking about?'

'Has it ever occurred to you,' said Wilt pointedly shoving the pork pie down the counter, 'what would have happened if Mrs Crippen, instead of being childless and bullying her husband and generally being in the way, had had quads? I can see it hasn't. Well, it has to me. Ever since I taught that course on Orwell and the Art of the English Murder, I have gone into the subject deeply on my way home to an Alternative Supper consisting of uncooked soya sausage and homegrown sorrel washed down with dandelion coffee and I've come to certain conclusions.'

'Henry, this is verging on paranoia,' said Braintree sternly.

'Is it? Then answer my question. If Mrs Crippen had had quads who would have ended up under the cellar floor? Dr Crippen. No, don't interrupt. You are not aware of the change that maternity has brought to Eva. I am. I live in an oversize house with an oversize mother and four daughters and I can tell you that I have had an insight into the female of the species which is denied more fortunate men and I know when I'm not wanted.'

'What the hell are you on about now?'

'Two more pints please,' Wilt told the barman, 'and kindly return that pie to its cage.'

'Now look here, Henry, you're letting your imagination run

45

away with you,' said Braintree. 'You're not seriously suggesting that Eva is setting out to poison you?'

'I won't go quite that far,' said Wilt, 'though the thought did cross my mind when Eva moved into Alternative Fungi. I soon put a stop to that by getting Samantha to taste them first. I may be redundant but the quads aren't. Not in Eva's opinion anyway. She sees her litter as being potential geniuses. Samantha is Einstein, Penelope's handiwork with a felt-pen on the sitting-room wall suggested she was a feminine Michelangelo, Josephine hardly needs an introduction with a name like that. Need I go on?'

Braintree shook his head.

'Right,' continued Wilt, despondently helping himself to the fresh beer. 'As a male I have performed my biological function and just when I was settling down relatively happily to pre-mature senility Eva, with an infallible intuition, which I might add I never suspected, brings to live under the same roof a woman who possesses all those remarkable qualities, intelli-gence, beauty, a spiritual sensitivity and a radiance . . . all I can say is that Irmgard is the epitome of the woman I should have married.'

'And didn't,' said Braintree emerging from the beer-mug where he had taken refuge from Wilt's ghastly catalogue. 'You are lumbered with Eva and . . .'

'Lumbered is exact,' said Wilt. 'When Eva gets into bed . . . I'll spare you the sordid details. Suffice it to say that she's twice the man I am. He relapsed into silence and finished his pint.

'Anyway, I still say you'd be making a hell of a mistake if you brought the Tech. any more bad publicity,' said Braintree, to change a distressing subject. 'Let sleeping dogs lie is my motto.'

'Mine too if people didn't sleep with crocs on film,' said Wilt. 'As it is that bastard Bilger has the gall to tell me I'm a deviationist swine and a lackey of capitalistic fascism . . . thank you, I will have another pint . . . and all the time I'm protecting the sod. I've half a mind to make a public issue of the whole damned thing. Only half a mind, because Toxted and his gang of National Front thugs are just waiting for a chance to have a punch-up and I'm not going to be their hero thank you very much.'

'I saw our little Hitler pinning up a poster in the canteen this morning,' said Braintree.

'Oh really, what's he advocating this time? Castration for coolies or bring back the rack?'

'Something to do with Zionism,' said Braintree. 'I'd have ripped the thing down if he hadn't had a bodyguard of Bedouins. He's moved in with the Arabs now, you know.'

'Brilliant,' said Wilt, 'absolutely brilliant. That's what I like about these maniacs of the right and left, they're so bloody inconsistent. There's Bilger who sends his children to a private school and lives in a ruddy great house his father bought him and he goes round advocating world revolution from the driving seat of a Porsche that must have cost six thousand if it cost a penny and he calls me a fascist pig. I'm just recovering from that one when I bang into Toxted who is a genuine fascist and lives in a council house and wants to send anyone with a pigmentation problem back to Islamabad even though they were actually born in Clapham and haven't been out of England since, and who does he team up with? A bunch of ruddy sheikhs with more oil dollars under their burnouses than he's had hot dinners, can't speak more than three words of English, and own half Mayfair. Add the fact that they're semites and he's so anti-semitic he makes Eichmann look like a Friend of Israel, and then tell me how his bloody mind ticks. I'm damned if I know. It's enough to drive a rational man to drink.'

As if to give point to this remark Wilt ordered two more pints.

'You've had six already,' said Braintree doubtfully. 'Eva will give you hell when you get home.'

'Eva gives me hell, period,' said Wilt. 'When I consider how my life is spent . . .'

'Yes, well I'd just as soon you didn't,' said Braintree, 'there's nothing worse than an introspective drunk.'

'I was quoting from the first line of "Testament of Beauty" by Robert Bridges,' said Wilt. 'Not that it's relevant. And I may be introspective but I am not introspectively drunk. I am merely pissed. If you'd had the sort of day I've had and were faced with the prospect of climbing into bed with Eva in a foul temper you would seek oblivion in beer too. Added to which is the knowledge that ten feet above my head, separated only by a ceiling, a floor and some wall-to-wall rush matting, will be lying the most beautiful, intelligent, radiant, sensitive creature . . .'

'If you mention the word Muse again, Henry . . .' said Braintree threateningly.

'I don't intend to,' said Wilt. 'Such ears as yours are far too coarse. Come to think of it, that almost rhymes. Has it ever occurred to you that English is a language most naturally fitted for poetry which rhymes?'

Wilt launched into this more agreeable topic and finished two more beers. By the time they left The Glassblower's Arms Braintree was too drunk to drive home.

'I'll leave the car here and fetch it in the morning,' he told Wilt, who was propping up a telegraph pole, 'and if I were you I'd ring for a taxi. You're not even fit to walk.'

'I shall commune with nature,' said Wilt, 'I have no intention of hastening the time between now and reality. With any luck it'll be asleep by the time I get back.'

And he wobbled off in the direction of Willington Road, stopping occasionally to steady himself against a gatepost and twice to pee into someone else's garden. On the second occasion he mistook a rosebush for a hydrangea and scratched himself rather badly and was sitting on the grass verge attempting to use a handkerchief as a tourniquet when a police car pulled up beside him. Wilt blinked into the flashlight which shone in his face before travelling down to the bloodstained handkerchief.

'Are you all right?' asked the voice behind the flashlight, rather too obsequiously for Wilt's taste.

'Does it look like it?' he asked truculently. 'You find a bloke sitting on the kerb tying a handkerchief round the remains of his once-proud manhood and you ask a bloody fool question like that?'

'If you don't mind, sir, I'd lay off the abusive language,' said the policeman. 'There's a law against using it on the public highway.'

'There ought to be a law about planting ruddy rosebushes next to the fucking pavement,' said Wilt.

'And may one ask what you were doing to the rose, sir?'

'One may,' said Wilt, 'if one can't bloody we'll surmise for one's ruddy self, one may indeed.'

48

'Mind telling me, then?' said the policeman taking out a notebook. Wilt told him with a wealth of description and a volubility that brought the lights on in several houses down the road. Ten minutes later he was helped out of the police car into the station. 'Drunk and disorderly, using abusive language, disturbing the peace . . .'

Wilt intervened. 'Peace my bloody foot,' he shouted. 'That was no Peace. We've got a Peace in our front garden and it hasn't got thorns a foot long. And anyway I wasn't disturbing it. You want to try partial circumcision on flaming floribunda to find out what disturbs what. All I was doing was quietly relieving myself or in plain language having a slash when that infernal thicket of climbing cat's claws took it into its vegetable head to have a slash at me and if you don't believe me, go back and try for yourselves . . .'

'Take him down to the cells,' said the desk sergeant to prevent Wilt upsetting an elderly woman who had come in to report the loss of her Pekinese. But before the two constables could drag Wilt away to a cell they were interrupted by a shout from Inspector Flint's office. The Inspector had been called back to the station by the arrest of a long-suspected burglar and was happily interrogating him when the sound of a familiar voice reached him. He erupted from his office and stared lividly at Wilt.

'What the hell is he doing here?' he demanded.

'Well, sir . . .' one constable began but Wilt broke loose.

'According to your goons I was attempting to rape a rosebush. According to me I was having a quiet pee . . .'

'Wilt,' yelled the Inspector, 'if you've come down here to make my life a misery again, forget it. And as for you two, take a good look at this bastard, a very good, long look and unless you catch him in the act of actually murdering someone, or better still wait until you've seen him do it, don't lay a finger on the brute. Now get him out of here.'

'But, sir—'

'I said out,' shouted Flint. 'I meant out. That thing you've just brought in is a human virus of infective insanity. Get him out of here before he turns this station into a madhouse.'

'Well, I like that,' Wilt protested. 'I get dragged down here on a trumped-up charge . . .'

He was dragged out again while Flint went back to his office and sat abstractedly thinking about Wilt. Visions of that damned doll still haunted his mind and he would never forget the hours he had spent interrogating the little sod. And then there was Mrs Eva Wilt whose corpse he had supposed to be buried under thirty tons of concrete while all the time the wretched woman was drifting down the river on a motor cruiser. Together the Wilts had made him look an idiot and there were jokes in the canteen about inflatable dolls. One of these days he would get his revenge. Yes, one of these days . . . He turned back to the burglar with a new sense of purpose.

On the doorstep of his house in Willington Road Wilt sat staring up at the clouds and meditating on love and life and the differing impressions he made on people. What had Flint called him? An infective virus . . . a human virus of infective . . . The word recalled Wilt to his own injury.

'Might get tetanus or something,' he muttered and fumbled in his pocket for the doorkey. Ten minutes later, still wearing his jacket but without trousers and pants, Wilt was in the bathroom soaking his manhood in a toothmug filled with warm water and Dettol when Eva came in.

'Have you any idea what time it is? It's—' She stopped and stared in horror at the toothmug.

'Three o'clock,' said Wilt, trying to steer the conversation back to less controversial matters, but Eva's interest in the time had vanished.

'What on earth are you doing with that thing?' she gasped. Wilt looked down at the toothmug.

'Well, now that you come to mention it, and despite all circum . . . circumstantial evidence to the contrary, I am not . . . well, actually I am trying to disinfect myself. You see—'

'Disinfect yourself?'

'Yes . . . well,' said Wilt conscious that there was an element of ambiguity about the explanation, 'the thing is . . .'

'In my toothmug,' shouted Eva. 'You stand there with your thingamajig in my toothmug and admit you're disinfecting yourself? And who was the woman, or didn't you bother to ask her name?'

'It wasn't a woman. It was . . .'

'Don't tell me. I don't want to know. Mavis was right about you. She said you didn't just walk home. She said you spent your evenings with some other woman.'

'It wasn't another woman. It was . . .'

'Don't lie to me. To think that after all these years of married life you have to resort to whores and prostitutes . . .'

'It wasn't a whore in that sense,' said Wilt. 'I suppose you could say hips and haws but it's spelt differently and . . .'

'That's right, try to wriggle out of it . . .'

'I'm not wriggling out of anything. I got caught in a rose-bush . . .'

'Is that what they call themselves nowadays? Rosebushes?' Eva stopped and stared at Wilt with fresh horror.

'As far as I know they've always called themselves rose-bushes,' said Wilt, unaware that Eva's suspicions had hit a new low. 'I don't see what else you can call them.'

'Gays? Faggots? How about them for a start?'

'What?' shouted Wilt, but Eva was not to be stopped.

'I always knew there was something wrong with you, Henry Wilt,' she bawled, 'and now I know what. And to think that you come back and use my toothmug to disinfect yourself. How low can you get?'

'Listen,' said Wilt, suddenly conscious that his Muse was privy to Eva's appalling innuendos, 'I can prove it was a rose-bush. Take a look if you don't believe me.'

But Eva didn't wait. 'Don't think you're spending another night in my house,' she shouted from the passage. 'Never again! You can take yourself back to your boyfriend and . . .'

'I have had about as much as I can take from you,' yelled Wilt emerging in hot pursuit. He was brought up short by the sight of Penelope standing wide-eyed in the passage.

'Oh, shit,' said Wilt and retreated to the bathroom again. Outside he could hear Penelope sobbing and Eva hysterically pretending to calm her. A bedroom door opened and closed. Wilt sat on the edge of the bath and cursed. Then he emptied the toothmug down the toilet, dried himself distractedly on a towel and used the Elastoplast. Finally he squeezed toothpaste onto the electric toothbrush and was busily brushing his teeth when the bedroom door opened again and Eva rushed out.

'Henry Wilt, if you're using that toothbrush to . . .'

'Once and for all,' yelled Wilt with a mouthful of foam, 'I am sick and tired of your vile insinuations. I have had a long and tiring day and—'

'I can believe that,' bawled Eva.

'For your information I am simply brushing my teeth prior to climbing into bed and if you think I am doing anything else . . .' He was interrupted by the toothbrush. The end jumped off and fell into the washbasin.

'Now what are you doing?' Eva demanded.

'Trying to get the brush out of the plughole,' said Wilt, an explanation that led to further recriminations, a brief and uneven encounter at the top of the stairs and finally a disgruntled Wilt being shoved out through the kitchen door with a sleeping-bag and told to spend the rest of the night in the summerhouse.

'I won't have you perverting the minds of the wee ones,' Eva shouted through the door, 'and tomorrow I'm seeing a lawyer.'

'As if I bloody care,' Wilt shouted back and wove down the garden to the summerhouse. For a while he stumbled about in the darkness trying to find the zip in the sleeping-bag. It didn't appear to have one. Wilt sat down on the floor and got his feet into the thing and was just wriggling his way down it when a sound from behind the summerhouse startled him into silence. Someone was making his way through the orchard from the field beyond. Wilt sat still in the darkness and listened. There could be no doubt about it. There was a rustle of grass, and a twig broke. Silence again. Wilt peered over the edge of the window and as he did so the lights in the house went out. Eva had gone to bed again. The sound of someone walking cautiously through the orchard began once more. In the summerhouse Wilt's imagination was toying with burglars and what he would do if someone tried to break into the house, when he saw close outside the window a dark figure. It was joined by a second. Wilt crouched lower in the summerhouse and cursed Eva for leaving him without his trousers and . . .

But a moment later his fears had gone. The two figures were moving confidently across the lawn and one of them had spoken in German. It was Irmgard's voice that reached Wilt and reassured him. And as the figures disappeared round the side of the house Wilt wriggled down into the sleeping-bag with the relatively comfortable thought that at least his Muse had been spared that insight into English family life which Eva's denunciations would have revealed. On the other hand, what was Irmgard doing out at this time of night and who was the other person? A wave of self-pitying jealousy swept over Wilt before being dislodged by more practical considerations. The summer-house floor was hard, he had no pillow and the night had suddenly become extremely chilly. He was damned if he was going to spend the rest of it outside. And anyway the keys to the front door were still in his jacket pocket. Wilt climbed out of the sleeping-bag and fumbled for his shoes. Then dragging the sleeping-bag behind him he made his way across the lawn and round to the front door. Once inside he took off his shoes and crossed the hall to the sitting-room and ten minutes later was fast asleep on the sofa.

When he awoke Eva was banging things about in the kitchen while the quads, evidently gathered round the breakfast table, were discussing the events of the night. Wilt stared at the curtains and listened to the muffled questions of his daughters and Eva's evasive answers. As usual she was garnishing down-right lies with mawkish sentimentality.

'Your father wasn't very well last night, darling,' he heard her say. 'He had the collywobbles in his tummy that's all and when he gets like that he says things . . . Yes, I know mumsy said things too, Hennypenny. I was . . . What did you say, Samantha? . . . I said that? . . . Well he can't have had it in the toothmug because tummies won't go in little things like that . . . Tummies, darling . . . You can't get collywobbles anywhere else . . . Where did you learn that word, Samantha? . . . No he didn't and if you go to playgroup and tell Miss Oates that daddy had his . . .'

Wilt buried his head under the cushions to shut out the conversation. The bloody woman was doing it again, lying through her teeth to four damned girls who spent so much of their time trying to deceive one another they could spot a lie a mile off. And harping on about Miss Oates was calculated to make them compete to see who could be the first to tell the old bag and twenty-five other toddlers that daddy spent the night with his penis in a toothmug. By the time that story had been disseminated through the neighbourhood it would be common

53

knowledge that the notorious Mr Wilt was some sort of tooth-mug fetishist.

He was just cursing Eva for her stupidity and himself for having drunk too much beer when the further consequences of too much beer made themselves felt. He needed a pee and badly. Wilt clambered out of the sleeping-bag. In the hall Eva could be heard hustling the quads into their coats. Wilt waited until the front door had closed behind them and then hobbled across the hall to the downstairs toilet. It was only then that full magnitude of his predicament became apparent. Wilt stared down at a large and extremely tenacious piece of sticking-plaster.

'Damn,' said Wilt, 'I must have been drunker than I thought. When the hell did I put that on?' There was a gap in his memory. He sat down on the toilet and wondered how on earth to get the bloody thing off without doing himself any more injury. From past experience of sticking-plaster he knew the best method was to wrench the stuff off with one swift jerk. It didn't seem advisable now.

'Might pull the whole bloody lot off,' he muttered. The safest thing would be to find a pair of scissors. Wilt emerged cautiously from the toilet and peered over the banisters. Just so long as he didn't meet Irmgard coming down from the flat in the attic. Considering the hour she had got back it was extremely unlikely. She was probably still in bed with some beastly boyfriend. Wilt went upstairs and into the bedroom. Eva kept some nail-scissors in the dressing table. He found them and was sitting on the edge of the bed when Eva returned. She headed upstairs, hesitated a moment on the landing and then entered the bedroom.

'I thought I'd find you here,' she said crossing the room to the curtains. 'I knew the moment my back was turned you'd sneak into the house. Well don't think you can worm your way out of this one because you can't. I've made up my mind.'

'What mind?' said Wilt.

'That's right. Insult me,' said Eva, pulling the curtains back and flooding the room with sunshine.

'I am not insulting you,' snarled Wilt, 'I am merely asking a question. Since I can't get it into your empty head that I am not a raving arse-bandit—'

'Language, language,' said Eva.

54

'Yes, language. It's a means of communication, not just a series of moos, coos and bleats the way you use it.'

But Eva was no longer listening. Her attention was riveted on the scissors. 'That's right. Cut the horrid thing off,' she squawked and promptly burst into tears. 'To think that you had to go and . . .'

'Shut up,' yelled Wilt. 'Here I am in imminent danger of bursting and you have to start howling like a banshee. If you had used your bloody head instead of a perverted imagination last night I wouldn't have been in this predicament.'

'What predicament?' asked Eva between sobs.

'This,' shouted Wilt waving his agonized organ.

Eva glanced at it curiously. 'What did you do that for?' she asked.

'To stop the damned thing from bleeding. I have told you repeatedly that I caught it on a rosebush but you had to jump to idiotic conclusions. Now I can't get this bloody sticking-plaster off and I've got a gallon of beer backed up behind it.'

'You really meant it about the rosebush then?'

'Of course I did. I spend my life telling the truth and nothing but the truth and nobody ever believes me. For the last time I was having a pee next to a rosebush and I got snagged in the fucking thing. That is the simple truth, unembroidered, ungarnished and unexaggerated.'

'And you want the sticking-plaster off?'

'What the hell have I been saying for the last five minutes? I not only want it off. I need it off before I burst.'

'That's easy,' said Eva. 'All you've got to do . . .'

Chapter 7

Twenty-five minutes later Wilt hobbled through the door of the Accident Centre at the Ipford Hospital, pale, pained and horribly embarrassed. He made his way to the desk and looked into the unsympathetic and obviously unimaginative eyes of the admissions clerk.

'I'd like to see a doctor,' he said with some difficulty.

'Have you broken something?' asked the woman.

'Sort of,' said Wilt, conscious that his conversation was being monitored by a dozen other patients with more obvious but less distressing injuries.

'What do you mean, sort of?'

Wilt eyed the woman and tried to convey wordlessly that his was a condition that required discretion. The woman was clearly extraordinarily obtuse.

'If it's not a break, cut or wound requiring immediate attention, or a case of poisoning you should consult your own doctor.' Wilt considered these options and decided that 'wound requiring immediate attention' fitted the bill.

'Wound,' he said.

'Where?' asked the woman picking up a ballpen and a pad of forms.

'Well . . .' said Wilt even more hoarsely than before. Half the other patients seemed to have brought their wives or mothers.

'I said where?' said the woman impatiently.

'I know you did,' whispered Wilt. 'The thing is . . .'

'I haven't got all day, you know.'

'I realize that,' said Wilt, 'it's just that . . . well I . . . Look, would you mind if I explained the situation to a doctor? You see . . .' But the woman didn't. In Wilt's opinion she was either a sadist or mentally deficient.

'I have to fill in this form and if you won't tell me where the wound is . . .' She hesitated and looked at Wilt suspiciously, 'I thought you said it was a break. Now you say it's a wound. You'd better make up your mind. I haven't got all day, you know.'

'Nor, at this rate, have I,' said Wilt irritated by the repetition. 'In fact if something isn't done almost immediately I may well pass out in front of you.'

The woman shrugged. People passing out in front of her were evidently part of her daily routine. 'I still have to state whether it is a wound or a break and its location and if you won't tell me what it is and where it is I can't admit you.'

Wilt glanced over his shoulder and was about to say that he had had his penis practically scalped by his bloody wife when he caught the eyes of several middle-aged women who were paying close attention to the exchange. He changed his tactic hastily.

'Poison,' he muttered.

'Are you quite sure?'

'Of course I'm sure,' said Wilt. 'I took the stuff, didn't I?'

'You also claimed you had a break and then a wound. Now you say you've taken all three . . . I mean you've taken poison. And it's no good looking at me like that. I'm only doing my job, you know.'

'At the speed you're doing it I wonder anyone gets in here at all before they're actually dead,' snapped Wilt, and instantly regretted it. The woman was staring at him with open hostility. The look on her face suggested that as far as Wilt was concerned he had just expressed her most ardent hope.

'Look,' said Wilt trying to pacify the bitch, 'I'm sorry if I seem agitated . . .'

'Rude, more like.'

'Have it your own way. Rude then. I apologize but if you had just swallowed poison, fallen on your arm and broken it and suffered a wound in your posterior you'd be a bit agitated.'

To lend some sort of credibility to this list of catastrophes he raised his left arm limply and supported it with his right hand. The woman regarded it doubtfully and took up the ballpen again.

'Did you bring the bottle with you?' she asked.

'Bottle?'

'The bottle containing the poison you claim to have taken.'

'What would I do that for?'

'We can't help you unless we know what sort of poison you took.'

'It didn't say what sort of poison it was on the bottle,' said Wilt. 'It was in a lemonade bottle in the garage. All I know is that it was poison.'

'How?'

'How what?'

'How do you know it was poison?'

'Because it didn't taste like lemonade,' said Wilt frantically, aware that he was getting deeper and deeper into a morass of diagnostic confusion.

'Because something doesn't taste like lemonade it doesn't necessarily mean it's poisonous,' said the woman, exercising an indefatigable logic. 'Only lemonade tastes like lemonade. Nothing else does.'

'Of course it doesn't. But this stuff didn't simply not taste like lemonade. It tasted like deadly poison. Probably cyanide.'

'Nobody knows what cyanide tastes like,' said the woman continuing to batter Wilt's defences. 'Death is instantaneous.'

Wilt glared at her bleakly. 'All right,' he said finally, 'forget the poison. I've still got a broken arm and a wound that requires immediate attention. I demand to see a doctor.'

'Then you'll have to wait your turn. Now where did you say this wound was?'

'On my backside,' said Wilt, and spent the next hour regretting it. To substantiate his claim he had to stand while the other patients were treated and the admissions clerk continued to eye him with a mixture of outright suspicion and dislike. In an effort to avoid her eye Wilt tried to read the paper over the shoulder of a man whose only apparent claim to be in need of urgent attention was a bandaged toe. Wilt envied him and, not for the first time, considered the perversity of circumstances which rendered him incapable of being believed.

It wasn't as simple as Byron had suggested with his 'Truth is stranger than fiction'. If his own experience was anything to go by, truth and fiction were equally unacceptable. Some element of ambiguity in his own character, perhaps the ability to see every side of every problem, created an aura of insincerity around him and made it impossible for anyone to believe what

58

he was saying. The truth, to be believed, had first to be plausible and probable, to fall into some easy category of predigested opinion. If it didn't conform to the expected, people refused to believe it. But Wilt's mind did not conform. It followed possibilities wherever they led in labyrinths of speculation beyond most people's ken. Certainly beyond Eva's. Not that Eva ever speculated. She leapt from one opinion to another without that intermediate stage of bewilderment which was Wilt's perpetual condition. In her world, every problem had an answer; in Wilt's, every problem had about ten, each of them in direct contradiction to all the others. Even now in this bleak waiting-room where his own immediate misery might have been expected to spare him concern for the rest of the world, Wilt's febrile intelligence found material to speculate upon.

The headlines in the paper OIL DISASTER: SEA BIRDS THREATENED dominated a page filled with apparently minor horrors. Apparently because they occupied such little space. There had been another terrorist raid on a security truck. The driver had been threatened with a rocket launcher and a guard had been callously shot through the head. The murderers had got away with £250,000 but this was of less importance than the plight of seagulls threatened by an oil slick off the coast. Wilt noted this distinction and wondered how the widow of the shot guard felt about her late husband's relegation to second place in public concern compared to the sea birds. What was it about the modern world that wildlife took precedence over personal misery? Perhaps the human species was so fearful of extinction that it no longer cared what happened to individuals, but closed collective ranks and saw the collision of two supertankers as a foretaste of its own eventual fate. Or perhaps . . .

Wilt was interrupted from this reverie by the sound of his name and looking up from the paper his eyes met those of a hatchet-faced nurse who was talking to the admissions clerk. The nurse disappeared and a moment later the admissions clerk was joined by an elderly and evidently important specialist, if his retinue of young doctors, a Sister and two nurses was anything to go by. Wilt watched unhappily while the man studied his record of injuries, looked over his spectacles at Wilt as at some specimen beneath his dignity to treat, nodded to one of the housemen and, smiling sardonically, departed.

'Mr Wilt,' called the young doctor. Wilt stepped cautiously forward.

'If you'll just go through to a cubicle and wait,' said the doctor.

'Excuse me, doctor,' said Wilt, 'I would like a word with you in private.'

'In due course, Mr Wilt, we will have words in private and now if you have nothing better to do kindly go through to a cubicle.' He turned on his heel and walked down the corridor. Wilt was about to hobble after him when the admissions clerk stopped him.

'Accident cubicles are that way,' she said pointing to curtains down another corridor. Wilt grimaced at her and went down to a cubicle.

At Willington Road Eva was on the telephone. She had called the Tech. to say that Wilt was unavoidably detained at home by sickness and was now in conference with Mavis Mottram.

'I don't know what to think,' said Eva miserably. 'I mean it seemed so unlikely and when I found out he was really hurt I felt so awful.'

'My dear Eva,' said Mavis, who knew exactly what to think, 'you are far too ready to blame yourself and of course Henry exploits that. I mean that doll business must have given you some indication that he was peculiar.'

'I don't like to think about that,' said Eva. 'It was so long ago and Henry has changed since then.'

'Men don't change fundamentally and Henry is at a dangerous age. I warned you when you insisted on taking that German au pair girl.'

'That's another thing. She's not an au pair. She's paying much more rent than I asked for the flat but she won't help in the house. She has enrolled in the Foreigners' Course at the Tech. and she speaks perfect English already.'

'What did I tell you, Eva? She never mentioned anything about the Tech. when she came to you for a room, did she?'

'No,' said Eva.

'It wouldn't surprise me to find that Henry knew her already and told her you were letting the attic.'

60

'But how could he? He seemed very surprised and angry when I told him.'

'My dear, I hate to say this but you always look on the good side of Henry. Of course he would pretend to be surprised and angry. He knows exactly how to manipulate you and if he had seemed pleased you'd have known there was something wrong.'

'I suppose so,' said Eva doubtfully.

'And as for knowing her before,' continued Mavis, waging war vicariously against her Patrick by way of Wilt, 'I seem to remember he spent a lot of time at the Tech. at the beginning of the summer vac and that's when the foreign students enrol.'

'But Henry doesn't have anything to do with that department. He was busy on the timetable.'

'He doesn't have to belong to the department to meet the slut, and for all you know when he was supposed to be doing the timetable the two of them were doing something quite different in his office.'

Eva considered this possibility only to dismiss it. 'Henry isn't like that, and anyway I would have noticed the change in him,' she said.

'My dear, what you have got to realize is that all men are like that. And I didn't notice any change in Patrick until it was too late. He'd been having an affair with his secretary for over a year before I knew anything about it,' said Mavis. 'And then it was only when he blew his nose on her panties that I got an inkling what was going on.'

'Blew his nose on her *what*?' said Eva, intrigued by the extraordinary perversion the statement conjured up.

'He had a streaming cold and at breakfast one morning he took out a pair of red panties and blew his nose on them,' said Mavis. 'Of course I knew then what he had been up to.'

'Yes, well you would, wouldn't you?' said Eva. 'What did he say when you asked him?'

'I didn't ask him. I knew. I told him that if he thought he could provoke me into divorcing him he was quite mistaken because . . .'

Mavis chattered on about her Patrick while Eva's mind turned slowly as she listened. There was something in her memory of the night that was coming to the surface. Something to do with

Irmgard Mueller. After that awful row with Henry she hadn't been able to sleep. She had lain awake in the darkness wondering why Henry had to . . . well of course now she knew he hadn't but at the time . . . Yes, that was it, the time. At four o'clock she had heard someone come upstairs very quietly and she had been sure it was Henry and then there had been sounds of creaking from the steps up to the attic and she had known it was Irmgard coming home. She remembered looking at the luminous dial of the alarm clock and seeing the hands at four and twelve and for a moment she had thought they pointed to twenty past twelve only Henry had come in at three and . . . She had drifted off to sleep with a question half-formed in her mind. Now, against Mavis' chatter, the question completed itself. Had Henry been out with Irmgard? It wasn't like Henry to come in so late. She couldn't remember when he had done it before. And Irmgard certainly didn't behave like an au pair girl. She was too old for one thing, and she had so much money. But Mavis Mottram interrupted this slow train of thought by stating the conclusion Eva was moving towards.

'I know I'd keep an eye on that German girl,' she said. 'And if you take my advice you'll get rid of her at the end of the month.'

'Yes,' said Eva. 'Yes, I'll think about that, Mavis. Thank you for being so sympathetic.'

Eva put the phone down and stared out of the bedroom window at the beech tree that stood on the front lawn. It had been one of the first things to attract her to the house, the copper beech in the front garden, a large comfortable solid tree with roots that stretched as far underground as the branches did above. She had read that somewhere, and the balance between branches seeking the light and roots searching for water had seemed so right and so, somehow, organic, as to explain what she wanted from the house and could give it in return.

And the house had seemed right too. A big house with high ceilings and thick walls and a garden and orchard in which the quads could grow up happily and at a further remove from unsettling reality than Parkview Road would have allowed. But Henry hadn't liked the move. She had had to force it on him and he had never succumbed to the call of the domesticated wildness of the orchard or the sense of social invulnerability she

62

had found in the house and Willington Road. Not that Eva was a snob but she didn't like anyone to look down on her and now they couldn't. Even Mavis didn't patronize her any longer and that story about Patrick and the panties was something Mavis would never have told her if she had still been living two streets away. Anyway, Mavis was a bitch. She was always running Patrick down and if he was unfaithful physically Mavis was morally disloyal. Henry had said she committed adultery by gossip, and there was something in what he said. But there was also something in what Mavis said about Irmgard Mueller. She would keep an eye on her. There was a strange coldness about her—and what did she mean by saying she would help around the house and then suddenly enrolling at the Tech?

With an unusual sense of depression Eva made herself some coffee and then polished the hall floor and Hoovered the stair-carpet and tidied the living-room and put the dirty clothes in the washing-machine and brushed the rim of the Organic Toilet and did all those jobs which had to be done before she collected the quads from play school. She had just finished and was brushing her hair in the bedroom when she heard the front door open and close and footsteps on the stairs. That couldn't be Henry. He never came up two at a time and anyway with his dooda in bandages he probably wouldn't come up at all. Eva crossed to the bedroom door and looked out at a startled young man on the landing.

'What do you think you're doing?' she asked in some alarm.

The young man raised his hands. 'Please, I am here for Miss Mueller,' he said with a thick foreign accent. 'She has borrowed me the key.' He held it up in front of him as evidence.

'She had no right to,' said Eva annoyed at herself for being so alarmed, 'I don't want people walking in and out without knocking.'

'Yes,' said the young man, 'I understand you. But Miss Mueller have told me I can work on my studies in her rooms. Where I am living too much noise.'

'All right, I don't mind you working here but I don't want any noise either,' said Eva and went back into the bedroom. The young man went on up the narrow steps to the attic while Eva finished brushing her hair with a suddenly lighter mind. If

Irmgard invited rather good-looking young men to her room, she was unlikely to be interested in Henry. And the young man had been decidedly handsome. With a sigh which combined regret that she was not younger and more attractive herself, and relief that her marriage wasn't threatened, she went downstairs.

Chapter 8

At the Tech. Wilt's absence from the weekly meeting of Heads of Departments met with mixed reactions. The Principal was particularly alarmed.

'What with?' he asked the secretary who brought Eva's message that Wilt was sick.

'She didn't make that clear. She just said he would be incapacitated for a few days.'

'Would it were years,' murmured the Principal, and called the meeting to order. 'I have no doubt you have all heard the distressing news about the ... er ... film made by a Liberal Studies lecturer,' he said. 'I can't see there's much to be gained from discussing its implications for the College.'

He looked cheerlessly round the room. Only Dr Board seemed inclined to disagree. 'What I haven't been able to make out is whether it was a male or a female crocodile,' he said.

The Principal regarded him with disgust. 'In actual fact it was a toy one. As far as I know, they are not noticeably differentiated by sex.'

'No, I suppose not,' said Dr Board. 'Still it raises an interesting point—'

'Which, I feel sure, the rest of us would prefer not to discuss,' said the Principal.

'On the grounds of least said, soonest mended?' said Board. 'Though for the life of me I can't understand how the star of this film could be induced to—'

'Board,' said the Principal with dangerous patience, 'we are here to discuss academic matters, not the obscene aberrations of lecturers in the Liberal Studies Department.'

'Hear, hear,' said the Head of Catering. 'When I think that some of my girls are exposed to the influence of such disgusting perverts I can only say that I think we should consider very seriously the possibility of doing away with Liberal Studies altogether.'

There was a general murmur of approval. Dr Board was the exception.

'I can't see why you should blame Liberal Studies as a whole,' he said, 'and having had a look at some of your girls I should say—'

'Don't, Board, don't,' said the Principal.

Dr Mayfield took up the issue. 'This deplorable incident only reinforces my opinion that we should extend the parameters of our academic content to include courses of wider intellectual significance.'

For once Dr Board agreed with him. 'I suppose we could run an evening class in Reptile Sodomy,' he said. 'It might have the side-effect, if that is the right expression, of attracting a number of crocophiliacs, and on a more theoretical level doubtless a course on Bestiality Down The Ages might have a certain eclectic appeal. Have I said something wrong, Principal?'

But the Principal was beyond speech. The V.-P. stepped into the breach.

'The first essential is to see that this regrettable affair doesn't become public knowledge.'

'Well, considering that it took place in Nott Road—'

'Shut up, Board,' shouted the Principal, 'I have stood just about all I can stand of your infernal digressions. One more word out of you and I shall demand either your resignation or my own from the Education Committee. And if need be both. You can make your choice. Shut up or get out.'

Dr Board shut up.

At the Accident Centre Wilt was finding he had no choice at all. The doctor who finally arrived at his cubicle to attend to him was accompanied by a formidable Sister and two male nurses. Wilt regarded him balefully from the couch on which he had been told to lie.

'You've taken your time,' he grumbled. 'I've been lying here in agony for the last hour and . . .'

'Then we must get a move on,' said the doctor. 'We'll start with the poison first. A stomach wash-out will . . .'

'What?' said Wilt, sitting up on the couch in horror.

'It won't take more than a minute,' said the doctor. 'Just lie back while Sister inserts the tube.'

66

'Oh no! Nothing doing,' said Wilt, bolting from the couch into a corner of the cubicle as the nurse closed in with a length of rubber pipe. 'I haven't taken poison.'

'It says on your admittance sheet that you have,' said the doctor. 'You are Mr Henry Wilt, I take it?'

'Yes,' said Wilt, 'but you needn't take it that I have taken poison. I can assure you . . .' He dodged round the couch to avoid the Sister, only to find himself grabbed from behind by the two male nurses.

'I swear that—' Wilt's denial died on his lips as he was pushed back onto the couch. The pipe hovered over his mouth. Wilt stared villainously at the doctor. The man seemed to be smiling in a singularly sadistic manner.

'Now then, Mr Wilt, you will kindly cooperate.'

'Won't,' grunted Wilt through clenched teeth. Behind him the Sister held his head and waited.

'Mr Wilt,' said the doctor, 'you arrived here this morning and stated quite adamantly and of your own free will that you had swallowed poison, broken your arm and had suffered a wound that required immediate attention. Is that not so?'

Wilt debated how to answer. It seemed safest not to open his mouth. He nodded and then tried to shake his head.

'Thank you. Not only that but you were impolite, to put it mildly, to the lady at the desk.'

'Wasn't,' said Wilt only to regret both his rudeness and this attempt to state his case. Two hands attempted to insert the tube. Wilt bit the thing.

'Have to use the left nostril,' said the doctor.

'No you fucking don't,' yelled Wilt, but it was too late. As the pipe slid up his nose and, by the feel of it, expanded in his throat, Wilt's protests came to an unintelligible end. He writhed and gurgled.

'You may find the next part slightly uncomfortable,' said the doctor with evident pleasure. Wilt stared at the man murderously and would, had the infernal pipe not prevented him, have stated forcibly that he found the present part bloody terrible. He was just burbling his protest when the curtains parted and the admissions clerk came in.

'I thought you might want to see this, Mrs Clemence,' said the doctor. 'Go ahead, Sister.' The Sister went ahead while

67

Wilt silently promised himself that if he didn't suffocate first or burst he would wipe the smile off that sadistic doctor's face just as soon as this ghastly experience was over. By the time it was Wilt's condition prevented him from doing anything except moan feebly. Only the Sister's suggestion that perhaps to be on the safe side they ought to give him an oil enema into the bargain provided him with the strength to state his case.

'I came here to have my penis attended to,' he whispered hoarsely.

The doctor consulted his record sheet. 'It doesn't make any mention of your penis here,' he said. 'It states quite clearly that . . .'

'I know what it states,' squeaked Wilt. 'I also know that if you were forced to go into a waiting-room filled with middle-class mothers and their skateboard-suicidal sons and had to announce at the top of your voice to that harridan there that you needed stitches in the top of your prick you'd have been less than reluctant to do it.'

'I'm not standing here listening to a lunatic call me a harridan,' said the clerk.

'And I wasn't standing out there shouting the odds about what had happened to my penis for all the bloody world to hear. I asked to see a doctor but you wouldn't let me. Deny that if you can.'

'I asked you if you had broken a limb, suffered a wound that required—'

'I know what you asked me,' yelled Wilt, 'don't I just. I can quote it word for word. Well, for your information a penis is not a limb, not in my case anyway. I suppose it comes into the category of an appendage and if I'd said I had damaged my appendage you'd have asked me which one and where and how and on what occasion and with whom and then sent me round to the VD clinic and . . .'

'Mr Wilt,' interrupted the doctor, 'we are extremely busy here and if you come and refuse to state exactly what is wrong with you . . .'

'I get a fucking stomach-pump stuffed down my gullet for my pains,' shouted Wilt. 'And what happens if some poor bugger who is deaf and dumb comes in? I suppose you let him die on the waiting-room floor or whip his tonsils out to teach him to speak up for himself in future. And they call this the National Health Service. It's a fucking bureaucratic dictatorship. That's what I call it.'

'Never mind what it's called, Mr Wilt. If there is something really the matter with your penis we're quite prepared to look at it.'

'I'm not,' said the admissions clerk firmly, and disappeared through the curtains. Wilt lay back on the couch and removed his pants.

The doctor observed him cautiously.

'Mind telling me what you've got wound round it?' he asked.

'Bloody handkerchief,' said Wilt and slowly untied the makeshift bandage.

'Good God,' said the doctor, 'I see what you mean about an appendage. Would it be asking too much to enquire how you got your penis into this condition?'

'Yes,' said Wilt, 'it would. Everyone I've told so far hasn't believed me and I'd rather not go through that drill again.'

'Drill?' asked the doctor pensively. 'You're surely not implying that this injury was inflicted by a drill? I don't know what you think, Sister, but from where I stand it looks as though our friend here had a rather too intimate relationship with a mincing machine.'

'And from where I lie it feels like it,' said Wilt. 'And if it will help to cut the badinage let me tell you that my wife was largely responsible.'

'Your wife?'

'Listen, doctor,' said Wilt, 'if it's all the same to you I'd just as soon not go into details.'

'Can't say I blame you,' said the doctor scrubbing his hands. 'If my wife did that to me I'd divorce the bitch. Were you having intercourse at the time?'

'No comment,' said Wilt deciding that silence was the best policy. The doctor donned surgical gloves and drew his own ghastly conclusions. He loaded a hypodermic.

'After what you've already been through,' he said approaching the couch, 'this isn't going to hurt at all.'

Wilt bounded off the couch again. 'Hold it,' he shouted. 'If you imagine for one moment that you're going to stick that surgical hornet into my private fucking parts you can think again. And what's that for?'

The Sister had picked up an aerosol can.

'Just a mild disinfectant and freezer. I'll spray it on first and you won't feel the little prick.'

'Won't I? Well let me tell you that I want to feel it. If I'd wanted anything else I'd have let nature take its course and I wouldn't be here now. And what's she doing with that razor?'

'Sterilizing it. We've got to shave you.'

'Have you just? I've heard that one before, and while we're on the subject of sterilizing I'd like to hear your views on vasectomy.'

'I'm pretty neutral on the subject,' said the doctor.

'Well I'm not,' snarled Wilt from the corner. 'In fact I am distinctly biased not to say prejudiced. What are you laughing about?' The muscular Sister was smiling. 'You're not some damned women's libber, are you?'

'I'm a working woman,' said the Sister, 'and my politics are my own affair. They don't enter into the matter.'

'And I'm a working man and I want to remain that way and politics do enter into the matter. I've heard what they get up to in India and if I walk out of here with a transistor, no balls and jabbering like an incipient mezzo-soprano I warn you I shall return with a meat cleaver and you'll both learn what social genetics are all about.'

'Well, if that is your attitude,' said the doctor, 'I suggest you try private medicine, Mr Wilt. You get what you pay for that way. I can only assure you . . .'

It took ten minutes to lure Wilt back onto the couch and five seconds to get him off it again clutching his scrotum.

'Freezer,' he squealed. 'My God, you meant it too. What the hell do you think I've got down there, a packet of freezable peas?'

'We'll just wait until the anaesthetic takes effect,' said the doctor. 'It shouldn't be long now.'

'It isn't,' squawked Wilt peering down. 'It's bloody disappearing. I came in here to have minor medication, not a sex-change operation, and if you think my wife is going to be happy having a husband with a clitoris you sorely misjudge the woman.'

'I'd say you had already misjudged her,' said the doctor

70

che :fully. 'Any woman who can inflict that sort of damage on her husband deserves what she gets.'

'She may but I don't,' said Wilt frantically. 'I happen . . . What's she doing with that tube?'

The Sister was unwrapping a catheter.

'Mr Wilt,' said the doctor, 'we are going to insert this . . .'

'No, you're not,' shouted Wilt. 'I may be shrinking rapidly in parts but I'm not Alice in Wonderland or a fucking dwarf with chronic constipation. I heard what she said about an oil enema and I'm not having one.'

'No one intends giving you an enema. This will simply enable you to pass water through the bandages. Now kindly get back on the couch before I have to call for assistance.'

'What do you mean pass water simply?' asked Wilt cautiously, climbing onto the couch. The doctor explained, and this time it took four male nurses to hold Wilt down. Throughout the operation he kept up a barrage of obscene observations and it was only the threat of a general anaesthetic that caused him to lower his voice. Even then his remark that the doctor and the Sister were less fitted for medicine than for off-shore oil drilling could be heard in the waiting-room.

'That's right, send me out into the world like a bleeding petrol pump,' he said when he was finally allowed to go. 'There's such a thing as the dignity of man, you know.'

The doctor looked at him sceptically. 'In the light of your behaviour I'll reserve my opinion on the matter. Call in again next week and we'll see how you're coming along.'

'The only reason I'll be back is if I don't come again,' said Wilt bitterly. 'From now on I'll see the family doctor.' He hobbled out to a telephone and called for a taxi.

By the time he got home the anaesthetic was beginning to wear off. He went wearily upstairs and climbed into bed. He was lying there staring at the ceiling and wondering why he was not as other men presumably were when it came to bearing pain manfully, and wishing he was, when Eva returned with the quads.

'You do look awful,' she said encouragingly as she stood by the bed.

'I am awful,' said Wilt. 'Why I should be married to a female circumcisionist, God alone knows.'

71

'Perhaps it will teach you not to drink so much in future.'

'It's already taught me not to let you get your mitts near my waterworks,' said Wilt. 'And I mean waterworks.'

Even Samantha had to contribute to his misery. 'When I grow up I'm going to be a nurse, daddy.'

'Bounce on the bed like that again and you won't grow up to be anything,' snarled Wilt on the recoil.

Downstairs the telephone rang.

'If it's the Tech. again, what shall I tell them?' asked Eva.

'Again? I thought I told you to say I was sick.'

'I did but they've phoned back several times.'

'Tell them I'm still sick,' said Wilt. 'Just don't mention what with.'

'They probably know anyway by now. I saw Rowena Blackthorn at play school and she said she was sorry to hear about your accident,' said Eva, going downstairs.

'And which of you quadraphonic loudspeakers blurted the good news about daddy's whatsit to Mrs Blackthorn's little prodigy?' asked Wilt, turning a terrible eye on the quads.

'I didn't,' said Samantha smugly.

'You just egged Penelope on to, I suppose. I know that look on your mug.'

'It wasn't Penny. It was Josephine. She played with Robin and they were playing mummies and daddies . . .'

'Well when you get a little older you'll learn that there's no such thing as playing mummies and daddies. You will find instead that there is a war between the sexes and that you, my sweethearts, being females of the species, invariably win.'

The quads retreated from the bedroom and could be heard conferring on the landing. Wilt edged his way out of bed in search of a book and was just getting back with *Nightmare Abbey*, which was sufficiently unromantic to suit his mood, when Emmeline was pushed into the room.

'What do you want now? Can't you see I'm ill?'

'Please daddy,' said Emmeline, 'Samantha wants to know why you've got that bag tied to your leg.'

'Oh she does, does she?' said Wilt with dangerous calmness. 'Well you can tell Samantha and through her Miss Oates and her animal minders that your daddy wears a bag on his leg and a pipe up his prick because your mummsyfuckingwumsy took it

72

into her empty head to try to rip off daddywaddy's genitalia on the end of a strip of fucking sticking-plaster. And if Miss Oates doesn't know what genitalia are tell her from me that they're the adult equivalent of a male stork only its spelt with a fucking L. Now get out of my sight before I add hernia, hypertension and multiple infanticide to my other infernal problems.'

The children fled. Downstairs Eva slammed the phone down and shouted.

'Henry Wilt. . . .'

'Shut up,' yelled Wilt. 'One more comment out of anybody in this house and I won't be responsible for my actions.'

And for once he was obeyed. Eva went through to the kitchen and put the kettle on for tea. If only Henry would be more masterful when he was up and about and well.

Chapter 9

For the next three days Wilt was off work. He mooched about the house, sat in the Spockery and speculated on the nature of a world in which Progress with a capital P conflicted with Chaos and man with a small M was continually at loggerheads with Nature. In Wilt's view it was one of life's great paradoxes that Eva, who was forever accusing him of being cynical and non-progressive, should succumb so readily to the recessive call of nature in the shape of compost heaps, Organic Toilets, home weaving and anything that smacked of the primitive while at the same time maintaining an unshakable optimism in the future. For Wilt there was only the eternal present, a succession of present moments, not so much moving forward as aggregating behind him like a reputation. And if in the past his reputation had suffered some nasty blows, his latest misfortune had already added to his legend. From Mavis Mottram the ripples of gossip had spread out across Ipford's educational suburbia, gaining fresh credence and additional attributes with each re-telling. By the time the story reached the Braintrees it had already incorporated the crocodile film by way of the Tech., Blighte-Smythe, and Mrs Chatterway, and rumour had it that Wilt was about to be arrested for grossly indecent behaviour with a circus alligator which had only managed to preserve its virginity by biting Wilt's member.

'That's typical of this bloody town,' Peter Braintree told his wife, Betty, when she brought this version home. 'Henry has merely to take a few days off from the Tech. and the grapevine is buzzing with absolute lies.'

'Grapevines don't buzz,' said Betty. 'There's no smoke—'

'Without some evil-minded moron adding two and two together and coming up with fifty-nine. There's a bloke called Bilger in Liberal Studies who did make a film in which a plastic crocodile figures largely as a rape victim. Point one. Henry has to give some explanation to the Education Committee that will prevent Comrade Bilger's numerous offspring having to leave their private school because daddy is on the dole. Point two. Point three is that Wilt is taken ill next day . . .'

'Not according to Rowena Braintree. It's common knowledge Henry's penis has been mauled.'

'Where?'

'Where what?'

'Where is it common knowledge?'

'At the play group. The quads have been reporting progress on papa's dingaling daily.'

'Great,' said Braintree. 'For once common knowledge about sums it up. Henry's dutiful daughters wouldn't know a penis from a marrow-bone. Eva sees to that. She may be into self-sufficiency but it doesn't extend to sex. Not after the Prings-heims, and I can't see Henry in the role of Flash Harry. If anything, he's a bit of a prude.'

'Not where his language is concerned,' said Betty.

'His use of "fucking" as an adjective is the simple consequence of years of teaching apprentices. In the average bloke's sentence it serves as a sort of hyphen. If you listened to me more carefully you'd hear it at least twenty times in an average day. As I was saying, whatever's the matter with Henry he is *not* into croco-diles. Anyway, I'll pop round this evening and see what is up.'

But when he arrived at Willington Road that evening there was no sign of Wilt. Several cars were parked in the driveway, among them an Aston-Martin which looked out of place in the company of the Nyes' methane-converted Ford and Mavis Mottram's battered Minor. Braintree made his way across the obstacle course of cast-off clothing and the quad's toys that cluttered the hall and found Eva in the conservatory, chairing what appeared to be a committee on the problems of the Third World.

'The issue that seems to be overlooked is that Marangan medicine has an important part to play in providing an alter-native to chemically derived drug treatment in the West,' Roberta Smott was saying as Braintree hesitated behind the bean flyscreen, 'I don't think we should forget that in helping the Marangans we are also helping ourselves in the long term.'

Braintree tiptoed away as John Nye launched into an im-passioned plea for the preservation of Marangan agricultural

75

methods and particularly the use of human excreta as fertilizer. 'It has all the natural goodness of . . .'

Braintree slipped through the kitchen door, skirted the Fertility Retainer or compost bin outside, and went down the Bio/Dynamic kitchen garden to the summerhouse where he found Wilt lurking behind a cascade of dried herbs. He was reclining on a deckchair and wearing what looked suspiciously like a muslin bell-tent.

'As a matter of fact it's one of Eva's maternity gowns,' he said when Braintree enquired. 'In its time it has doubled as a wigwam, the interior sheet of a kingsize sleeping-bag, and the canopy of the camping loo. I rescued it from the mountain of clothing Eva's inflicting on her equatorial village.'

'I wondered what they were on about in there. Is this some sort of Oxfam exercise?'

'You're out of date. Eva's into Alternative Oxfam. Personal Assistance for Primitive People. Appropriately P.A.P.P. for short. You adopt some tribe in Africa or New Guinea and then load them with overcoats that would be unsuitably hot on a windy day in February here, write letters to the local witch-doctor asking his advice about herbal cures for chilblains, or better still frostbite, and generally twin Willington Road and the Ipford Brigade of the Anti-Male Chauvinist League with a cannibal community who go in for female circumcision with a rusty flint.'

'I didn't know you could circumcise females and anyway a rusty flint is out,' said Braintree.

'So are clitorises in Maranga,' said Wilt. 'I've tried to tell Eva but you know what she is. The noble savage is the latest vogue and it's nature worship run riot. If the Nyes had their way they'd import cobras to keep down rats in central London.'

'He was on about human faeces as a substitute for Growmore when I passed through. The man's an anal fanatic.'

'Religious,' said Wilt, 'I swear they sing Nearer My Turd to Thee before taking herbal communion at the compost heap every Sunday morning.'

'On a more personal note,' said Braintree, 'just exactly what is the matter with you?'

'I'd prefer not to discuss it,' said Wilt.

76

'All right, but why the . . . er . . . maternity drag?'

'Because it has none of the inconvenience of trousers,' said Wilt. 'There are depths of suffering you have yet to plumb. I use that word advisedly.'

'What, suffering?'

'Plumb,' said Wilt. 'If it hadn't been for all that beer we drank the other night I wouldn't be in this awful condition.'

'I notice you're not drinking your usual foul home-brewed lager.'

'I am not drinking anything in large quantities. In fact I am rationing myself to a thimble every four hours in the hope that I can sweat it out instead of peeing razor blades.'

Braintree smiled. 'Then there is some truth in the rumour,' he said.

'I don't know about the rumour,' said Wilt, 'but there's certainly truth in the description. Razor blades is exact.'

'Well, you'll be interested to hear that the gossip-mongers are thinking of awarding a medal to the croc that took the bit between its teeth. That's the version that's going the rounds.'

'Let it,' said Wilt. 'Nothing could be further from the truth.'

'Christ, you haven't got syphilis or something ghastly like that, have you?'

'Unfortunately not. I understand the modern treatment for syphilis is relatively painless. My condition isn't. And I've had all the fucking treatment I can stand. There are a number of people in this town I could cheerfully murder.'

'Oh dear,' said Braintree, 'things do sound grim.'

'They are,' said Wilt. 'They reached their nadir of grimness at four o'clock this morning when that little bitch Emmeline climbed into bed and stepped on my septic tank. It's bad enough being a human hose pipe but to be awakened in the dead hours of the night to find yourself peeing backwards is an experience that throws a new and terrible light on the human condition. Have you ever had a non-euphemistically wet dream in reverse?'

'Certainly not,' said Braintree with a shudder.

'Well I have,' said Wilt. 'And I can tell you that it destroys what few paternal feelings a father has. If I hadn't been in convulsions I'd have been charged with quadricide by now. Instead I have added volumes to Emmeline's vile vocabulary and Miss Mueller must be under the impression that English

77

sex life is sado-masochistic in the extreme. God alone knows what she thought of the din we made last night.'

'And how is our Inspiration these days? Still musing?' asked Braintree.

'Evasive. Distinctly evasive. Mind you in my present condition I try not to be too conspicuous myself.'

'If you will go around in Eva's maternity gowns I can't say I'm surprised. It's enough to make anyone wonder.'

'Well, I'm puzzled too,' said Wilt. 'I can't make the woman out. Do you know she has a succession of disgustingly rich young men traipsing through the house?'

'That accounts for the Aston-Martin,' said Braintree. 'I wondered who had inherited a fortune.'

'Yes, but it doesn't account for the wig.'

'What wig?'

'The car belongs to some Casanova from Mexico. He wears a walrus moustache, Chanel Number something or other, and worst of all a wig. I have observed it closely through the binoculars. He takes it off when he gets up there.'

Wilt handed Braintree the binoculars and indicated the attic flat.

'I can't see anything. The venetian blinds are down,' said Braintree after a minute's observation.

'Well I can tell you he does wear a wig and I'd like to know why.'

'Probably because he's bald. That's the usual reason.'

'Which is precisely why I ask the question. Lothario Zapata isn't. He has a perfectly good head of hair, and yet when he gets up to the flat he takes his wig off.'

'What sort of wig?'

'Oh, a black shaggy thing,' said Wilt. 'Underneath he's blond. You've got to admit it's peculiar.'

'Why don't you ask your Irmgard? Could be she has a penchant for blond young men with wigs.'

But Wilt shook his head. 'In the first place because she leaves the house before I'm up and relatively about, and secondly because my sense of self-preservation tells me that anything in the way of sexual stimulation could have the most dire and possibly irreversible consequences. No, I prefer to speculate from afar.'

78

'Very wise,' said Braintree. 'I hate to think what Eva would do if she found you knew you were passionately in love with the au pair.'

'If what she has done for lesser reasons is anything to go by so do I,' said Wilt and left it at that.

'Any message for the Tech?' asked Braintree.

'Yes,' said Wilt, 'just tell them that I'll be back in circulation . . . Christ, what a word . . . when it's safe for me to sit down without back-firing.'

'I doubt if they'll understand what you mean.'

'I don't expect them to. I have emerged from this ordeal with the firm conviction that the last thing anyone will believe is the truth. It is far safer to lie in this vile world. Just say I am suffering from a virus. Nobody knows what a virus is but it covers a multitude of ailments.'

Braintree went back to the house leaving Wilt thinking dark thoughts about the truth. In a godless, credulous, violent and random world it was the only touchstone he had ever possessed and the only weapon. But like all his weapons it was double-edged and, from recent experience, served as much to harm him as to enlighten others. It was something best kept to oneself, a personal truth, probably meaningless in the long run but at least providing a moral self-sufficiency more effective than Eva's practical attempts to the same end in the garden. Having reached that conclusion and condemned Eva's world concern and P.A.P.P., Wilt turned these findings on their head and accused himself of a quietism and passivity in the face of an underfed and deprived world. Eva's actions might not be more than sops to a liberal conscience but for all that they helped to sustain conscience and set an example to the quads which his own apathy denied. Somewhere there had to be a golden mean between charity beginning at home and improving the lot of starving millions. Wilt was damned if he knew where that mean was. It certainly wasn't to be found in doctrinaire shits like Bilger. Even John and Bertha Nye were trying to make a better world, not destroy a bad one. And what was he, Henry Wilt, doing? Nothing. Or rather, turning into a beer-swilling, self-pitying Peeping Tom without a worthwhile achievement to his credit. As if to prove that he had at least the courage of his garb, Wilt left the summerhouse and walked back to the house in full view of the conservatory, only to discover that the meeting had ended and Eva was putting the quads to bed.

When she came downstairs she found Wilt sitting at the kitchen table stringing runner beans.

'Wonders never cease,' she said. 'After all these years you're actually helping in the kitchen. You're not feeling ill or something?'

'I wasn't,' said Wilt, 'but now you mention it . . .'

'Don't go. There's something I want to discuss with you.'

'What?' said Wilt, stopping in the doorway.

'Upstairs,' said Eva, raising her eyes to the ceiling meaningfully.

'Upstairs?'

'You know what,' said Eva, increasing the circumspection.

'I don't,' said Wilt. 'At least I don't think I do, and if your tone of voice means anything, I don't want to. If you suppose for one moment I'm mechanically capable of . . .'

'I don't mean us. I mean them.'

'Them?'

'Miss Mueller and her friends.'

'Oh, them,' said Wilt and sat down again. 'What about them?'

'You must have heard,' said Eva.

'Heard what?' said Wilt.

'Oh, you know. You're just being difficult.'

'Lord,' said Wilt, 'we're back in Winnie-The-Pooh language. If you mean has it dawned on my semi-consciousness that they occasionally copulate, why don't you say so?'

'It's the children I'm thinking of,' said Eva. 'I'm not sure it's good for them to live in an environment where there's so much of what you just said going on.'

'If it didn't they wouldn't be here at all. And anyway your primitive penfriends are great ones for a bit of icketyboo, to use an expression that will suitably baffle Josephine. She usually comes straight out with—'

'Henry,' said Eva warningly.

'Well she does. Frequently. I heard her only yesterday tell Penelope to go—'

'I don't want to hear,' said Eva.

'I didn't either, come to that,' said Wilt, 'but the fact remains

80

that the younger generation mature rather more rapidly in words and deeds than we did. When I was ten I still thought fuck was something father did with a hammer when he hit his thumb instead of the nail. Now it's common parlance at four . . .'

'Never mind that,' said Eva. 'Your father's language left much to be desired.'

'At least in my father's case it was his language. In your old man it was the whole person. I've often wondered how your mother could bring herself . . .'

'Henry Wilt, you'll leave my family out of this. I want to know what you think we should do about Miss Mueller.'

'Why ask me? You invited her to come and live here. You didn't consult me. And I certainly didn't want the damned woman. Now that she's turned out to be some sort of international sex fiend, according to you, who's likely to infect the children with premature nymphomania, I get dragged in . . .'

'All I want is your advice,' said Eva.

'Then here it is,' said Wilt. 'Tell her to get the hell out.'

'But that's the difficulty. She's given a month's rent in advance. I haven't put it in the bank yet, but still . . .'

'Well, give it back to her for Christ's sake. If you don't want the bag give her the boot.'

'It seems so inhospitable really,' said Eva. 'I mean she's foreign and far from home.'

'Not far enough from my home,' said Wilt, 'and all her boyfriends seem to be Croesus Juniors. She can shack up with them or stay at Claridges. My advice is to give her money back and bung her out.' And Wilt went through to the living-room and sat in front of the television until supper was ready.

In the kitchen Eva made up her mind. Mavis Mottram had been wrong again. Henry wasn't in the least interested in Miss Mueller and she could give the money to P.A.P.P. So there was no need to ask the lodger to leave. Perhaps if she just suggested that things could be heard through the ceiling or . . . Anyway it was nice to know Henry hadn't been up to anything nasty. Which only went to show that she shouldn't listen to what Mavis had to say. Henry was a good husband in spite of his funny ways. It was a happy Eva who called Wilt to his supper that evening.

Chapter 10

It was a surprisingly happy Wilt who left Dr Scally's surgery the following Wednesday. After an initial bout of jocularity about Wilt's injuries the removal of the bandages and the pipeline had proceeded comparatively painlessly.

'Absolutely no need for all this in my opinion,' said the doctor, 'but those young fellows up at the hospital like to make a thorough job of things while they're about it.'

A remark that almost persuaded Wilt to lodge an official complaint with the Health Ombudsman. Dr Scally was against it.

'Think of the scandal, my dear fellow, and strictly speaking they were within their rights. If you will go round saying you've been poisoned . . .'

It was a persuasive argument and with the doctor's promise that he'd soon be as right as rain provided he didn't overdo things with his missus, Wilt emerged into the street feeling, if not on top of the world, at least half-way up it. The sun was shining on autumnal leaves, small boys were collecting conkers underneath the chestnuts in the park, and Dr Scally had given him a doctor's certificate keeping him away from the Tech. for another week. Wilt strolled into town, spent an hour browsing in the second-hand bookshop, and was about to go home when he remembered he had to deposit Miss Mueller's advance in the bank. Wilt turned bankwards and felt even better. His brief infatuation for her had evaporated. Irmgard was just another silly foreign student with more money than sense, a taste for expensive cars and young men of every nationality.

And so he walked up the bank steps airily and went to the counter where he wrote out a deposit slip and handed it to the cashier. 'My wife has a special account,' he explained. 'It's a deposit account in the name of Wilt. Mrs H. Wilt. I've forgotten the number but it's for an African tribe and I think it's called . . .' But the cashier was clearly not listening. He was busy counting the notes and while Wilt watched he stopped several times.

Finally with a brief 'Excuse me, sir,' he opened the hatch at the back of his cubicle and disappeared through it. Several customers behind Wilt moved to the next cashier, leaving him with that vague sense of unease he always felt when he cashed a cheque and the clerk before stamping the back glanced at a list of customers who were presumably grossly overdrawn. But this time he was paying money in, not taking it out, and it wasn't possible for notes to bounce.

It was. Wilt was just beginning to work up some resentment at being kept waiting when a bank messenger approached him.

'If you wouldn't mind stepping into the manager's office, sir,' he said with a slightly threatening politeness. Wilt followed him across the foyer and into the manager's office.

'Mr Wilt?' said the manager. Wilt nodded. 'Do take a seat.' Wilt sat and glared at the cashier who was standing beside the manager's desk. The notes and the deposit slip lay on the blotting pad in front of him.

'I'd be glad if you would tell me what this is all about,' said Wilt with growing alarm. Behind him the bank messenger had taken up a position by the door.

'I think we'll reserve any comment until the police arrive,' said the manager.

'What do you mean "the police arrive"?'

The manager said nothing. He stared at Wilt with a look that managed to combine sorrow and suspicion.

'Now look here,' said Wilt, 'I don't know what's going on but I demand . . .'

Wilt's protest died away as the manager eyed the pile of notes on the desk.

'Good Lord, you're not suggesting they're forged?'

'Not forged, Mr Wilt, but as I said before when the police arrive you'll have a chance to explain matters. I'm sure there's some perfectly reasonable explanation. Nobody for one moment suspects you . . .'

'Of what?' said Wilt.

But again the bank manager said nothing. Apart from the noise of traffic outside there was silence and the day which only a few minutes before had seemed full of good cheer and hope suddenly became grey and horrid. Wilt searched his mind frantically for an explanation but could think of nothing, and he was about to protest that they had no right to keep him there when there was a knock on the door and the bank messenger opened it cautiously. Inspector Flint, Sergeant Yates and two sinister plainclothes men entered.

'At last,' said the manager. 'This is really very awkward. Mr Wilt here is an old and respected customer . . .'

His defence died out. Flint was staring at Wilt.

'I didn't think there could be two Wilts in the same town,' he said triumphantly. 'Now then—'

But he was interrupted by the older of the two plainclothes men. 'If you don't mind, Inspector, we'll handle this,' he said with a brisk authority and almost a charm of manner that was even more alarming than the bank manager's previous coolness. He moved to the desk, picked up some of the notes and studied them. Wilt watched him with increasing concern.

'Would you mind telling us how you came by these five-pound notes, sir?' said the man. 'By the way, my name is Misterson.'

'They're a month's rent in advance from our lodger,' said Wilt. 'I came here to deposit them in my wife's P.A.P.P. account. . . .'

'Pap, sir? Pap account?' said the smooth Mr Misterson.

'It stands for Personal Assistance for Primitive People,' said Wilt. 'My wife is the treasurer of the local branch. She's adopted a tribe in Africa and . . .'

'I understand, Mr Wilt,' said Misterson, casting a cold eye on Inspector Flint who had just muttered 'Typical'. He sat down and hitched his chair closer to Wilt. 'You were saying that this money came from the lodger and was destined for your wife's deposit account. What sort of lodger is this?'

'Female,' said Wilt slipping into cross-examination brevity.

'And her name, sir?'

'Irmgard Mueller.'

The two plainclothes men exchanged a look. Wilt followed it and said hastily, 'She's German.'

'Yes sir. And would you be able to identify her?'

'Identify her?' said Wilt. 'I'd be hard put not to. She's been living in the attic for the last month.'

'In which case if you'll kindly come to the station we'd be glad if you would look at some photographs,' said Misterson pushing back his chair.

'Now wait a moment. I want to know what this is all about,' said Wilt. 'I've been to that police station and frankly I don't want to go there again.' He stayed resolutely in his chair.

Mr Misterson reached in his pocket and took out a plastic licence which he opened.

'If you'll take a good look at this.'

Wilt did and felt sick. It stated that Superintendent Misterson of the Anti-Terrorist Branch was empowered . . . Wilt got up unsteadily and moved towards the door. Behind him the Superintendent was giving Inspector Flint, Sergeant Yates and the bank manager their orders. No one was to leave the office, there were to be no outgoing phone calls, maximum security and business as usual. Even the bank messenger was to remain where he was.

'And now Mr Wilt if you'll just walk out quite normally and follow me. We don't want to attract attention.'

Wilt followed him out and across the bank to the door and was hesitating there wondering what to do when a car drew up. The Superintendent opened the door and Wilt got in. Five minutes later he was sitting at a table being handed photographs of young women. It was twenty past twelve when he finally picked Miss Irmgard Mueller out.

'Are you absolutely certain?' asked the Superintendent.

'Of course I am,' said Wilt irritably. 'Now I don't know who she is or what the wretched woman has done but I'd be glad if you would go and arrest her or something. I want to get home to my lunch.'

'Quite so, sir. And is your wife in the house?'

Wilt looked at his watch. 'I don't see what that's got to do with it. As a matter of fact she will now be on her way back from play school with the children and . . .'

The Superintendent sighed. It was a long ominous sigh. 'In that case I'm afraid there won't be any question of an arrest just yet,' he said. 'I take it that Miss . . . er . . . Mueller is in the house.'

'I don't know,' said Wilt, 'she was when I left this morning, and today being Wednesday she doesn't have any lectures, so she probably is. Why don't you go round and fin.¹ out?'

'Because, sir, your lodger just happens to be one of the most

85

dangerous woman terrorists in the world. I think that is self-explanatory.'

'Oh my God,' said Wilt, suddenly feeling very weak.

Superintendent Misterson leant across the desk. 'She has at least eight killings to her credit and she's suspected of being the mastermind . . . I'm sorry to use such melodramatic terms but in the event they happen to fit. As I was saying she has organized several bombings and we now know she's been involved in the hijacking of a security van in Gantrey last Tuesday. A man died in the attack. You may have read about the case.'

Wilt had. In the waiting-room at the Accident Centre. It had seemed then one of those remote and disgusting acts of gratuitous violence which made the morning paper such depressing reading. And yet because he read about it the murder of a security guard had been invested with a reality which it lacked in the present circumstances. Mastermind, terrorist, killings—words spoken casually in an office by a bland man with a paisley tie and a brown tweed suit. Like some country solicitor, Superintendent Misterson, was the last person he would have expected to use such words and it was this incongruity which was so alarming. Wilt stared at the man and shook his head.

'I'm afraid it's true,' said the Superintendent.

'But the money . . .'

'Marked, sir. Marked and numbered. Bait in a trap.'

Wilt shook his head again. The truth was unbearable. 'What are you going to do? My wife and children are at home by now and if she's there . . . and there are all those other foreigners in the house too.'

'Would you mind telling us how many other . . . er . . . foreigners are there, sir?'

'I don't know,' said Wilt, 'it varies from day to day. There's a stream of them coming and going. Jesus wept.'

'Now, sir,' said the Superintendent briskly, 'what's your usual routine? Do you normally go home for lunch?'

'No. I usually have it at the Tech. but just at the moment I'm off work and yes, I suppose I do.'

'So your wife will be surprised if you don't come home?'

'I doubt it,' said Wilt. 'Sometimes I drop into a pub for sandwiches.'

'And you don't telephone first?'

'Not always.'

'What I am trying to ascertain, sir, is whether your wife will evince any alarm were you not to come home now or contact her.'

'She won't,' said Wilt. 'The only time she'll be alarmed is when she knows we've been providing accommodation for . . . What is the name of this bloody woman anyway?'

'Gudrun Schautz. And now, sir, I'll have some lunch sent up from the canteen and we'll make preparations.'

'What preparations?' asked Wilt but the Superintendent had left the room and the other plainclothes man seemed disinclined to talk. Wilt regarded the slight bulge under the man's right armpit and tried to stifle his growing feeling of insanity.

In the kitchen at Willington Road Eva was busy giving the quads their lunch.

'We won't wait for daddy,' she said, 'he'll probably be back a little later.'

'Will he bring his bagpipe home?' asked Josephine.

'Bagpipe, dear? Daddy doesn't have a bagpipe.'

'He's been wearing one,' said Penelope.

'Yes, but not the sort you play.'

'I saw some men in dresses playing bagpipes at the show,' said Emmeline.

'Kilts, dear.'

'I saw daddy playing with his pipe in the summerhouse,' said Penelope, 'and he was wearing mummy's dress too.'

'Well he wasn't playing with it in the same way, Penny,' argued Eva, wondering privately what way Wilt had been playing with it.

'Bagpipes make a horrid noise anyway,' maintained Emmeline.

'And daddy made a horrid noise when you got into bed . . .'

'Yes, dear, he was having a bad dream.'

'He called it a wet dream, mummy. I heard him.'

'Well that's a bad dream too,' said Eva. 'Now then, what did you do at school today?'

But the quads were not to be diverted from the absorbing topic of their father's recent misfortune. 'Roger's mummy told him daddy must have something wrong with his bladder to have a pipe,' said Penelope. 'What's a bladder, mummy?'

'I know,' shouted Emmeline, 'it's a pig's tummy and that's what they make bagpipes out of because Sally told me.'

'Daddy's not a pig . . .'

'That's enough of that,' said Eva firmly, 'we won't talk about daddy any more. Now eat your cod's roe.'

'Roger says cod's roe is baby fishes,' said Penelope. 'I don't like it.'

'Well it's not. Fishes don't have babies. They lay eggs.'

'Do sausages lay eggs, mummy?' asked Josephine.

'Of course they don't, darling. Sausages aren't alive.'

'Roger says his daddy's sausage lays eggs and his mummy wears something . . .'

'I don't care to hear what Roger says any more,' said Eva torn between curiosity about the Rawstons and revulsion at her offsprings' encyclopedic knowledge. 'It's not nice to talk about such things.'

'Why not, mummy?'

'Because it isn't,' said Eva unable to think of a suitably progressive argument to silence them. Caught between her own indoctrinated sense of niceness and her opinion that children's innate curiosity should never be thwarted, Eva struggled through lunch wishing that Henry were there to put a stop to their questions with a taciturn growl. But Henry still wasn't there at two o'clock when Mavis phoned to remind her that she had promised to pick her up on the way to the Symposium on Alternative Painting in Thailand.

'I'm sorry but Henry isn't back,' said Eva. 'He went to the doctor's this morning and I expected him home for lunch. I can't leave the children.'

'Patrick's got the car today,' said Mavis, 'his own is in for a service and I was relying on you.'

'Oh well, I'll go and ask Mrs de Frackas to baby-sit for half an hour,' said Eva, 'she's always volunteering to sit and Henry's bound to be back shortly.'

She went next door and presently old Mrs de Frackas was sitting in the summerhouse surrounded by the quads reading them the story of Rikki Tikki Tavi. The widow of Major-General de Frackas, at eighty-two her memories of girlhood days in India were rather better than on topics of more recent occurrence. Eva drove off happily to pick up Mavis.

By the time Wilt had finished his lunch he had picked out two more terrorists from the mug shots as being frequent visitors to the house, and the police station had seen the arrival of several large vans containing a large number of surprisingly agile men in a motley of plain clothes. The canteen had been turned into a briefing centre and Superintendent Misterson's authority had been superseded by a Major (name undisclosed) of Special Ground Services.

'The Superintendent here will explain the initial stages of the operation,' said the Major condescending, 'but before he does I want to stress that we are dealing with some of the most ruthless killers in Europe. They must on no account escape. At the same time we naturally want to avoid bloodshed if at all possible. However, it has to be said that in the circumstances we are entitled to shoot first and ask questions afterwards if the target is able to answer. I have that authority from the Minister.' He smiled bleakly and sat down.

'After the house has been surrounded,' said the Superintendent, 'Mr Wilt will enter and hopefully effect the exit of his family. I want nothing done to prevent that first essential requirement. The second factor to take into account is that we have a unique opportunity to arrest at least three leading terrorists and possibly more, and again, hopefully, Mr Wilt will enable us to know how many members of the group are in the house at the moment of time of his exit. I'll go ahead with my side and leave the rest to the Major.'

He left the canteen and went up to the office where Wilt was finishing his Queen's pudding with the help of mouthfuls of coffee. Outside the door he met the SGS surgeon and parapsychologist who had been studying Wilt covertly.

'Nervous type,' he said gloomily. 'Couldn't be worse material. Sort of blighter who'd funk a jump from a tethered balloon.'

'Fortunately he doesn't have to jump from a tethered balloon,' said the Superintendent. 'All he has to do is enter the house and find an excuse for taking his family out.'

'All the same I think he ought to have a shot of something

to stiffen his backbone. We don't want him dithering on the doorstep. Give the game away.'

He marched off to fetch his bag while the Superintendent went in to Wilt. 'Now then,' he said with alarming cheerfulness, 'all you've got to do . . .'

'Is enter a house filled with killers and ask my wife to come out. I know,' said Wilt.

'Nothing very difficult about that.'

Wilt looked at him incredulously. 'Nothing difficult?' said Wilt in a vaguely soprano voice. 'You don't know my bloody wife.'

'I haven't had the privilege yet,' admitted the Superintendent.

'Precisely,' said Wilt. 'Well, when and if you do you'll discover that if I go home and ask her to come out she'll think of a thousand reasons for staying in.'

'Difficult woman, sir?'

'Oh no, nothing difficult about Eva. Not at all. She's just bloody awkward, that's all.'

'I see, sir, and if you suggested she didn't go out you think she might in fact do so?'

'If you want my opinion,' said Wilt, 'if I do that she'll think I'm off my rocker. I mean what would you do if you were sitting peacefully at home and your wife came in and suggested out of the blue that you didn't go out when it had never occurred to you to go out in the first place? You'd think there was something fucking odd going on, wouldn't you?'

'I suppose I would,' said the Superintendent. 'Never thought of it like that before.'

'Well you'd better start now,' said Wilt, 'I'm not going . . .' He was interrupted by the entrance of the Major and two other officers wearing jeans, T-shirts with UP THE I.R.A. printed on them, and carrying rather large handbags.

'If we might just interrupt a moment,' said the Major, 'we would like Mr Wilt to draw a detailed plan of the house, vertical section and then horizontal.'

'What for?' said Wilt unable to take his eyes off the T-shirts.

'In the event that we have to storm the house, sir,' said the Major, 'we need to get the killing angles right. Don't want to go in and find the loo's in the wrong place and what not.'

90

'Listen, mate,' said Wilt, 'you go down Willington Road with those T-shirts and handbags you won't reach my house. You'll be bloody lynched by the neighbours. Mrs Fogin's nephew was blown up in Belfast and Professor Ball's got a thing about gays. His wife married one.'

'Better change into the KEEP CLAPHAM WHITE shirts, chaps,' said the Major.

'Better not,' said Wilt. 'Mr and Mrs Bokani at Number 11 would be onto Race Relations like the clappers. Can't you think of something neutral?'

'Mickey Mouse, sir?' suggested one of the officers.

'Oh, all right,' said the Major grumpily, 'one Mickey Mouse and the rest Donald Ducks.'

'Christ,' said Wilt, 'I don't know how many men you've got but if you're going to flood the neighbourhood with Donald Ducks armed to the teeth with whatever you have in those gigantic handbags you'll have a whole lot of schizophrenic infants on your conscience.'

'Never mind that,' said the Major, 'you leave the tactical angle to us. We've had experience before of this sort of operation and all we want from you is a detailed plan of the domestic terrain.'

'Talk about calling a spade an earth-inverting horticultural implement,' said Wilt. 'I never thought I'd live to hear my home called a domestic terrain.'

He picked up a pencil but the Superintendent intervened. 'Look, if we don't get Mr Wilt back to the house soon, someone may begin wondering where he is,' he protested.

As if to reinforce this argument the phone rang.

'It's for you,' said the Major. 'Some bugger called Flint who says he's holed up in the bank.'

'I thought I told you not to make any outgoing calls,' the Superintendent said angrily into the phone. 'Relieve themselves? Of course they can . . . An appointment at three with Mr Daniles? Who's he? . . . Oh shit . . . Where? . . . Well, empty the wastepaper basket for Chrissake . . . I don't have to tell you where. I should have thought that was patently obvious . . . What do you mean it's going to look peculiar? . . . Do they have to cross the entire bank? . . . I know all about the smell. Get hold of an aerosol or something . . . Well if he objects detain the sod. And Flint, see if someone has a bucket and use that in future.'

He slammed down the phone and turned back to the Major. 'Things are steaming up at the bank and if we don't move swiftly—'

'Someone's going to smell a rat?' suggested Wilt. 'Now, do you want me to draw my house or not?'

'Yes,' said the Major, 'and fast.'

'There's no need to adopt that tone,' said Wilt. 'You may be eager to have a battle on my property but I want to know who's going to pay for the damage. My wife's a very particular woman and if you start killing people all over the carpet in the living-room . . .'

'Mr Wilt,' said the Major with determined patience, 'we shall do everything we can to avoid any violence on your property. It is for precisely that reason we need a detailed plan of the domestic . . . er . . . the house.'

'I think if we leave Mr Wilt to draw the plan . . .' said the Superintendent and nodded towards the door. The Major followed him out and they conferred in the corridor.

'Listen,' said the Superintendent, 'I've already had a report from your trick-cyclist that the little bastard's a mass of nerves and if you're going to start bullying him . . .'

'Superintendent,' said the Major, 'it may interest you to know that I have a casualty allowance of ten on this op and if he's one of them I shan't be sorry. War Office approval.'

'And if we don't get him in there, and his wife and children out, you'll have used up six of your quota,' snapped the Superintendent.

'All I can say is that a man who puts his living-room carpet before his country and the Western World . . .' He would have said a lot more had it not been for the arrival of the para-psychologist with a cup of coffee.

'Fixed him a spot of nervebracer,' he said cheerfully. 'Should see him through.'

'I certainly hope so,' said the Superintendent. 'I could do with something myself.'

'No need to worry about it working,' said the Major. 'Used it myself once in County Armagh when I had to defuse a bloody

92

great bomb. Bugger went off before I could get to it but by God I felt good all the same.'

The medic went into the office and presently reappeared with the empty cup. 'In like a lamb, out like a lion,' he said. 'No trouble at all.'

Chapter 11

Ten minutes later Wilt lived up to the prediction. He left the police station of his own free will and entered the Superintendent's car quite cheerfully.

'Just drop me off at the bottom of the road and I'll find my own way home,' he said. 'No need for you to bother to drive right up to the house.'

The Superintendent looked at him doubtfully. 'I hadn't intended to. The object of the exercise is for you to go into the house without arousing suspicion and persuade your wife to come out by telling her you've met this herbalist in a pub and he's invited you all round to look at his collection of plants. You've got that straight?'

'Wilco,' said Wilt.

'Wilco?'

'And what's more,' continued Wilt, 'if that doesn't flush the bitch out I'll take the children and leave her to stew in her own juice.'

'Stop the car, driver,' said the Superintendent hastily.

'What for?' said Wilt. 'You don't expect me to walk two miles? When I said you could drop me off I didn't mean here.'

'Mr Wilt,' said the Superintendent, 'I must impress on you the seriousness of the situation. Gudrun Schautz is undoubtedly armed and she won't hesitate to shoot. The woman is a professional killer.'

'So what? Bloody woman comes into my house having killed people all over the place and expects me to give her bed and board. Like hell I will. Driver, drive on.'

'Oh God,' said the Superintendent, 'trust the army to cock this one up.'

'Want me to turn back, sir?' asked the driver.

'Certainly not,' said Wilt. 'The sooner I can get my family out and the army in the better. No need to look like that. Everything's going to be roger over and out.'

'I wouldn't be at all surprised,' said the Superintendent

despondently. 'All right, drive on. Now then, Mr Wilt, for God's sake stick to your story about the herbalist. The fellow's name is . . .'

'Falkirk,' said Wilt automatically. 'He lives at Number 45 Barrabas Road. He has recently returned from South America with a collection of plants including tropical herbs previously uncultivated in this country . . .'

'At least he knows his lines,' muttered the Superintendent as they turned into Farringdon Avenue and pulled into the kerb. Wilt got out, slammed the car door with unnecessary violence and marched off down Willington Road. Behind him the Superintendent watched miserably and cursed the parapsychologist.

'Must have given him some sort of chemical kamikaze mixture,' he told the driver.

'There's still time to stop him, sir,' said the driver. But there wasn't. Wilt had dived into the gate of his house and disappeared. As soon as he had gone a head popped out of the hedge beside the car.

'Don't want to give the game away, old boy,' said an officer wearing the uniform of a Gas Inspector. 'If you'll just toddle along I'll call HQ and tell them the subject has entered the danger zone . . .'

'Oh no you won't,' snarled the Superintendent as the officer twiddled with the knobs of his walkie-talkie, 'there's to be strict radio silence until the family are safely out.'

'My orders are . . .'

'Countermanded as of now,' said the Superintendent. 'Innocent lives are at stake and I'm not having them jeopardized.'

'Oh all right,' said the officer. 'Anyway we've got the area sealed off. Not even a rabbit could get out of there now.'

'It's not simply a question of anyone getting out. We want as many to get in before we move.'

'Rightho, want to bag the lot of them eh? Nothing like going the whole hog, what!'

The officer disappeared into the hedge and the Superintendent drove on.

'Lions, lambs, and now fucking rabbits and hogs,' he told the driver, 'I wish to heaven the Special Ground Services hadn't been called in. They seem to have animals on the brain.'

'Comes of recruiting them from the huntin' an' shootin' set, I expect, sir,' said the driver. 'Wouldn't like to be in that bloke Wilt's shoes.'

In the garden of Number 9 Willington Road Wilt did not share his apprehensions. Stiffened by the parapsychologist's nervebracer he was in no mood to be trifled with. Bloody terrorists coming into his house without so much as a by-your-leave. Well, he'd soon show them the door. He marched resolutely up to the house and opened the front door before realizing that the car wasn't outside. Eva must be out with the quads. In which case there was no need for him to go in. 'To hell with that,' said Wilt to himself, 'this is my house and I'm entitled to do what I damned well please in it.' He went into the hall and shut the door. The house was silent and the living-room empty. Wilt went through the kitchen and wondered what to do next. In normal circumstances he would have left, but circumstances were not normal. To Wilt's intoxicated way of thinking they called for stern measures. The bloody army wanted a battle on his domestic terrain, did they? Well, he'd soon put a stop to that. Domestic terrain indeed! If people wanted to kill one another they could jolly well do it somewhere else. Which was all very fine, but how to persuade them? Well, the simplest way was to go up to the attic and heave Miss Bloody Schautz/Mueller's suitcases and clobber out into the front garden. That way when she came home she'd get the message and take herself off to someone else's domestic terrain.

With this simple solution in mind Wilt went upstairs and climbed the steps to the attic door only to find it locked. He went down to the kitchen, found the spare key and went back. For a moment he hesitated outside the door before knocking. There was no reply. Wilt unlocked the door and went inside.

The attic flat consisted of three rooms, a large bedsitter with the balcony looking down onto the garden, a kitchenette and beyond it a bathroom. Wilt shut the door behind him and looked around. The bedsitter which had occupied his former Muse was unexpectedly tidy. Gudrun Schautz might be a ruthless terrorist but she was also house-proud. Clothes hung neatly in a wall closet and the cups and saucers in the kitchen were all washed and set on shelves. Now, where would she have put her suit-cases? Wilt looked round and tried another cupboard before remembering that Eva had moved the cold-water cistern to a higher position under the roof when the bathroom had been put in. There was a door to it somewhere.

He found it beside the stove in the kitchenette and crawled through only to discover that he had to stoop along under the eaves on a narrow plank to reach the storage space. He groped about in the darkness and found the lightswitch. The suitcases were in a row beside the cistern. Wilt made his way along and grabbed the handle of the first bag. It felt incredibly heavy. Also distinctly lumpy. Wilt dragged it down from the shelf and it dropped with a metallic thud onto the plank at his feet. He wasn't going to lug that back across the rafters. Wilt fumbled with the catches and finally opened the bag.

All his doubts about Miss Schautz/Mueller's profession vanished. He was looking down on some sort of sub-machine gun, a mound of revolvers, boxes of ammunition, a typewriter and what appeared to be grenades. And as he looked he heard the sound of a car outside. It had pulled into the drive and even to his untrained ear it sounded like the Aston-Martin. Cursing himself for not listening to his innate cowardice, Wilt struggled to get back along the plank to the door but the bag was in the way. He banged his head on the rafters above and was about to crawl over the bag when it occurred to him that the sub-machine gun might be loaded and could well go off if he prodded it in the wrong place. Best get the damned thing out. Again, that was easier said than done. The barrel got caught in the end of the bag and by the time he had disentangled it he could hear foot-steps on the wooden stairs below. Too late to do anything now except switch the light off. Leaning forward across the bag and holding the machine gun at arm's length Wilt joggled the switch up with the muzzle before crouching down in the darkness.

Outside in the garden the quads had had a marvellous after-noon with old Mrs de Frackas. She had read them the story about Rikki Tikki Tavi, the mongoose, and the two cobras, and had then taken them into her house to show them what a stuffed cobra looked like (she had one in a glass case and it bared its fangs most realistically) and had told them about her own childhood in India before sitting them down to tea in her conservatory. For once the quads had behaved themselves. They had picked up from Eva a proper sense of Mrs de Frackas' social standing and in any case the old lady's voice had a distinctly firm ring to it—or as Wilt had once put it, if at eighty-two she could no longer break a sherry glass at fifty paces she could still make a guard dog whimper at forty. It was certainly true that the milkman had long since given up trying to collect his payment on a weekly basis. Mrs de Frackas belonged to a generation that had paid when it felt so inclined; the old lady sent her cheque only twice a year, and then it was wrong. The milk company did not dispute it. The widow of the late Major-General de Frackas, D.S.O. etcetera was a personage to whom people deferred and it was one of Eva's proudest boasts that she and the old lady got on like a house on fire. Nobody else in Willington Road did and it was almost entirely because Mrs de Frackas loved children and considered Eva, in spite of her obvious lack of breeding, to be an excellent mother that she smiled on the Wilts. To be precise, she seldom smiled on Wilt, evidently regarding him as an accident in the family process and one that, if her observation of his activities in the summerhouse of an evening was correct, drank. Since the Major-General had died of cirrhosis or as she bluntly said, hob-nailed liver, Wilt's solitary communion with the bottle only increased her regard for Eva and concern for the children. Being also rather deaf she thought them delightful girls, an opinion that was shared by no one else in the district.

And so this bright sunny afternoon Mrs de Frackas sat the quads in her conservatory and served tea, happily unaware of the gathering drama next door. Then she allowed them to play with the tiger rug in her drawing-room and even to knock over a potted palm before deciding it was time to go home. The little procession went out of the front gate and into Number 9 just as Wilt began his search in the attic. In the bushes on the opposite side of the road the officer whom the Superintendent had warned not to use his radio watched them enter the house and was desperately praying that they would come out again straightaway when the Aston-Martin drove up. Gudrun Schautz and two young men got out, opened the boot and took out several suitcases while the officer dithered but before he could make up his mind to tackle them in the open they had hurried in the front door. Only then did he break radio silence.

'Female target and two males have entered the zone,' he told the Major who was making a round of the S.G.S. men posted at the bottom of the Wilts' garden. 'No present withdrawal of civilian occupants. Request instructions.'

In response the Major threaded his way through the gardens of Numbers 4 and 2 and accompanied by two privates carrying a theodolite and a striped pole promptly set this up on the pavement and began to take sightings down Willington Road while carrying on a conversation with the officer in the hedge.

'What do you mean you couldn't stop them?' demanded the Major when he learnt that the quads and an old lady had left the house next door and gone into the Wilts'. But before the officer could think of an answer they were interrupted by Professor Ball.

'What's the meaning of all this?' he demanded, regarding the two long-haired privates and the theodolite with equal distaste.

'Just making a survey for the new road extension,' said the Major improvising hastily.

'Road extension? What road extension?' said the Professor transferring his disgust to the handbag the Major had over his shoulder.

'The proposed road extension to the by-pass,' said the Major.

Professor Ball's voice rose. 'By-pass? Did I hear you say there's a proposal to put a road through here to the by-pass?'

'Only doing my job, sir,' said the Major, wishing to hell the old fool would get lost.

'And what job is that?' demanded the Professor, taking a notebook from his pocket.

'Surveyor's Department, Borough Engineering.'

'Really? And your name?' asked the Professor with a nasty glint in his eye. He wetted the end of his ballpen with his tongue while the Major hesitated.

'Palliser, sir,' said the Major. 'And now, sir, if you don't mind, we've got to get on.'

'Don't let me disturb you, Mr Palliser.' The Professor turned and stalked into his house. He returned a moment later with a heavy stick.

'It may interest you to know, Mr Palliser,' he said brandishing the stick, 'that I happen to sit on the Highways and Planning Committee of the City Council. Note the word "city", Mr Palliser. And we don't have a Borough Engineering Department. We have a City one.'

'Slip of the tongue, sir,' said the Major trying to keep one eye on the Wilts' house while conscious of the threat of the stick.

'And I suppose it was another slip of the tongue that you said that the City of Ipford was proposing to build an extension of this road to the by-pass . . .'

'It's just a vague idea, sir,' said the Major.

Professor Ball laughed dryly. 'It must indeed be vague considering we don't yet have a by-pass and that as Chairman of the Highways and Planning Committee I would be the first to hear of any proposed alterations to the existing roads. What's more, I happen to know a great deal about the use of theodolites and you don't look through the wrong end. Now then, you will kindly remain where you are until the police arrive. My housekeeper has already phoned . . .'

'If I could have a word with you in private,' said the Major fumbling frantically in his handbag for his credentials. But Professor Ball knew an impostor when he saw one and, as Wilt had predicted, his reaction to men who carried handbags was violent. With the descent of his stick the Major's credentials tipped from his handbag and clattered on the ground. They included one walkie-talkie, two revolvers and a teargas grenade.

'Fuck,' said the Major, stooping to retrieve his armoury, but Professor Ball's stick was in action again. This time it caught the Major on the back of the neck and sent him sprawling in the gutter. Behind him the private in charge of the theodolite moved swiftly. Throwing himself on the Professor he pinned his left arm behind his back and with a karate chop knocked the stick from his right hand.

'If you'll just come quietly, sir,' he said, but that was the last thing Professor Ball intended to do. Safety, from men pretending to be surveyors who carried revolvers and grenades, lay in

100

making as much noise as he could and Willington Road was aroused from its suburban torpor by yells of 'Help! Murder! Call the police!'

'For God's sake gag the old bastard,' shouted the Major still scrabbling for his revolvers but it was too late. Across the road a face appeared at the attic skylight, was followed by a second, and before the Professor could be removed in silence they had disappeared.

Squatting in the darkness beside the water tank Wilt was only dimly aware that something odd was happening in the street. Gudrun Schautz had decided to take a bath and the tank was rumbling and hissing but he could hear the reactions of her companions clearly enough.

'Police!' one of them yelled. 'Gudrun, the police are here.'

Another voice shouted from the balcony room. 'There are more in the garden with rifles.'

'Downstairs quickly. We take them on the ground.'

Footsteps clattered down the wooden staircase while Gudrun Schautz from the bathroom shouted instructions in German and then remembered to bawl them in English.

'The children,' she shouted, 'hold the children.'

It was too much for Wilt. Disregarding the bag and the machine gun he was holding he hurled himself at the door, fell through it into the kitchen and promptly sprayed the ceiling with bullets by accidentally pulling the trigger. The effect was quite remarkable. In the bathroom Gudrun Schautz screamed, downstairs the terrorists began firing into the back garden and at the little group including Professor Ball across the street, and from both the street and the back garden the S.G.S. returned their fire fourfold, smashing windows, adding new holes in the leaves of Eva's Swiss Cheese plant and generally pock-marking the walls of the living-room where Mrs de Frackas and the quads were enjoying a Western on TV until the Mexican rug on the wall behind them was dislodged and covered their heads.

'Now then, children,' she said calmly, 'there's no need to be alarmed. We'll just lie on the floor until whatever's happening stops.' But the quads were not in the least alarmed. Inured by continual gunfights on television they were perfectly at home in the middle of a real one.

The same could hardly be said for Wilt. As the plaster from the perforated ceiling drifted down onto him he scrambled to his feet and was making for the stairs when a burst of small-arms fire heading through the back windows of the landing and out the front deterred him. Still clutching the sub-machine gun, he stumbled back into the kitchen and then realized that the infernal Fräulein Schautz was behind him in the bathroom. She had stopped screaming and might at any moment emerge with a gun. 'Lock the bitch in,' was his first thought but since the key was on the inside . . . Wilt looked round for an alternative and found it in a kitchen chair which he jammed under the door handle. To make this doubly secure he tore the flex from a table-lamp in the main room and dragged it through before tying a loop to the handle and attaching the other end to the leg of the electric stove. Then having secured his rear he made another sortie to the stairs, but the battle below still raged. He was just about to risk going down when a head appeared on the landing, a head and shoulders carrying the same sort of weapon he had just used. Wilt didn't hesitate. He slammed the door of the flat, pushed up the safety lock and then dragged a bed from the wall and lodged it against the door. Finally he picked up his own gun and waited. If anyone tried to come through the door he would pull the trigger. But then just as suddenly as the battle had begun it ceased.

Silence reigned in Willington Road, a short, blissful, healthy silence. Wilt stood in the attic and listened breathlessly, wondering what to do next. It was decided for him by Gudrun Schautz trying the door of the bathroom. He edged into the kitchen and pointed the gun at the door.

'One more move in there and I fire,' he said, and even to Wilt his voice had a strange and unnaturally menacing, almost unrecognizable sound to it. To Gudrun Schautz it held the authentic tone of a man behind a gun. The doorhandle stopped wriggling. On the other hand there was someone at the top of the stairs trying to get into the flat. With a facility that astonished him Wilt turned and pulled the trigger and once more the flat resounded to a burst of gunfire. None of the bullets hit the door. They spattered the wall of the bedsitter while the sub-machine gun juddered in Wilt's hands. The bloody thing seemed to have a will of its own and it was a horrified Wilt who finally took his finger off the trigger and put the gun gingerly down on the kitchen table. Outside someone descended the stairs with remarkable rapidity but there was no other sound.

Wilt sat down and wondered what the hell was going to happen next.

Chapter 12

Much the same question was occupying Superintendent Misterson's mind.

'What the hell's going on?' he demanded of the dishevelled Major who arrived with Professor Ball and the two pseudo-surveyors at the corner of Willington Road and Farringdon Avenue. 'I thought I told you nothing must be done until the children were safely out of the house.'

'Don't look at me,' said the Major. 'This old fool had to poke his fucking nose in.'

He fingered the back of his neck and eyed the Professor with loathing.

'And who might you be?' Professor Ball asked the Superintendent.

'A police officer.'

'Then kindly do your duty and arrest these bandits. Come down the road with a damned theodolite and handbags filled with guns and tell me they're from the Roads Department and indulge in gun battles . . .'

'Anti-Terrorist Squad, sir,' said the Superintendent and showed him his pass. Professor Ball regarded it bleakly.

'A likely story. First I'm assaulted by . . .'

'Oh, get the old bugger out of here,' snarled the Major. 'If he hadn't interfered we'd have—'

'Interfered? Interfered indeed! I was exercising my right to make a citizen's arrest of these impostors when they start shooting into a perfectly ordinary house across the street and . . .' Two uniformed constables arrived to escort the Professor, still protesting angrily, to a waiting police car.

'You heard the damned man,' said the Major in response to the Superintendent's reiterated request for someone to please tell him what the hell had gone wrong. 'We were waiting for the children to come out when he arrives on the scene and blows the gaff. That's what happened. The next thing you know the sods

104

were firing from the house, and by the sound of it using some damnably powerful weapons.'

'Right, so what you are saying is that the children are still in the house, Mr Wilt is still there, and so are a number of terrorists. Is that correct?'

'Yes,' said the Major.

'And all this in spite of your guarantee that you wouldn't do anything to jeopardize the lives of innocent civilians?'

'I didn't do a damned thing. I happened to be lying in the gutter when the balloon went up. And if you expect my men to sit quietly and let themselves be shot at by thugs using automatic weapons you're asking too much of human nature.'

'I suppose so,' the Superintendent conceded. 'Oh well, we'll just have to go into the usual siege routine. Any idea how many terrorists were in there?'

'Too bloody many for my liking,' said the Major looking to his men for confirmation.

'One of them was firing through the roof, sir,' said one of the privates. 'A burst of fire came through the tiles right at the beginning.'

'And I wouldn't say they were short of ammo. Not the way they were loosing off.'

'All right. First thing is to evacuate the street,' said the Superintendent. 'Don't want any more people involved than we can help.'

'Sounds as if someone else is already involved,' said the Major as the muffled burst of Wilt's second experiment with the machine gun echoed from Number 9. 'What the hell are they doing firing inside the house?'

'Probably started on the hostages,' said the Superintendent gloomily.

'Hardly likely, old chap. Not unless one of them tried to escape. Oh by the way I don't know if I mentioned it but there's a little old lady in there too. Went in with the four girls.'

'Went in with the four—' the Superintendent began lividly before being interrupted by his driver with the message that Inspector Flint had called from the bank to know if it was all right for him to leave now as it was closing time and the bank staff . . .

The Superintendent unleashed his fury on Flint via the driver,

105

and the Major made good his escape. Presently little groups of refugees from Willington Road were making their way circuitously out of the area while more armed men moved in to take their place. An armoured car with the Major perched safely on its turret rumbled past.

'HQ and Communications Centre are at Number 7,' he shouted. 'My signal chappies have rigged you up with a direct line in.'

He drove on before the Superintendent could think of a suitable retort. 'Damned military getting in the way all the time,' he grumbled and gave orders for parabolic listening devices to be brought up and for tape recorders and voiceprint analysers to be installed at the Communications Centre. In the meantime Farringdon Avenue was cordoned off by uniformed police at road blocks and a Press Briefing Room established at the Police Station.

'Got to give the public their pound of vicarious flesh,' he told his men, 'but I don't want any TV cameramen inside the area. The sods inside the house will be watching and frankly if I had my way there would be press and TV silence. These swine thrive on publicity.'

Only then did he make his way down Willington Road to Number 7 to begin the dialogue with the terrorists.

Eva drove home from Mavis Mottram's in a bad temper. The Symposium on Alternative Painting in Thailand had been cancelled because the artist-cum-lecturer had been arrested and was awaiting extradition proceedings for drug smuggling and instead Eva had had to sit through two hours of discussion on Alternative Childbirth about which, since she had given birth to four overweight infants in the course of forty minutes, she considered she knew more than the lecturer. To add to her irritation, several ardent advocates of abortion had used the occasion to promote their views and Eva had violent feelings about abortion.

'It's unnatural,' she told Mavis afterwards in the Coffee House with that simplicity her friends found so infuriating. 'If people don't want children they shouldn't have them.'

'Yes, dear,' said Mavis, 'but it's not as easy as all that.'

'It is. They can have their babies adopted by parents who

106

can't have any. There are thousands of couples like that.'

'Yes but in the case of teenage girls . . .'

'Teenage girls shouldn't have sex. I didn't.'

Mavis looked at her thoughtfully. 'No, but you're the exception, Eva. The modern generation is much more demanding than we were. They're physically more mature.'

'Perhaps they are, but Henry says they're mentally retarded.'

'Of course, he would know,' said Mavis but Eva was impervious to such slights.

'If they weren't they would take precautions.'

'But you're the one who is always going on about the pill being unnatural.'

'And so it is. I just meant they wouldn't allow boys to go so far. After all once they're married they can have as much as they like.'

'That's the first time I've heard you say that, dear. You're always complaining that Henry is too tired to bother.'

In the end Eva had had to riposte with a reference to Patrick Mottram and Mavis had seized the opportunity to catalogue his latest infidelities.

'Anyone would think the whole world revolved round Patrick,' Eva grumbled to herself as she drove away from Ms Mottram's house. 'And I don't care what anyone thinks, I still say abortion is wrong.' She turned into Farringdon Avenue and was immediately stopped by a policeman. A barrier had been erected across the road and several police cars were parked against the kerb.

'Sorry, ma'am, but you'll have to go back. No one is allowed through,' a uniformed constable told her.

'But I live here,' said Eva. 'I'm only going as far as Willington Road.'

'That's where the trouble is.'

'What trouble?' asked Eva, her instincts suddenly alert. 'Why have they got that barbed wire across the road?'

A sergeant walked across as Eva opened the door of the car and got out.

'Now then, if you'll kindly turn round and drive back the way you came,' he said.

'Says she lives in Willington Road,' the constable told him. At that moment two S.G.S. men armed with automatic weapons came round the corner and entered Mrs Granberry's garden by way of her flowerbed of prize begonias. If anything was needed to confirm Eva's worst fears this was it.

'Those men have got guns,' she said. 'Oh my God, my children! Where are my children?'

'You'll find everyone from Willington Road in the Memorial Hall. Now what number do you live at?'

'Number 9. I left the quads with Mrs de Frackas and—'

'If you'll just come this way, Mrs Wilt,' said the sergeant gently and started to take her arm.

'How did you know my name?' Eva asked, staring at the sergeant with growing horror. 'You called me Mrs Wilt.'

'Now please keep calm. Everything is going to be all right.'

'No, it isn't.' And Eva threw his hand aside and began running down the road before being stopped by four policemen and dragged back to a car.

'Get the medic and a policewoman,' said the sergeant. 'Now you just sit in the back, Mrs Wilt.' Eva was forced into a police car.

'What's happened to the children? Somebody tell me what's happened.'

'The Superintendent will explain. They're quite safe so don't worry.'

'If they're safe why can't I go to them? Where's Henry? I want my Henry.'

But instead of Wilt she got the Superintendent who arrived with two policewomen and a doctor.

'Now then, Mrs Wilt,' said the Superintendent, 'I'm afraid I've got some bad news for you. Not that it couldn't be worse. Your children are alive and quite safe, but they're in the hands of several armed men and we're trying to get them out of the house safely.'

Eva stared at him wildly. 'Armed men? What armed men?'

'Some foreigners.'

'You mean they're being held *hostage*?'

'We can't be too sure just yet. Your husband is with them.'

The doctor intervened. 'I'm just going to give you a sedative, Mrs Wilt,' he began but Eva recoiled in the back seat.

'No you aren't. I'm not taking anything. You can't make me.'

'If you'll just calm down . . .'

But Eva was adamant, and too strong to be easily given an injection in the confined space. After the doctor had had the hypodermic syringe knocked from his hand for the second time he gave up.

'All right, Mrs Wilt, you needn't take anything,' said the Superintendent. 'If you'll just sit still we'll drive you back to the police station and keep you fully informed of any developments.'

And in spite of Eva's protests that she wanted to stay where she was or even go down to the house she was driven away with an escort of two policewomen.

'Next time you want me to sedate that damned woman I'll get a tranquillizer gun from the Zoo,' said the doctor, nursing his wrist. 'And if you're sensible you'll keep her in a cell. If she gets loose she could foul things up properly.'

'As if they weren't already,' said the Superintendent and made his way back to the Communications Centre. It was situated in Mrs de Frackas' drawing-room and there incongruously, set among mementos of life in Imperial India, antimacassars, potted plants and beneath the ferocious portrait of the late Major-General, the S.G.S. and the Anti-Terrorist Squad had collaborated to install a switchboard, a telephone amplifier, tape recorders and the voiceprint analyser.

'All ready to go, sir,' said the detective in charge of the apparatus. 'We've hooked into the line next door.'

'Have you got the listening devices in position?'

'Can't do that yet,' said the Major. 'No windows on this side and we can't move in across the lawn. Have a shot after dark, provided those buggers haven't got night sights.'

'Oh well, put me through,' said the Superintendent. 'The sooner we begin the dialogue the sooner everyone will be able to go home. If I know my job they'll start with a stream of abuse. So everyone stand by to be called a fascist shit.'

In the event he was mistaken. It was Mrs de Frackas who answered.

'This is Ipford 23 . . . I'm afraid I haven't got my glasses with me but I think it's . . . Now, young man . . .'

There was a brief pause during which Mrs de Frackas was evidently relieved of the phone.

109

'My name is Misterson, Superintendent Misterson,' said the Superintendent finally.

'Lying pig of a fascist shit,' shouted a voice, at last fulfilling his prediction. 'You think we are going to surrender, shitface, but you are wrong. We die first, you understand. Do you hear me, pig?'

The Superintendent sighed and said he did.

'Right. Get that straight in your pigshit fascist head. No way we surrender. If you want us you come in and kill us and you know what that means.'

'I don't think anyone wants . . .'

'What you want, pig, you don't get. You do what we want or people get hurt.'

'That's what I'm waiting to hear, what you want,' said the Superintendent, but the terrorists were evidently in consultation and after a minute the phone in the house was slammed down.

'Well, at least we know the little old lady hasn't been hurt and by the sound of things the children are all right.'

The Superintendent crossed to a coffee-dispenser and poured himself a cup.

'Bit of a bore being called a pig all the time,' said the Major sympathetically. 'You'd think they could come up with something slightly more original.'

'Don't you believe it. They're on a marxist millennium ego-trip, kamikaze style, and what few brains they have they laundered years ago. That sounded like Chinanda, the Mexican.'

'Intonation and accent was right,' said the sergeant on the tape recorder.

'What's his record?' asked the Major.

'The usual. Rich parents, good education, flunked University and decided to save the world by knocking people off. To date, five. Specializes in car bombs, and crude ones at that. Not a very sophisticated laddie, our Miguel. Better get that tape through to the analysts. I want to hear their verdict on his stress pattern. And now we settle down to the long slog.'

'You expect him to call back with demands?'

'No. Next time we'll have the charming Fräulein Schautz. She's the one with the brains up top.'

It was an unintentionally apt description. Trapped in the

bathroom, Gudrun Schautz had spent much of the afternoon wondering what had happened and why no one had either killed her or come to arrest her. She had also considered methods of escape but was hampered by the lack of her clothes, which she had left in the bedsitter, and by Wilt's threat that if she made one more move he would fire. Not that she knew it was Wilt who had made it. What she had heard of his domestic life through the floor above his bedroom had done nothing to suggest he was capable of any sort of heroism. He was simply an effete, degenerate and cowardly little Englishman who was bullied by his stupid wife.

Fräulein Schautz might speak English fluently but her understanding of the English was hopelessly deficient. Given the chance Wilt would have agreed in large measure with this assessment of his character but he was too preoccupied to waste time on introspection. He was trying to guess what had happened downstairs during the shooting. He had no way of knowing if the quads were still in the house, and only the presence of armed men at the bottom of the garden and across the road in front of the house told him that the terrorists were still on the ground floor. From the balcony window he could look down at the summerhouse where he had spent so many idle evenings regretting his wasted gifts and longing for a woman who turned out in reality to be less a Muse than a private executioner. Now the summerhouse was occupied by men with guns while the field beyond was ringed with coils of barbed wire. The view from the skylight over the kitchen was even less encouraging. An armoured car had stationed itself outside the front gate with its gun turret turned towards the house, and there were more armed men in Professor Ball's garden.

Wilt climbed down and was wondering rather hysterically what the hell to do next when the telephone rang. He went into the main room and picked the extension up in time to hear Mrs de Frackas end her brief statement. Wilt listened to the tide of abuse wash over the uncomplaining Superintendent and felt briefly for the man. It sounded just like Bilger in one of his tirades, only this time the men downstairs had guns. They probably had the quads too. Wilt couldn't be certain but Mrs de Frackas' presence suggested as much. Wilt listened to see if his own name was mentioned and was relieved that it wasn't. When

111

the one-sided conversation ended Wilt replaced his receiver very cautiously and with a slight feeling of optimism. It was very slight, a mere reaction from the tension and from a sudden sense of power. It wasn't the power of the gun but rather that of knowledge, what he knew and what nobody else apparently knew; that the attic was occupied by a man whose killing capacity was limited to flies and whose skill with firearms was less murderous than suicidal. About the only thing Wilt knew about machine guns and revolvers was that bullets came out the barrel when you pulled the trigger. But if he knew nothing about the workings of firearms the terrorists clearly had no idea what had happened in the attic. For all they knew the place was filled with armed policemen and the shots he had fired so accidentally could have killed Fräulein Bloody Schautz. If that were the case they would make no attempt to rescue her. Anyway, the illusion that the flat was held by desperate men who could kill without a moment's hesitation seemed definitely worth maintaining. He was just congratulating himself when the opposite thought occurred to him. What the hell would happen if they *did* discover he was up there?

Wilt slumped into a chair and considered this frightful possibility. If the quads were downstairs . . . Oh God . . . and all it needed was that blasted Superintendent to get on the phone and ask if Mr Wilt was all right. The mere mention of his name would be enough. The moment the swine downstairs realized he was up there they would kill the children. And even if they didn't they would threaten to unless he came down, which was much the same thing. Wilt's only answer to such an ultimatum would be to threaten to kill the Schautz bitch if they touched the children. That would be no sort of threat. He was incapable of killing anyone and even if he were it wouldn't save the children. Lunatics who supposed that they were adding to the sum total of human happiness by kidnapping, torturing and killing politicians and businessmen and who, when cornered, sheltered behind women and children, wouldn't listen to reason. All they wanted was maximum publicity for their cause and the murder of the quads would guarantee they got it. And then there was the theory of terrorism. Wilt had heard Bilger expound it in the staff-room and had been sickened by it then. Now he was panic-stricken. There had to be something he could do.

Well, first he could get the rest of the guns out of the bag in the storeroom and try to find out how to use them. He got up and went through the kitchen to the cupboard door and dragged the bag down. Inside were two revolvers, an automatic, four spare magazines for the sub-machine gun, several boxes of ammunition and three hand grenades. Wilt put the collection on the table, decided he didn't like the look of the hand grenades and put them back in the bag. It was then that he spotted a scrap of paper in the side pocket of the bag. He pulled it out and saw that he was holding what purported to be a COMMUNIQUE OF THE PEOPLE'S ARMY GROUP 4. That at least was the title but the space underneath was blank. Evidently no one had bothered to fill in the details. Probably nothing to communicate.

All the same it was interesting, very interesting. If this bunch were Group 4 it suggested that Groups 1, 2 and 3 were somewhere else and that there were possibly Groups 5, 6 and 7. Even more perhaps. On the other hand there might not be. The tactics of self-aggrandizement were not lost on Wilt. It was typical of tiny minorities to claim they were part of a much larger organization. It boosted their morale and helped to confuse the authorities. Then again it was just possible that a great many other groups did exist. How many? Ten, twenty? And with this sort of cell structure, one group would not know the members of another group. That was the whole point about cells. If one was captured and questioned there was no way of betraying anyone else. And with this realization Wilt lost interest in the arsenal on the table. There were more effective weapons than guns.

Wilt took out a pen and began to write. Presently he closed the kitchen door and picked up the phone.

113

Chapter 13

Superintendent Misterson was enjoying a moment of quiet and comfortable relaxation on the mahogany seat of Mrs de Frackas' toilet when the telephone rang in the drawing-room and the sergeant came through to say that the terrorists were back on the line.

'Well, that's a good sign,' said the Superintendent, emerging hurriedly. 'They don't usually start the dialogue quite so quickly. With any luck we'll get them to listen to reason.'

But his illusions on that score were quickly dispersed. The squawk that issued from the amplifier was strange in the extreme. Even the Major's face, usually a blank mask of calculated inanity, registered bewilderment. Made weirdly falsetto by fear and guttural by the need to sound foreign, and preferably German, Wilt's voice alternately whimpered and snarled a series of extraordinary demands.

'Zis is communiqué Number Vun of ze People's Alternative Army. Ve demand ze immediate release of all comrades held illegally in British prisons vizout trial. You understand?'

'No,' said the Superintendent, 'I certainly don't.'

'Fascistic schweinfleisch,' shouted Wilt. 'Zecond, ve demand . . .'

'Now hold on,' said the Superintendent, 'we don't have any of your . . . er . . . comrades in prison. We can't possibly meet your . . .'

'Lying pigdog,' yelled Wilt, 'Günther Jong, Erica Grass, Friederich Böll, Heinrich Musil to namen eine few. All in British prisons. You release wizin funf hours. Zecond, ve demand ze immediate haltings of all false reportings on television, transistor radios und der newspapers financed by capitalistic-militarische-liberalistic-pseudo-democratische-multi-nazionalistische und finanzialistische conspirationalistische about our fightings here for freedom, ja. Dritte, ve demand ze immediate withdrawal of alles militaristic truppen aus der garden unter den linden und die strasse Villington Road.

Vierte, ve demand ze safe conduct for ze People's Alternative Army cadres and ze exposing of ze deviationist and reformist class treachery of ze C.I.A.-Zionist-nihilistische murderers naming zemselves falsely People's Army Group Four who are threatening ze lives of women and children in ze propaganda attempt to deceive ze proletarian consciousness for ze true liberationist struggle for world freedom. End of communiqué.'

The line went dead.

'What the fuck was all that about?' asked the Major.

'I'm buggered if I know,' said the Superintendent with a glazed look in his eyes. 'Something's definitely screwy. If my ears and that sod's ghastly accent didn't deceive me he seemed to think Chinanda and the Schautz crowd are CIA agents working for Israel. Isn't that what he seemed to be saying?'

'It's what he said, sir,' said the sergeant. 'People's Army Group Four are the Schautz brigade and this bloke was blasting off at them. Could be we've got a splinter group in the People's Alternative Army.'

'Could be we've got a raving nut,' said the Superintendent. 'Are you positive that little lot came from the house?'

'Can't have come from anywhere else, sir. There's only one line in and we're hooked to it.'

'Somebody's got their wires crossed if you ask me,' said the Major, 'unless the Schautz crowd have come up with something new.'

'It's certainly new for a terrorist group to demand no TV or press coverage. That's one thing I do know,' muttered the Superintendent. 'What I don't know is where the hell he got that list of prisoners we're supposed to release. To the best of my knowledge we're not holding anyone called Günther Jong.'

'Might be worth checking that out, old boy. Some of these things are kept hush-hush.'

'If it's that top secret I can't see the Home Office blurting the fact out now. Anyway, let's hear that gobbledygook again.'

But for once the sophisticated electronic equipment failed them.

'I can't think what's wrong with the recorder, sir,' said the sergeant, 'I could have sworn I had it on.'

'Probably blew a fuse when that maniac came on the line,' said the Major, 'I know I damned near did.'

115

'Well, see the bloody thing works next time,' snapped the Superintendent, 'I want to get a voiceprint of this other bunch.' He poured himself another cup of coffee and sat waiting.

If there was confusion among the Anti-Terrorist Squad and the S.G.S. following Wilt's extraordinary intervention, there was chaos in the house. On the ground floor Chinanda and Baggish had barricaded themselves into the kitchen and the front hall while the children and Mrs de Frackas had been bundled down into the cellar. The telephone in the kitchen was on the floor out of the line of fire and it had been Baggish who had picked it up and listened to the first part. Alarmed by the look on Baggish's face, Chinanda had grabbed the receiver and had heard himself described as an Israeli nihilistic murderer working for the C.I.A. in a propaganda attempt to deceive proletarian consciousness.

'It's a lie,' he shouted at Baggish who was still trying to square a demand by the People's Alternative Army for the release of comrades held in British prisons with his previous belief that the attic flat was occupied by men from the Anti-Terrorist Squad.

'How do you mean a lie?'

'What they say. That we are C.I.A.-Zionists.'

'A lie?' yelled Baggish, desperately searching for a more extreme word to describe such a gross distortion of the truth. 'It's . . . Who said that?'

'Someone saying he was the People's Alternative Army.'

'But the People's Alternative Army demanded the release of prisoners held illegally by the British imperialists.'

'They did?'

'I heard them. First they say that and then they attack the false reporting on TV and then they demand all troops to be withdrawn.'

'Then why call us C.I.A.-Zionist murderers?' demanded Chinanda. 'And where are these people?'

They looked suspiciously at the ceiling.

'They're up there, you think?' asked Baggish.

But, like the Superintendent, Chinanda didn't know what to think.

'Gudrun is up there. When we came down there was shooting.'

116

'So maybe Gudrun is dead,' said Baggish. 'Is a trick to fool us.'

'Could be,' said Chinanda, 'British intelligence is clever. They know how to use psycho-warfare.'

'So what we do now?'

'We make our own demands. We show them we are not fooled.'

'If I might just interrupt for a moment,' said Mrs de Frackas, emerging from the cellar, 'it's time I gave the quadruplets their supper.'

The two terrorists looked at her lividly. It was bad enough having the house ringed with troops and police, but when to add to their troubles they had to cope with incomprehensible demands from someone representing the People's Alternative Army and at the same time were confronted by Mrs de Frackas' imperturbable self-assurance, they felt the need to assert their superior authority.

'Listen, old woman,' said Chinanda waving an automatic under her nose for emphasis, 'we give the orders here and you do what we say. You don't we kill you.'

But Mrs de Frackas was not to be so easily deterred. Over a long lifetime in which she had been bullied by governesses, shot at by Afghans, bombed out of two houses in two World Wars and had had to face an exceedingly liverish husband across the breakfast table for several decades, she had developed a truly remarkable resilience and, more usefully, a diplomatic deafness.

'I'm sure you will,' she said cheerfully, 'and now I'll see where Mrs Wilt keeps the eggs. I always think that children can't have enough eggs, don't you? So good for the digestive system.' And ignoring the automatic she bustled about the kitchen peering into cupboards. Chinanda and Baggish conferred in undertones.

'I kill the old bitch now,' said Baggish. 'That way she learns we're not bluffing.'

'That way we don't get out of here. We keep her and the children we got a chance and we keep up the propaganda war.'

'Without TV we got no propaganda war to keep up,' said Baggish. 'That was one of the demands of People's Alternative Army. No TV, no radio, no newspapers.'

'So we demand the opposite, full publicity,' said Chinanda, and picked up the phone. Upstairs Wilt who had been lying on the floor with the telephone to his ear answered it.

'Zis is People's Alternative Army. Communiqué Two. Ve demand . . .'

'No you don't. We do the demanding,' shouted Chinanda, 'we know British psycho-warfare.'

'Zionist pigs. Ve know CIA murderers,' countered Wilt. 'Ve are fighting for ze liberation of all peoples.'

'We are fighting for the liberation of Palestine . . .'

'So are ve. All peoples ve fight for.'

'If you would kindly make up your minds who is fighting for what,' intervened the Superintendent, 'we might be able to talk more reasonably.'

'Fascist police pig,' bellowed Wilt. 'Ve no discuss viz you. Ve know who ve are dealing viz.'

'I wish to God I did,' said the Superintendent, only to be told by Chinanda that the People's Army Group was—

'Revisionistic-deviationist lumpen schwein,' interjected Wilt. 'Ze revolutionary army of ze people rejects ze fascistic holding of hostages und . . .' He was interrupted by bangs from the bathroom which tended to contradict his argument and gave Chinanda the opportunity to state his demands. They included five million pounds, a jumbo jet and the use of an armoured car to take them to the airport. Wilt, having shut the kitchen door to drown out Gudrun Schautz's activities, came back in time to up the ante.

'Six million pounds and two armoured cars . . .'

'You can make it a round ten million for all I care,' said the Superintendent, 'it won't make any difference. I'm not bargaining.'

'Seven million or we kill the hostages. You have till eight in the morning to agree or we die with the hostages,' shouted Chinanda, and slammed down the phone before Wilt could make a further bid. Wilt replaced his own receiver with a sigh and tried to think what on earth to do now. There was no doubt in his mind that the terrorists downstairs would carry out their threat unless the police gave way. And it was just as certain that the police had no intention of providing an armoured car or a jet. They would simply play for time in the hope of breaking

118

the terrorists' morale. If they didn't succeed and the children died along with their captors it would hardly matter to the authorities. Public policy dictated that terrorists' demands must never be met. In the past Wilt had agreed. But now private policy dictated anything that would save his family. To reinforce the need for some new plan, Fräulein Schautz sounded as though she was ripping up the linoleum in the bathroom. For a moment Wilt considered threatening to fire through the doorway if she didn't stop, but decided against it. It was no damned use. He was incapable of killing anyone except by accident. There had to be some other way.

In the Communications Centre ideas were in short supply too. As the echo of the last conflicting demands died away the Superintendent shook his head wearily.

'I said this was a bag of maggots and by God it is. Will someone kindly tell me what the hell is going on in there?'

'No use looking at me, old boy,' said the Major, 'I'm simply here to hold the ring while you Anti-Terrorist chappies establish rapport with the blighters. That's the drill.'

'It may be the drill but considering we seem to be dealing with two competing sets of world-changers it's fucking near impossible. Isn't there some way we can get a separate line to each group?'

'Don't see how, sir,' said the sergeant. 'The People's Alternative Army seem to be using the extension phone from upstairs and the only way would be to get into the house.'

The Major studied Wilt's clumsy map. 'I could call a chopper up and land some of my lads on the roof to take the bastards out.'

Superintendent Misterson looked at him suspiciously. 'By "take out" I don't suppose you mean literally?'

'Literally? Oh, see what you mean. No. Doubt it. Bound to be a bit of schemozzle, what!'

'Which is precisely what we've got to avoid. Now, if someone can come up with a scheme whereby I can talk to one group without being drowned out by the other I'd be grateful.'

But instead there was a buzz on the intercom. The sergeant listened and then spoke. 'The psychos and the idiot brigade on the line, sir. Want to know if it's OK to move in.'

119

'I suppose so,' said the Superintendent.

'Idiot brigade?' said the Major.

'Ideological Warfare Analysis and the Psychological Advisers. Home Office insists we use them and sometimes they come up with a sensible suggestion.'

'Christ,' said the Major. 'Damned if I know what the world is coming to. First they call the army a peace-keeping force and now Scotland Yard has to have psychoanalysts to do their sleuthing for them. Rum.'

'The People's Alternative Army are back on the line,' said the sergeant. Once more a barrage of abuse issued from the telephone amplifier but this time Wilt had changed his tactics. His guttural German had been doing things to his vocal cords and his new accent was a less demanding but equally less convincing Irish brogue.

'Bejasus it will be nobody's fault but your own if we have to shoot the poor innocent creature Irmgard Mueller herself before eight in the morning if the wee babies are not returned to their mam, look you.'

'What?' said the Superintendent baffled by this new threat.

'I wouldn't want to be repeating meself for the likes of reactionary pigs like yourself but if you're deaf I'll say it again.'

'Don't,' said the Superintendent firmly, 'We got the message first time.'

'Well I'll be hoping those Zionist spalpeens will have got the message too begorrah.'

A muffled flow of Spanish seemed to indicate that Chinanda had heard.

'Well then that'll be all. I wouldn't want to be running up too big a telephone bill now would I?' And Wilt slammed the phone down. It was left to the Superintendent to interpret this ultimatum to Chinanda as best he could, a difficult process made almost impossible by the terrorist's insistence that the People's Alternative Army was a gang of fascist police pigs under the Superintendent's command.

'We know you British use psychological warfare. You are experts,' he shouted, 'we are not to be so easily deceived.'

'But I assure you, Miguel . . .'

'Don't try bluffing me by calling me Miguel so I think you

120

are my friend. We understand your tactics. First you threaten and then you keep us talking . . .'

'Well as a matter of fact I'm not keeping . . .'

'Shut your mouth, pig. I'm doing the talking now.'

'That's all I was going to say,' protested the Superintendent. 'But I want you to know there are no police . . .'

'Bullshit. You tried to trap us and now you threaten to kill Gudrun. Right, we do not respond to your threats. You kill Gudrun, we kill the hostages.'

'I'm not in a position to stop whoever is holding Fräulein Schautz . . .'

'You keep trying the bluff but it doesn't work. We know how clever you British imperialists are.' And Chinanda too slammed the phone down.

'I must say he seems to have a rather higher opinion of the British Empire than I have,' said the Major. 'I mean I can't actually see where we've got one, unless you count Gibraltar.'

But the Superintendent was in no mood to discuss the extent of the Empire. 'There's something demented about this bloody siege,' he muttered. 'First we need to get a separate telephone link through to the lunatics in that top flat. That's number one priority. If they shoot . . . What on earth did he call the Schautz woman, sergeant?'

'I think the expression was "the poor innocent creature Irmgard Mueller", sir? Do you want me to play the tape back?'

'No,' said the Superintendent, 'we'll wait for the analysts. In the meantime request use of helicopter to drop a field telephone onto the balcony of the flat. That way we'll at least get some idea who's up there.'

'Field telephone incorporating TV camera, sir?' asked the sergeant.

The Superintendent nodded. 'Second priority is to move the listening devices into position.'

'Can't do that until it gets dark,' said the Major. 'Not having my chaps shot down unless they're allowed to shoot back.'

'Well, we'll just have to wait,' said the Superintendent. 'That's always the way with these beastly sieges. Just a question of

121

sitting and waiting. Though I must say this is the first time I've had to deal with two lots of terrorists at once.'

'Makes you feel sorry for those poor children,' said the Major. 'What they must be going through doesn't bear thinking about.'

Chapter 14

But for once his sympathy was wasted. The quads were having a wonderful time. After the initial excitement of windows being shattered by bullets and the terrorists firing from the kitchen and the front hall, they had been bundled down into the cellar with Mrs de Frackas. Since the old lady refused to be flustered and seemed to regard the events upstairs as perfectly normal, the quads had taken the same attitude. Besides the cellar was usually forbidden territory, Wilt objecting to their visiting it on the ostensible grounds that the Organic Toilet was insanitary and dangerously explosive, while Eva barred the quads because she kept her stock of preserved fruit down there and the chest freezer was filled with homemade ice cream. The quads had made a bee-line for the ice cream and had finished a large carton before Mrs de Frackas' eyes had got accustomed to the dim light. By then the quads had found other interesting things to occupy their attention. A large coal bunker and a pile of logs gave them the opportunity to get thoroughly filthy. Eva's store of organically grown apples provided them with a second course after the ice cream, and they would undoubtedly have drunk themselves into a stupor on Wilt's homebrew if Mrs de Frackas hadn't put her foot down on a broken bottle first.

'You're not to go into that part of the cellar,' she said looking severely at the evidence of Wilt's inexpert brewing in the shape of several exploded bottles. 'It isn't safe.'

'Then why does daddy drink it?' asked Penelope.

'When you get a little older you'll learn that men do a great many things that aren't very sensible or safe,' said Mrs de Frackas.

'Like wearing a bag on the end of their wigwags?' asked Josephine.

'Well I wouldn't quite know about that, dear,' said Mrs de Frackas evidently torn between curiosity and a desire not to enquire too closely into the Wilts' private life.

'Mummy said the doctor made him wear it,' continued

123

Josephine adding an unmentionable disease to the old lady's dossier of Wilt's faults.

'And I stepped on it and daddy screamed,' said Emmeline proudly. 'He screamed ever so loudly.'

'I'm sure he did, dear,' said Mrs de Frackas, trying to imagine the reaction of her late and liverish husband had any child been so unwise as to step on his penis. 'Now let's talk about something nice.'

The distinction was wasted on the quads. 'When daddy comes home from the doctor mummy says his wigwag will be better and he won't say "Fuck" when he goes weewee.'

'Say what, dear?' asked Mrs de Frackas, adjusting her hearing aid in the hope that it rather than Samantha had been at fault. The quads in unison disillusioned her.

'Fuck, fuck, fuck,' they squealed. Mrs de Frackas turned her hearing aid down.

'Well, really,' she said, 'I don't think you should use that word.'

'Mummy says we mustn't too but Michael's daddy told him . . .'

'I don't want to hear,' said Mrs de Frackas hastily. 'In my young days children didn't talk about such things.'

'How did babies get born then?' asked Penelope.

'In the usual way, dear, only we were brought up not to mention such things.'

'What things?' demanded Penelope.

Mrs de Frackas regarded her dubiously. It was beginning to dawn on her that the Wilt quads were not quite such nice children as she had supposed. In fact they were distinctly unnerving. 'Just things,' she said finally.

'Like cocks and cunts?' asked Emmeline.

Mrs de Frackas eyed her with disgust. 'You could put it like that, I suppose,' she said stiffly. 'Though frankly I'd prefer it if you didn't.'

'If you don't put it like that how do you put it?' asked the indefatigable Penelope.

Mrs de Frackas searched her mind in vain for an alternative. 'I don't quite know,' she said, surprised at her own ignorance. 'I suppose the matter never arose.'

'Daddy's does,' said Josephine, 'I saw it once.'

124

Mrs de Frackas turned her disgusted attention on the child and tried to stifle her own curiosity. 'You did?' she said involuntarily.

'He was in the bathroom with mummy and I looked through the keyhole and daddy's . . .'

'It's time you had baths too,' said Mrs de Frackas, getting to her feet before Josephine could divulge any further details of the Wilts' sexual life.

'We haven't had supper yet,' said Samantha.

'Then I'll get you some,' said Mrs de Frackas and went up the cellar steps to hunt for eggs. By the time she returned with a tray the quads were no longer hungry. They had finished a jar of pickled onions and were halfway through their second packet of dried figs.

'You've still got to have scrambled eggs,' said the old lady resolutely. 'I didn't go to the trouble of making them to have them wasted, you know.'

'You didn't make them,' said Penelope. 'Mummy hens made them.'

'And daddy hens are called cocks,' squealed Josephine but Mrs de Frackas, having just outfaced two armed bandits, was in no mood to be defied by four foul-minded girls.

'We won't discuss that any further, thank you,' she said, 'I've had quite enough.'

It was shortly apparent that the quads had too. As she shooed them up the cellar steps Emmeline was complaining that her tummy hurt.

'It will soon stop, dear,' said Mrs de Frackas, 'and it doesn't help to hiccup like that.'

'Not hiccuping,' retorted Emmeline, and promptly vomited on the kitchen floor. Mrs de Frackas looked around in the semi-darkness for the light switch and had just found it and turned it on when Chinanda cannoned into her and switched it off.

'What are you trying to do? Get us all killed?' he yelled.

'Not all of us,' said Mrs de Frackas, 'and if you don't look where you're going . . .'

A crash as the terrorist slid across the kitchen floor on a mixture of half-digested pickled onions and dried figs indicated that Chinanda hadn't.

'It's no use blaming me,' said Mrs de Frackas, 'and you shouldn't use language like that in front of children. It sets a very bad example.'

'I set an example all right,' shouted Chinanda, 'I spill your guts.'

'I rather think somebody is doing that already,' retorted the old lady as the other three quads, evidently sharing Emmeline's inability to cope with quite so eclectic a diet, followed her example. Presently the kitchen was filled with four howling and vomit-stained small girls, a very unappetizing smell, two demented terrorists and Mrs de Frackas at her most imperious. To add to the confusion Baggish had deserted his post in the front hall and had dashed in threatening to kill the first person who moved.

'I have no intention of moving,' said Mrs de Frackas, 'and since the only person who is happens to be that creature grovelling in the corner I suggest you put him out of his misery.'

From the direction of the sink Chinanda could be heard disentangling himself from Eva's Kenwood mixer which had joined him on the floor.

Mrs de Frackas turned the light on again. This time no one objected, Chinanda because he had been momentarily stunned and Baggish because he was too dismayed by the state of the kitchen.

'And now,' said the old lady, 'if you've quite finished I'll take the children up for their bath before putting them to bed.'

'Bed?' yelled Chinanda getting unsteadily to his feet. 'Nobody goes upstairs. You all sleep down in the cellar. Go down there now.'

'If you really suppose for one moment that I am going to allow these poor children to go down that cellar again in their present condition and without being thoroughly washed you're very much mistaken.'

Chinanda jerked the cord on the venetian blind and cut out the view from the garden.

'Then you wash them in here,' he said pointing to the sink.

'And where do you propose to be?'

'Where we can see what you are doing.'

Mrs de Frackas snorted derisively. 'I know your sort, and if

126

you think I am going to expose their pure little bodies to your lascivious gaze . . .'

'What the hell is she saying?' demanded Baggish.

Mrs de Frackas turned her contempt on him. 'And yours too, don't I just. I haven't been through the Suez Canal and Port Said for nothing you know.'

Baggish stared at her. 'Port Said? The Suez Canal? I never been to Egypt in my life.'

'Well I have. And I know what I know.'

'So what are we talking about? You know what you know. I don't know what you know.'

'Postcards,' said Mrs de Frackas. 'I don't think I need say any more.'

'You haven't said anything yet. First the Suez Canal, then Port Said and now postcards. Will someone tell me what the hell these things have to do with washing children?'

'Well if you must know, I mean dirty postcards. I might also mention donkeys but I won't. And now if you'll both leave the room . . .'

But the implications of Mrs de Frackas' imperial prejudices had slowly dawned on Baggish.

'You mean pornography? What century you think you're living in? You want pornography you go to London. Soho is full—'

'I don't want pornography and I don't intend to discuss the matter further.'

'Then you go down the cellar before I kill you,' yelled the enraged Baggish. But Mrs de Frackas was too old to be persuaded by mere threats and it took bodily pressure to shove her through the cellar door with the quads. As they went down the steps Emmeline could be heard asking why the nasty man didn't like donkeys.

'I tell you the English are mad,' said Baggish. 'Why did we have to choose this crazy house?'

'It chose us,' said Chinanda miserably, and switched out the light.

But if Mrs de Frackas had decided to ignore the fact that her life was in danger, upstairs in the flat Wilt was now acutely aware that his previous tactics had backfired on him. To have invented the People's Alternative Army had served to confuse things for a while, but his threat to execute, or more accurately to murder Gudrun Schautz had been a terrific mistake. It put a time limit on his bluff. Looking back over forty years Wilt's record of violence was limited to the occasional and usually unsuccessful bout with flies and mosquitoes. No, to have issued that ultimatum had been almost as stupid as not getting out of the house when the going was good. Now it was distinctly bad, and the sounds coming from the bathroom suggested that Gudrun Schautz had torn up the lino and was busy on the floorboards. If she escaped and joined the men below she would add an intellectual fervour to their evidently stupid fanaticism. On the other hand he could think of no way of stopping her short of threatening to fire through the bathroom door, and if that didn't work . . . There had to be an alternative method. What if he opened the door himself and somehow persuaded her that it wasn't safe to go downstairs? In that way he could keep the two groups separate and provided they couldn't communicate with one another Fräulein Schautz would be hard put to it to influence her blood-brothers down below. Well, that was easy enough to do.

Wilt crossed to the telephone and jerked the cord from the wall. So far so good but there was still the little matter of the guns. The notion of sharing the flat with a woman who had cold-bloodedly murdered eight people was not an attractive one in any circumstances, but when that flat contained enough firearms to eliminate several hundred it became positively suicidal. The guns would have to go too. But where? He could hardly drop the damned things out of the window. The effect of a shower of revolvers, grenades and a sub-machine gun on the terrorists was likely to encourage them to come up and find out what the hell was going on. Anyway, the grenades might go off and there were enough misunderstandings floating around already without adding exploding grenades. The best thing would be to hide them. Very gingerly Wilt put his armoury back into the flight bag and went through the kitchen to the attic space. Gudrun Schautz was now definitely busy on the floorboards and under cover of the noise Wilt climbed up and edged his way along to the water cistern. There he lowered the bag into the water before replacing the cover. Then, having checked to make quite sure that he hadn't missed a gun, he steeled himself for the next move. It was, he considered, about as safe as opening the cage of a tiger at the zoo and inviting the thing to come out, but it had to be done and in an insane situation only an act of total lunacy could save the children. Wilt went through the kitchen to the bathroom door.

'Irmgard,' he whispered. Miss Schautz went on with her work of demolishing the bathroom floor. Wilt took another deep breath and whispered more loudly. Inside work ceased and there was silence.

'Irmgard,' said Wilt, 'is that you?'

There was a movement and then a quiet voice spoke. 'Who is there?'

'It's me,' said Wilt, sticking to the obvious and wishing to hell it wasn't, 'Henry Wilt.'

'Henry Wilt?'

'Yes. They've gone.'

'Who have gone?'

'I don't know. Whoever they were. You can come out now.'

'Come out?' asked Gudrun Schautz in a tone of voice that suggested the total bewilderment Wilt wanted.

'I'll undo the door.'

Wilt began to remove the flex from the doorhandle. It was difficult in the growing darkness but after several minutes he had undone the wire and removed the chair.

'It's OK now,' he said. 'You can come out.'

But Gudrun Schautz made no move. 'How do I know it's you?' she asked.

'I don't know,' said Wilt, glad of this opportunity to delay matters, 'it just is.'

'Who is with you?'

'No one. They've gone downstairs.'

'You keep saying "They". Who are these "They"?'

'I've no idea. Men with guns. The whole house is filled with men with guns.'

'So why are you here?' asked Miss Schautz.

'Because I can't be somewhere else,' said Wilt truthfully. 'You don't think I want to be here? They've been shooting at one another. I could have been killed. I don't know what the hell's going on.'

There was a silence from the bathroom. Gudrun Schautz was having difficulty working out what was going on too. In the darkness of the kitchen Wilt smiled to himself. Keep this up and he'd have the bitch bombed out of her mind.

'And no one is with you?' she asked.

'Of course not.'

'Then how did you know I was in the bathroom?'

'I heard you having a bath,' said Wilt, 'and then all these people started shouting and shooting and . . .'

'Where were you?'

'Look,' said Wilt deciding to change his tactics, 'I don't see why you keep asking me these questions. I mean I've taken the trouble to come up here and undo the door and you won't come out and you keep on about who they are and where I was and all that as if I knew. As a matter of fact I was having a nap in the bedroom and . . .'

'A nap? What is a nap?'

'A nap? Oh, a nap. Well it's a sort of after-lunch snooze. Sleep, you know. Anyway when all the hullabaloo started, the shooting and so on, and I heard you shout "Get the children," and I thought how jolly kind of you that was . . .'

'Kind of me? You thought that kind of me?' asked Miss Schautz with a distinctly strangulated disbelief.

'I mean putting the children first instead of your own safety. Most people wouldn't have thought of saving the children, would they?'

A gurgling noise from the bathroom indicated that Gudrun Schautz hadn't thought of this interpretation of her orders and was having to make readjustments in her attitude to Wilt's intelligence.

'No, that is so,' she said finally.

'Well naturally after that I couldn't leave you locked up here, could I?' continued Wilt, realizing that talking like some idiotic chinless wonder had its advantages. 'Noblesse oblige and all that, what!'

'Noblesse oblige?'

'You know, one good turn deserves another and whatnot,' said Wilt. 'So as soon as the coast was clear I sort of came out from under the bed and hopped up here.'

'What coast?' demanded Miss Schautz suspiciously.

130

'When the blighters up here decided to go downstairs,' said Wilt. 'Seemed the safest place to be. Anyway, why don't you come out and have a chair. It must be jolly uncomfortable in there.'

Miss Schautz considered this proposition and the fact that Wilt sounded like a congenital idiot and took the risk.

'I haven't any clothes on,' she said opening the door an inch.

'Gosh,' said Wilt, 'I'm awfully sorry. Hadn't thought of that. I'll go and get you something.'

He went into the bedroom and rummaged in a cupboard and having found what felt like a raincoat in the darkness took it back.

'Here's a coat,' he said handing it through the doorway. 'Don't like to turn the bedroom light on in case those blokes downstairs see it and start pooping off again with their guns. Mind you I've locked the door and barricaded it so they'd have a job getting in.'

In the bathroom Miss Schautz put on the raincoat and cautiously came out to find Wilt pouring boiling water from the electric kettle into a teapot.

'Thought you'd like a nice cup of tea,' he said. 'Know I would.'

Behind him Gudrun Schautz tried to comprehend what had happened. From the moment she had been locked in the bathroom she had been convinced that the flat was occupied by policemen. Now it seemed whoever had been there had gone and this weak and stupid Englishman was making tea as if nothing was wrong. Wilt's admission that he had spent the afternoon cowering under the bed in the room below had been convincingly ignominious and had helped to confirm the impression she had gathered from his previous nocturnal exchanges with Frau Wilt that he was no sort of threat. On the other hand she had to find out how much he knew.

'These men with guns,' she said, 'what sort of men are they?'

'Well I wasn't really in a very good position to see them,' said Wilt, 'being under the bed and so on. Some of them were wearing boots and some weren't, if you see what I mean.'

Gudrun Schautz didn't. 'Boots?'

'Not shoes. Do you take sugar, by the way?'

'No.'

131

'Very wise,' said Wilt, 'awfully bad for the teeth. Anyway here's your cup. Oh I am sorry. Here, let me get a cloth and wipe you down.'

And in the close confines of the little kitchen Wilt groped for a cloth and presently was mopping Gudrun Schautz's coat down where he had deliberately spilt the tea.

'You can stop now,' she said as Wilt transferred the attentions of the towel from her breasts to lower areas.

'Righto, and I'll pour another cup.'

She squeezed past him into the bedroom while Wilt considered what other domestic accidents he could provoke to distract her attention. There was always sex, of course, but in the circumstances it hardly seemed likely that the bitch would be particularly interested in it and, even if she were, the notion of making love with a professional murderess would make arousal extremely difficult. Whisky droop was bad enough, terror droop was infinitely worse. Still, flattery might help, and she certainly had nice boobs. Wilt took another cup of tea through to the bedroom and found her looking out of the balcony window into the garden.

'I shouldn't go over there,' he said, 'there are more maniacs outside with Donald Duck shirts on.'

'Donald Duck shirts?'

'And guns,' said Wilt. 'If you ask me the whole bloody place has gone loony.'

'And have you no idea what is happening?'

'Well I heard somebody shouting about Israelis, but it doesn't seem likely somehow, does it? I mean what on earth would Israelis want to come swarming all over Willington Road for?'

'Oh my God,' said Gudrun Schautz. 'So what do we do?'

'Do?' said Wilt. 'I don't see there is much we can do really. Except drink our tea and make ourselves inconspicuous. It's all probably some ghastly mistake or other. I can't think what else it can be, can you?'

Gudrun Schautz could, and did, but to admit it to this idiot before she had the power to terrify him into doing what she wanted didn't seem a good idea. She headed for the kitchen and began to climb into the attic space. Wilt followed, sipping his tea. 'Of course I did try phoning the police,' he said, dropping his chin even more gormlessly.

132

Miss Schautz stopped in her tracks. 'The police? You phoned the police?'

'Couldn't actually,' said Wilt, 'some blighter had pulled the phone out of the wall. Can't think why. I mean with all that shooting going on . . .'

But Gudrun Schautz was no longer listening. She was clambering along the plank towards the luggage and Wilt could hear her rummaging among the suitcases. So long as the bitch didn't look in the water tank. To distract her attention Wilt poked his head through the door and switched off the light.

'Better not show a light,' he explained as she stumbled about in the pitch darkness cursing, 'don't want anyone to know we're up here. Best just to lie low until they go away.'

A stream of incomprehensible but evidently malevolent German greeted this suggestion, and after fruitlessly groping about for the bag for several more minutes Gudrun Schautz climbed down into the kitchen, breathing heavily.

Wilt decided to strike again. 'No need to be so upset, my dear. After all, this is England and nothing nasty can happen to you here.'

He placed a comforting arm round her shoulders. 'And anyway you've got me to look after you. Nothing to worry about.'

'Oh my God,' she said and suddenly began to shake with silent laughter. The thought that she had only this weak and stupid little coward to look after her was too much for the murderess. Nothing to worry about! The phrase suddenly took on a new and horribly inverted meaning and like a revelation she saw its truth, a truth she had been fighting against all her life. The only thing she had to worry about was nothing. Gudrun Schautz looked into oblivion, an infinity of nothingness and was filled with terror. With a desperate need to escape the vision she clung to Wilt and her raincoat hung open.

'I say . . .' Wilt began, realizing this new threat but Gudrun Schautz's mouth closed over his, her tongue flickering, while her hand dragged his fingers up to a breast. The creature who had brought only death into the world was now turning in her panic to the most ancient instinct of all.

133

Chapter 15

Gudrun Schautz was not the only person in Ipford to look oblivion in the face. The manager of Wilt's bank had spent an exceedingly disturbing afternoon with Inspector Flint who kept assuring him that it was of national importance that he shouldn't phone his wife to cancel their dinner engagement and refusing to allow him to communicate with his staff and several clients who had made appointments to see him. The manager had found these aspersions on his discretion insulting and Flint's presence positively lethal to his reputation for financial probity.

'What the hell do you imagine the staff are thinking with three damned policemen closeted in my office all day?' he demanded, dropping the diplomatic language of banking for more earthy forms of address. He had been particularly put out by having to choose between urinating in a bucket procured from the care-taker or suffer the indignity of being accompanied by a police-man every time he went to the toilet.

'If a man can't pee in his own bank without having some bloody gendarme breathing down his neck all I can say is that things have come to a pretty pass.'

'Very aptly put, sir,' said Flint, 'but I'm only acting under orders and if the Anti-Terrorist Squad say a thing's in the national interest then it is.'

'I can't see how it's in the national interest to stop me relieving myself in private,' said the manager. 'I shall see that a complaint goes to the Home Office.'

'You do that small thing,' said Flint, who had his own reasons for feeling disgruntled. The intrusion of the Anti-Terrorist Squad into his patch had undermined his authority. The fact that Wilt was responsible only maddened him still further and he was just speculating on Wilt's capacity for disrupting his life when the phone rang.

'I'll take it if you don't mind,' he said and lifted the receiver.

'Mr Fildroyd of Central Investment on the line, sir,' said the telephonist.

Flint looked at the bank manager. 'Some bloke called Fildroyd. Know anyone of that name?'

'Fildroyd? Of course I do.'

'Is he to be trusted?'

'Good Lord, man, Fildroyd to be trusted? He's in charge of the entire bank's investment policy.'

'Stocks and shares, eh?' asked Flint who had once had a little flutter in Australian bauxite and wasn't likely to forget the experience. 'In that case I wouldn't trust him further than I could throw him.'

He relayed this opinion in only slightly less offensive terms to the girl on the switchboard. A distant rumble suggested that Mr Fildroyd was on the line.

'Mr Fildroyd wants to know who's speaking,' said the girl.

'Well you just tell Mr Fildroyd that it's Inspector Flint of the Fenland Constabulary and if he knows what's good for him he'll keep his trap shut.'

He put the phone down and turned to the manager who was looking distinctly seedy. 'What's the matter with you?' Flint asked.

'Matter? Nothing, nothing at all. Only that you've just led the entire Central Investment Division to suppose I'm suspected of some serious crime.'

'Landing me with Mr Henry Wilt is a serious crime,' said Flint bitterly, 'and if you want my opinion this whole thing's a put-up job on Wilt's part to get himself another slice of publicity.'

'As I understood it Mr Wilt was the innocent victim of—'

'Innocent victim my foot. The day that sod's innocent I'll stop being a copper and take holy fucking orders.'

'Charming way of expressing yourself, I must say,' said the bank manager.

But Flint was too engrossed in a private line of speculation to note the sarcasm. He was recalling those hideous days and nights during which he and Wilt had been engaged in a dialogue on the subject of Mrs Wilt's disappearance. There were still dark hours before dawn when Flint would wake sweating at the memory of Wilt's extraordinary behaviour and swearing that one day he would catch the little sod out in a serious crime. And today had seemed the ideal opportunity, or would have done if the Anti-Terrorist Squad hadn't intervened. Well, at least they were having to cope with the situation but if Flint had had his way he would have discounted all that talk about German au pairs as so much hogwash and remanded Wilt in custody on a charge of being in possession of stolen money, never mind where he said he had got it from.

But when at five he left the bank and returned to the police station it was to discover that Wilt's account seemed yet again to correspond, however implausibly, with the facts.

'A siege?' he said to the desk sergeant. 'A siege at Willington Road? At Wilt's house?'

'Proof of the pudding's in there, sir,' said the sergeant indicating an office. Flint crossed to the window and glanced in.

Like some monolith to maternity Eva Wilt sat motionless on a chair staring into space, her mind evidently absent and with her children in the house in Willington Road. Flint turned away and for the umpteenth time wondered what it was about this woman and her apparently insignificant husband that had brought them together and by some strange fusion of incompatibility had turned them into a catalyst for disaster. It was a recurring enigma, this marriage between a woman whom Wilt had once described as a centrifugal force and a man whose imagination fostered bestial fantasies involving murder, rape, and those bizarre dreams that had come to light during the hours of his interrogation. Since Flint's own marriage was as conventionally happy as he could wish, the Wilts' was less a marriage in his eyes than some rather sinister symbiotic arrangement of almost vegetable origin, like mistletoe growing on an oak tree. There was certainly a vegetable-looking quality about Mrs Wilt sitting there in silence in the office and Inspector Flint shook his head sadly.

'Poor woman's in shock,' he said, and hurried away to discover for himself what was actually happening at Willington Road.

But as usual his diagnosis was wrong. Eva was not in a state of shock. She had long since realized that it was pointless telling the policewomen who were sitting with her that she wanted to go home, and now her mind was calmly and rather menacingly working on practical things. Out there in the gathering darkness her children were at the mercy of murderers and Henry was probably dead. Nothing was going to stop her from joining the quads and saving them. Beyond that goal she had not looked, but a brooding violence seeped through her.

'Perhaps you would like some friend to come and sit with you,' one of the policewomen suggested. 'Or we could come with you to a friend's house.'

But Eva shook her head. She didn't want sympathy. She had her own reserves of strength to cope with her misery. In the end a social worker arrived from the welfare hostel.

'We've got a nice warm room for you,' she said with an extruded cheerfulness that had served in the past to irritate a number of battered wives, 'and you needn't worry about nighties and toothbrushes and things like that. Everything you want will be provided for you.'

'It won't,' thought Eva but she thanked the policewomen and followed the social worker out to her car and sat docilely beside her as they drove away. And all the time the woman chattered on, asking questions about the quads and how old they were and saying how difficult it must be bringing up four girls at the same time as if the continually repeated assumption that nothing extraordinary had happened would somehow re-create the happy, humdrum world Eva had seen disintegrate round her that afternoon. Eva hardly heard her. The trite words were so grotesquely at odds with the instincts moving within her that they merely added anger to her terrible resolve. No silly woman who didn't have children could know what it meant to have them threatened and she wasn't going to be lulled into a passive acceptance of the situation.

At the corner of Dill Road and Persimmon Street she caught sight of a billboard outside a newsagent's shop. TERRORIST SIEGE LATEST.

'I want a newspaper,' said Eva abruptly and the woman pulled to the kerb.

'It won't tell you anything you don't know already,' she said.

'I know that. I just want to see what they're saying,' said Eva and opened the door of the car. But the woman stopped her.

'You just sit here and I'll get one for you. Would you like a magazine too?'

'Just the paper.'

And with the sad thought that even in terrible tragedies some people found solace by seeing their names in print the social worker crossed the pavement to the shop and went in. Three minutes later she came out and had opened the car door before she realized that the seat beside her was empty. Eva Wilt had disappeared into the night.

By the time Inspector Flint had made his way past the road blocks in Farringdon Avenue and with the help of an S.G.S. man had clambered across several gardens to the Communications Centre he had begun to have doubts about his theory that the whole business was yet another hoax on Wilt's part. If it was it had gone too far this time. The armoured car in the road and the spotlights that had been set up round Number 9 indicated how seriously the Anti-Terrorist Squad and Special Ground Services were taking the siege. In the conservatory at the back of Mrs de Frackas' house men were assembling strange looking equipment.

'Parabolic listening devices. P.L.D.s for short,' explained a technician. 'Once we've installed them we'll be able to hear a cockroach fart in any room in the house.'

'Really? I had no idea cockroaches farted,' said Flint. 'One lives and learns.'

'We'll learn what those bastards are saying and just where they are.'

Flint went through the conservatory into the drawing-room and found the Superintendent and the Major listening to the adviser on International Terrorist Ideology who was discussing the tapes.

'If you want my opinion,' said Professor Maerlis gratuitously, 'I would have to say that the People's Alternative Army represents a sub-faction or splinter group of the original cadre known as the People's Army Group. I think I would go so far.'

Flint took a seat in a corner and was pleased to note that the Superintendent and Major seemed to share his bewilderment.

'Are you saying that they're actually part of the same group?' asked the Superintendent.

'Specifically, no,' said the Professor. 'I can only surmise from the inherent contradictions expressed in their communiqués that there is a strong difference of opinion as to the tactical approach

138

while at the same time the two groups share the same underlying ideological assumptions. Owing, however, to the molecular structure of terrorist organizations the actual identification of a member of one group by another member of another group or sub-faction of the same group remains extremely problematical.'

'The whole fucking situation is extremely problematical, come to that,' said the Superintendent. 'So far we've had two communiqués from what sounds like a partially castrated German, one from an asthmatic Irishman, demands from a Mexican for a jumbo jet and six million quid, a counter-demand from the Kraut for seven million, not to mention a stream of abuse from an Arab and everyone accusing everyone else of being a CIA agent working for Israel and who's fighting for whose freedom.'

'Beats me how they can begin to talk about freedom when they're holding innocent children and an old lady hostage and threatening to kill them,' said the Major.

'There I must disagree with you,' said the Professor. 'In terms of Neo-Hegelian post-Marxist political philosophy the freedom of the individual can only reside within the parameters of a collectively free society. The People's Army Groups regard themselves as in the forefront of total freedom and equality and as such are not bound to observe the moral norms which restrict the actions of lackeys of imperialist, fascist and neo-colonialist oppression.'

'Listen, old boy,' said the Major angrily removing his Afro wig, 'just whose side are you on anyway?'

'I am merely stating the theory. If you want a more precise analysis . . .' began the Professor nervously, only to be interrupted by the Head of the Psychological Warfare team who had been working on the voiceprints.

'From our analysis of the stress factors revealed in these tape recordings we are of the opinion that the group holding Fräulein Schautz are emotionally more disturbed than the two other terrorists,' he announced, 'and frankly I think we should concentrate on reducing their anxiety level.'

'Are you saying the Schautz woman is likely to be shot?' asked the Superintendent.

The Psychologist nodded. 'It's rather baffling actually. We've hit something rather odd with that lot, a variation from the normal pattern of speech reactions and I must admit I think she's the one who's most likely to get it in the neck.'

'No skin off my nose if she does,' said the Major, 'she's had it coming to her.'

'There'll be skin off everyone's nose if that happens,' said the Superintendent. 'My instructions are to keep this thing cool and if they start killing their hostages all hell will be let loose.'

'Yes,' said the Professor, 'a very interesting dialectical situation. You must understand that the theory of terrorism as a progressive force in world history demands the exacerbation of class warfare and the polarizing of political opinion. Now in terms of simple effectiveness we must say that the advantage lies with People's Army Group Four and not with the People's Alternative Army.'

'Say that again,' said the Major.

The Professor obliged. 'Put quite simply it is politically better to kill these children than eliminate Fräulein Schautz.'

'That may be your opinion,' said the Major, his fingers twitching on the butt of his revolver, 'but if you know what's good for you you won't express it round here again.'

'I was talking only in terms of political polarization,' said the Professor nervously. 'Only a very small minority will be perturbed if Fräulein Schautz dies but the effect of liquidating four small children, and coterminously conceived female siblings at that, would be considerable.'

'Thank you, Professor,' said the Superintendent hastily. And before the Major could decipher this sinister pronouncement he had ushered the adviser on Terrorist Ideologies out of the room.

'It's blasted eggheads like him who've ruined this country,' said the Major. 'To hear him talk you'd think there were two sides to every damned question.'

'Which is exactly the opposite of what we're getting on the voiceprints,' said the psychologist. 'Our analysis seems to indicate that there's only one spokesman for the People's Alternative Army.'

'One man?' said the Superintendent incredulously. 'Didn't sound like one man to me. More like half-a-dozen insane ventriloquists.'

'Precisely. Which is why we think you should try to lower

140

the anxiety level of that group. We may well be dealing with a split personality. I'll play the tapes again and perhaps you'll see what I mean.'

'Must you? Oh well . . .'

But the sergeant had switched the recorder on and once again the cluttered drawing-room echoed to guttural snarls and whimpers of Wilt's communiqués. In a dark corner Inspector Flint who had been on the point of dozing off suddenly sprang to his feet.

'I knew it,' he shouted triumphantly, 'I knew it. I just knew it had to be and by God it is!'

'Had to be what?' asked the Superintendent.

'Henry Fucking Wilt who was behind this foul-up. And there's the proof on those tapes.'

'Are you sure, Inspector?'

'I'm more than that. I'm positive. I'd know that little sod's voice if he imitated an Eskimo in labour.'

'I don't think we have to go that far,' said the psychological adviser. 'Are you telling us you know the man we've just heard?'

'Know him?' said Flint. 'Of course I know the bastard. I ought to after what he did for me. And now he's having you lot on.'

'I must say I find it hard to believe,' said the Superintendent. 'A more inoffensive little man you couldn't wish to meet.'

'I could,' said Flint with feeling.

'But he had to be drugged up to the eyeballs before we could get him to go back in,' said the Major.

'Drugged? What with?' said the psychologist.

'No idea. Some little concoction our medic brews up for blighters with a streak of yellow. Works wonders with the bomb-disposal chappies.'

'Well it wouldn't appear to have worked quite so well in this case,' said the psychologist nervously, 'but it certainly accounts for the remarkable readings we've been getting. We could well have a case of chemically induced schizophrenia on our hands.'

'I wouldn't bother too much about the "chemically induced" if I were you,' said Flint. 'Wilt's a nutter anyway. I'll give a hundred to one he set this thing up from the start.'

'You can't seriously be suggesting that Mr Wilt deliberately went out of his way to put his own children in the hands of a bunch of international terrorists,' said the Superintendent. 'When I discussed the matter with him he seemed genuinely astonished and disturbed.'

'What Wilt seems and what Wilt is are two entirely separate things. I can tell you this much though. Any man who can dress an inflatable doll up in his wife's clothes and ditch the thing at the bottom of a pile hole under thirty tons of quick-set concrete isn't—'

'Excuse me, sir,' interrupted the sergeant, 'message just come through from the station that Mrs Wilt has flown the coop.'

The four men looked at him in despair.

'She's what?' said the Superintendent.

'Escaped from custody, sir. Nobody seems to know where she is.'

'It fits,' said Flint, 'it fits and no mistake.'

'Fits? What fits for Chrissake?' asked the Superintendent, who was beginning to feel distinctly peculiar himself.

'The pattern, sir. Next thing we'll hear is that she was last seen on a motor cruiser going down the river, only she won't be.'

The Superintendent stared at him dementedly. 'And you call that a pattern? Oh my God.'

'Well, it's the sort of the thing Wilt would come up with, believe me. That little bugger can think up more ways of taking a perfectly sane and sensible situation and turning it into a raving nightmare than any villain I've ever met.'

'But there's got to be some motive for his actions.'

Flint laughed abruptly. 'Motive? With Henry Wilt? Not on your life. You can think of a thousand good motives, ten thousand if you like, for what he does but at the end of the day he'll come up with the one explanation you never even dreamt of. Wilt's the nearest thing to Ernie you could wish to meet.'

'Ernie?' said the Superintendent. 'Who the hell is Ernie?'

'That ruddy computer they use for the premium bonds, sir. You know, the one that picks numbers out at random. Well, Wilt's a random man, if you know what I mean.'

'I don't think I want to,' said the Superintendent. 'I thought all I had to cope with was a nice simple ordinary siege, instead of which this thing is developing into a madhouse.'

'While we're on that subject,' said the psychologist, 'I really do think it's very important to resume communications with the people in the top flat. Whoever is up there and holding the Schautz woman is in a highly disturbed state. She could be in grave danger.'

'No "could" about it,' said Flint. 'Is.'

'All right. I suppose we'll have to risk it,' said the Superintendent. 'Give the go-ahead for the helicopter to move in with a field telephone, sergeant.'

'Any orders regarding Mrs Wilt, sir?'

'You'd better ask the Inspector here. He seems to be the expert on the Wilt family. What sort of woman is Mrs Wilt? And don't say she's a random one.'

'I wouldn't really like to say,' said Flint, 'except that she's a very powerful woman.'

'What do you think she plans to do then? She obviously didn't leave the police station without some aim in mind.'

'Well, knowing Wilt as well as I do, sir, I have to admit I've grave doubts about her having a mind at all. Any normal woman would have been in a nut-house years ago living with a man like that.'

'You're not suggesting she's some sort of psychopath as well?'

'No, sir,' said Flint, 'all I'm saying is that she can't have any nerves worth speaking about.'

'That's a big help. So we've got a bunch of terrorists armed to the teeth, some sort of nutter in the shape of Wilt and a woman on the loose with a hide like a rhino. Put that little lot together and we've got ourselves one hell of a combination. All right, sergeant, put out an alert for Mrs Wilt and see that they take her into custody before anyone else gets hurt.'

The Superintendent crossed to the window and looked at the Wilts' house. Under the glare of the floodlights it stood out against the night sky like a monument erected to commemorate the stolidity and unswerving devotion to boredom of English middle-class life. Even the Major was moved to comment.

'Sort of suburban son-et-lumière, what?' he murmured.

'Lumière perhaps,' said the Superintendent, 'but at least we're spared the son.'

But not for long. From somewhere seemingly close at hand there came a series of terrible wails. The Wilt quads were giving tongue.

143

Chapter 16

A mile away Eva Wilt moved towards her home with a fixed resolve that was wholly at variance with her appearance. The few people who noticed her as she bustled down narrow streets saw only an ordinary housewife in a hurry to fix her husband's supper and put the children to bed. But beneath her homely look Eva Wilt had changed. She had shed her cheerful silliness and her borrowed opinions and had only one thought in mind. She was going home and no one was going to stop her. What she would do when she got there she had no idea, and in a vague way she was aware that home was not simply a place. It was also what she was, the wife of Henry Wilt and mother of the quads, a working woman descended from a line of working women who had scrubbed floors, cooked meals and held families together in spite of illnesses and deaths and the vagaries of men. It wasn't a clearly defined thought but it was there driving her forward almost by instinct. But with instinct there came thought.

They would be waiting for her in Farringdon Avenue so she would avoid it. Instead she would cross the river by the iron footbridge and go round by Barnaby Road and then across the fields where she had taken the children blackberrying only two months ago and enter the garden at the back. And then? She would have to wait and see. If there was any way of entering the house and joining the children she would take it. And if the terrorists killed her it was better than losing the quads. The main thing was that she would be there to protect them. Beneath this uncertain logic there was rage. Like her thoughts it was vague and diffuse and focused as much on the police as on the terrorists. If anything she blamed the police more. To her the terrorists were criminals and murderers and the police were there to save the public from such people. That was their job, and they hadn't done it properly. Instead they had allowed her children to be taken hostage and were now playing a sort of game in which the quads were merely pieces. It was

144

a simple view but Eva's mind saw things simply and straight-forwardly. Well, if the police wouldn't act she would.

It was only when she reached the footbridge over the river that she saw the full magnitude of the problem facing her. Half a mile away the house in Willington Road stood in an aura of white light. Around it the street lamps glimmered dimly and the other houses were black shadows. For a moment she paused, gripping the handrail and wondering what to do, but there was no point in hesitating. She had to go on. She went down the iron steps and along Barnaby Road until she came to the footpath across the field. She went through and followed it until she reached the muddy patch by the next gate. A group of bullocks stirred in the darkness near her but Eva had no fear of cattle. They were part of the natural world to which she felt she properly belonged.

But on the far side of the gate everything was unnatural. Against the sinister white glare of the floodlights she could see men with guns and when she had climbed the gate she stooped down and spotted the coils of barbed wire. They ran right across the field from Farringdon Avenue. Willington Road had been sealed off. Again instinct provoked cunning. There was a ditch to her left and if she made her way along it . . . But there would be a man there to stop her. She needed something to divert his attention. The bullocks would do. Eva opened the gate and then trudging through the mud shooed the beasts into the next field before closing the gate again. She shooed them still further and the bullocks scattered and were presently moving slowly forward in their usual inquisitive way. Eva scrambled down into the ditch and began to wade along it. It was a muddy ditch, half filled with water and as she went weeds gathered round her knees and the occasional bramble scratched her face. Twice she put her hand into clumps of stinging-nettles but Eva hardly felt them. Her mind was too occupied with other problems. Mainly the lights. They glared at the house with a brilliance that made it seem unreal and almost like looking at a photographic negative where all the tones were reversed and windows which should have shone with light were black squares against a lighter background. And all the time from somewhere across the field there came the incessant beat of an engine. Eva peered over the edge of the ditch and made

145

out the dark shape of a generator. She knew what it was because John Nye had once explained how electricity was made when he had been trying to persuade her to install a Savonius rotor which ran off windpower. So that was how they were lighting the house. Not that it helped her. The generator was out in the middle of the field and she couldn't possibly reach it. Anyway, the bullocks were proving a useful distraction. They had gathered in a group round one of the armed men and he was trying to get rid of them. Eva went back into the ditch and stumbling along came to the barbed wire.

As she had expected it coiled down into the water and it was only by reaching down the full length of her arm that she could find the bottom strand. She pulled it up and then stooping down so that she was almost submerged managed to wriggle her way underneath. By the time she reached the hedge that ran along the backs of all the gardens she was soaked to the skin and her hands and legs were covered with mud, but the cold didn't affect her. Nothing mattered except the fear that she would be stopped before she reached the house. And there were bound to be more armed men in the garden.

Eva stood knee-deep in the mud and waited and watched. Noises came to her out of the night. There was certainly some-one in Mrs Haslop's garden. The smell of cigarette smoke told her so but her main attention was fixed on her own back garden and the lights that blazed her home into a fearful isolation. A man moved from the back of the summerhouse and crossed to the gate into the field. Eva watched him stroll away towards the generator. And still she waited with the cunning that sprang from some deep instinct. Another man moved behind the summerhouse, a match flared in the darkness as he lit a cigarette, and Eva, like some primeval amphibian, climbed slowly from the ditch and on her hands and knees crawled forward along the hedge. All the time her eyes were fixed on the glowing tip of the cigarette. By the time she reached the gate she could see the man's face each time he took a deep puff, and the gate was open. It swung slightly in the breeze, never quite shutting. Eva began to crawl through it when her knee touched something cylindrical and slippery. She felt down with a hand and found a thick plastic-coated cable. It ran through the gateway to the three floodlights stationed on the

146

lawn. All she had to do was cut it and the lights would go off. And there were secateurs in the greenhouse. But if she used them she might electrocute herself. Better to take the axe with the long handle and that was by the woodpile on the far side of the summerhouse. If only the man with the cigarette would go she could reach it in no time. But what would make him move? If she threw a stone at the greenhouse he would certainly investigate.

Eva felt around on the path and had just found a piece of flint when the need for throwing it ended. A loud chattering noise was coming from behind her and turning her head she could make out the shape of a helicopter coming low over the field. And the man had moved. He was on his feet and had walked round the summerhouse so that his back was towards her. Eva crawled through the gate, got to her feet and ran for the woodpile. On the other side of the summerhouse the man didn't hear her. The helicopter was nearer now and its rotors drowned her movements. Already Eva had the axe and had returned to the cable and as the helicopter passed overhead she swung the axe down. A moment later the house had disappeared and the night had become intensely dark. She stumbled forward, trampled across the herb garden and reached the lawn before she realized that she seemed to be in the middle of a tornado. Above her the helicopter blades thrashed the air, the machine veered sideways, something swung past her head and a moment later there came the sound of breaking glass. Mrs de Frackas' conservatory was being demolished. Eva stopped in her tracks and threw herself flat on the lawn. From inside the house there came the rattle of automatic fire, and bullets riddled the summerhouse. She was in the middle of some awful battle and everything had suddenly gone horribly wrong.

In Mrs de Frackas' conservatory Superintendent Misterson had been watching the helicopter moving in towards the balcony window with the field telephone dangling beneath it, when the world had suddenly vanished. After the brilliance of the floodlights he could see nothing but he could still feel and hear and before he could grope his way back into the drawing-room he both felt and heard. He certainly felt the field telephone on the side of his head and he vaguely heard the sound of breaking glass. A second later he was on the tiled floor and the whole damned place seemed to be cascading glass, potted geraniums, *begonia semperflorens* and soilless compost. It was the latter that prevented him from expressing his true feelings.

'You bleeding maniac . . .' he began before choking in the dust storm. The Superintendent rolled onto his side and tried to avoid the debris but things were still falling from the shelves and Mrs de Frackas' treasured Cathedral Bell plant had detached itself from the wall and had draped him with tendrils. Finally as he tried to fight his way out of this home-grown jungle a large Camellia 'Donation' in a heavy clay pot toppled from its pedestal and put an end to his misery. The Head of the Anti-Terrorist Squad lay comfortably unconscious on the tiles and made no comment.

But in the Communications Centre comments flew thick and fast. The Major yelled orders to the helicopter pilot while two operators wearing headphones were clutching their ears and screaming that some fucking lunatic was bouncing on the parabolic listening devices. Only Flint remained cool and comparatively detached. Ever since he had first learnt that Wilt was involved in the case he had known that something appalling was bound to happen. In Flint's mind the name Wilt spelt chaos, a sort of cosmic doom against which there was no protection, except possibly prayer, and now that catastrophe had struck he was secretly pleased. It proved his premonition right and the Superintendent's optimism entirely wrong. And so while the Major ordered the helicopter pilot to get the hell out, Flint picked his way through the rubble in the conservatory and disentangled his unconscious superior from the foliage.

'Better call an ambulance,' he told the Major as he dragged the injured man into the Communications Centre, 'the Super looks as if he's bought it.'

The Major was too busy to be concerned. 'That's your business, Inspector,' he said. 'I've got to see those swine don't get away.'

'Sounds as though they're still in the house,' said Flint as the sporadic firing continued from Number 9, but the Major shook his head.

148

'Doubt it. Could have left a suicide squad to cover their retreat, or rigged up a machine gun with a timing device to fire at intervals. Can't trust the buggers an inch.'

Flint radioed for medical help and ordered two constables to carry the Superintendent through the neighbouring gardens to Farringdon Avenue, a process that was impeded by the S.G.S. men searching for escaping terrorists. It was half an hour before silence descended on Willington Road and the listening devices had confirmed that there was still human presence in the house.

There was also apparently something vertebrate lying on the Wilts' lawn. Flint, returning from the ambulance, found the Major grasping a revolver and preparing to make a sortie.

'Got one of the bastards by the sound of things,' he said as a massive heartbeat issued from an amplifier linked to a listening device. 'Going out to bring him in. Probably wounded in the cross-fire.'

He dashed out into the darkness and a few minutes later there was a yell, the sound of a violent struggle involving an extremely vigorous object and sections of the fence between the two gardens. Flint switched the amplifier off. Now that the massive heartbeat had gone there were other even more disturbing sounds coming from the machine. But what was finally dragged through the shattered conservatory was worst of all. Never the most attractive of women in Flint's eyes, Eva Wilt daubed in mud, weeds and soaked to the skin which showed through her torn dress in several places, now presented a positively prehistoric appearance. She was still struggling as the six S.G.S. men bundled her into the room. The Major followed with a black eye.

'Well at least we've got one of the swine,' he said.

'I'm not one of the swine,' shouted Eva, 'I'm Mrs Wilt. You've no right to treat me like this.'

Inspector Flint retreated behind a chair. 'It's certainly Mrs Wilt,' he said. 'Mind telling us what you were trying to do?'

From the carpet Eva regarded him with loathing.

'I was trying to join my children. I've got a right to.'

'I've heard that one before,' said Flint. 'You and your rights. I suppose Henry put you up to this?'

'He did nothing of the sort. I don't even know what's

149

happened to him. For all I know he's dead.' And she promptly burst into tears.

'All right, you can let her go now, chaps,' said the Major at last convinced that his captive was not one of the terrorists. 'You could have got yourself killed, you know.'

Eva ignored him and got to her feet. 'Inspector Flint, you're a father yourself. You must know what it means to be separated from your loved ones in their hour of need.'

'Yes, well . . .' said the Inspector awkwardly. Weeping Neanderthal women aroused mixed emotions in him and in any case his particular loved ones were two teenage louts with an embarrassing taste for vandalism. He was grateful for an interruption from one of the technicians in charge of the listening devices.

'Getting something peculiar, Inspector,' he said. 'Want to hear it?'

Flint nodded. Anything was better than appeals for sympathy from Eva Wilt. It wasn't. The technician switched the amplifier on.

'That's coming from Boom Number 4,' he explained as a series of grunts, groans, ecstatic cries and the insistent creaking of bedsprings issued from the loudspeaker.

'Boom Number 4? That's not a boom, that's a . . .'

'Sounds like a fucking sex maniac, begging the lady's pardon,' said the Major. But Eva was listening too intently to care.

'Where's it coming from?'

'Attic flat, sir. The one where you-know-who is.'

But the subterfuge was wasted on Eva. 'Yes, I do,' she shrieked, 'that's my Henry. I'd know that moan anywhere.'

A dozen disgusted eyes turned on her but Eva was unabashed. After all she had been through in so short a time this new revelation destroyed the last vestiges of her social discretion.

'He's making love to some other woman. Just wait till I lay my hands on him,' she screamed in fury and would have dashed out into the night again if she hadn't been seized.

'Handcuff the bitch,' shouted the Inspector, 'and take her back to the station and see she doesn't get out again. I want maximum security this time and I don't mean maybe.'

'Doesn't sound as if her husband does either, come to that,' said the Major as Eva was dragged off and the unequivocal evidence of Wilt's first affair continued to pulsate through the Communications Centre. Flint emerged from behind the chair and sat down.

'Well at least she's proved me right. I said the little bastard was in this thing up to his eyeballs.'

The Major shuddered. 'I can think of pleasanter ways of putting it, but it rather sounds as if you're right.'

'Of course I am,' said Flint smugly. 'I know friend Wilt's little tricks.'

'I'm glad I don't,' said the Major. 'If you ask me we ought to get the psycho to analyse this little lot.'

'It's all going down on the tape, sir,' said the radio man.

'In that case turn that filthy din off,' said Flint. 'I've got enough on my hands without having to listen to Wilt having it off.'

'Couldn't agree more,' said the Major, struck by the accuracy of the term, 'the fellow must have nerves of steel. Dashed if I could get it up in the circumstances.'

'You'd be surprised what that little bugger can get up to in any circumstances,' said Flint, 'and married to that maternal mastodon of his, is it any wonder? I'd just as soon go to bed with a giant clam as climb in with Eva Wilt.'

'I suppose there's something in that,' said the Major fingering his black eye cautiously. 'She certainly packs one hell of a punch. Can't stay around. Got to go and get those floodlights going again.'

He wandered out and Flint sat on wondering what to do. Now that the Superintendent was out of action he supposed he must be in charge of the case. It was not a promotion he wanted. About the only consolation he could find was the thought that Henry Wilt was about to get his final come-uppance.

In fact Wilt was concentrating his mind on just the opposite. The state of his manhood, so recently repaired, demanded it. Besides, adultery was not his forte and he had never found the process of making love when he didn't feel up to it at all appealing. And since when he felt like it Eva usually didn't, reserving her moments of passion until the quads were safely asleep and Wilt would have been given half a chance, he had become accustomed to a sort of split sexuality in which he did

151

one thing while thinking about another. Not that Eva was satisfied with one thing. Her interest, while more single-minded than his, was infinitely eclectic in matters of procedure and Wilt had learnt to accept being bent, crushed, twisted and generally contorted along lines suggested by the manuals Eva consulted. They had titles like *How to Keep your Marriage Young* or *Making Love the Natural Way*. Wilt had objected that their marriage wasn't young and that there was nothing natural about risking strangulated hernia by using the coitus position advocated by Dr Eugene van Yonk. Not that his arguments ever did any good. Eva replied by making unpleasant references to his adolescence and unwarranted accusations about what he did in the bathroom when she wasn't there and in the end he had been driven to prove his normality by doing what he considered thoroughly abnormal. But if Eva had been vigorously experimental in bed Gudrun Schautz was a demented carnivore.

From the moment in the kitchen when she had first latched onto him in a frenzy of blatant lust, Wilt had been bitten, scratched, licked, chewed and sucked with a violence and lack of discrimination that was frankly insulting, not to say dangerous, and which had led him to wonder why the bitch bothered to shoot people when she could just as easily have done them to death in more lawful and decidedly nastier ways. Anyway, nobody in his right mind could sensibly accuse him of being an unfaithful husband. If anything, quite the opposite; only the most dutiful and conscientious family man would have put himself so much at risk as to get voluntarily into bed with a wanted murderess. Wilt found the adjective singularly inappropriate and it was only by concentrating his imagination on Eva when he had first met her that he could evoke a modicum of desire. It was this flaccid response that provoked Gudrun Schautz. The bitch was not only a murderess; she managed to combine political terror with the expectation that Wilt was a male chauvinist pig who would launch himself into her without a second thought.

Wilt's views on the matter were different. It was one of the tenets of his confused philosophy that you didn't mess about with other women once you were married. And bouncing up and down on an extremely nubile young woman undoubtedly came into the category of messing about. On the other hand

152

there was the interesting paradox that he was spiritually closer to Eva now than when he was actually making love to her and thinking about something else. More practically there wasn't a hope in hell of having an orgasm. The catheter had put paid to that for the time being. He could bounce away until the cows came home, but he was no more going to put his penis to the test of a genuine erection than fly. To prevent this dreadful possibility he alternated his vision of a youthful Eva with images of himself and the execrable Schautz lying on the autopsy table in a terminal coitus interruptus. Considering the din they were making it seemed all too likely and it was certainly a most effective anti-aphrodisiac. Besides, it had the additional advantage of confusing the Schautz woman. She was evidently accustomed to more committed lovers and Wilt's erratic fervour threw her.

'You like it some other way, Liebling?' she asked as Wilt receded for the umpteenth time.

'In the bath,' said Wilt who had suddenly become conscious that the terrorists below might decide to take a hand and that baths were more bulletproof than beds. Gudrun Schautz laughed. 'So funny, ja. In the bath!'

At that moment the floodlights went out and the roar of the helicopter could be heard. The noise seemed to spur her to a new frenzy of lust.

'Quick, quick,' she moaned, 'they're coming.'

'Buggered if I am,' muttered Wilt but the murderess was too busy trying to exorcise oblivion to hear him and as Mrs de Frackas' conservatory disintegrated and rapid gunfire sounded below he was hurtled once more into a maelstrom of lust that had nothing to do with real sex at all. Death was going through the motions of life and Wilt, unaware that his part in this grisly performance was being monitored for posterity, did his best to play his role. He tried thinking about Eva again.

Chapter 17

Downstairs in the kitchen Chinanda and Baggish were having a hard time thinking at all. All the complexities of life from which they had tried to escape into the idiotic and murderous fanaticism of terror seemed suddenly to have combined against them. They fired frantically into the darkness, and for one proud moment imagined they had hit the helicopter. Instead, the thing had apparently bombed the house next door. When they finally stopped shooting they were assailed by the yells of quads in the cellar. To make matters worse, the kitchen had become a health hazard. Eva's highly polished tiles were a slick of vomit and after Baggish had twice landed on his backside they had retreated to the hall to consider their next move. It was then that they heard the extraordinary noises emanating from the attic.

'They're raping Gudrun,' said Baggish and would have gone to her rescue if Chinanda hadn't stopped him.

'It's a trap the police pigs are setting. They want to get us upstairs and then they rush the house and rescue the hostages. We stay down here.'

'With that noise? How long do you think we can go on with all that yelling? We each need to sleep by turns and with them crying is impossible.'

'So we stop them,' said Chinanda and led the way down to the cellar where Mrs de Frackas was sitting on a wooden chair while the quads demanded mummy.

'Shut up, you hear me! You want to see your mummy you stop that noise,' Baggish shouted. But the quads only yelled the louder.

'I should have thought coping with small children would have been an essential part of your training,' said Mrs de Frackas unsympathetically. Baggish rounded on her. He still hadn't got over her suggestion that his proper métier was selling dirty postcards in Port Said.

154

'You make them quiet yourself,' he told her, waving his automatic in her face, 'or else we—'

'My dear boy, there are some things you have yet to learn,' said the old lady. 'By the time you reach my age dying is so imminent that I can't be bothered to worry about it. In any case I have always been an advocate of euthanasia. So much more sensible, don't you think, than putting one on a drip or one of those life-support machines or whatever they call them. I mean, who wants to keep a senile old person alive when she's no use to anyone?'

'I don't,' said Baggish fervently. Mrs de Frackas looked at him with interest.

'Besides, being a Moslem, you'd be doing me a favour. I've always understood that death in battle was a guarantee of salvation according to the Prophet, and while I can't say I'm actually battling I should have thought being shot by a murderer amounts to the same thing.'

'We are not murderers,' shouted Baggish, 'we are freedom fighters against international imperialism!'

'Which serves to prove my point,' continued Mrs de Frackas imperturbably. 'You're fighting and I am self-evidently a product of the Empire. If you kill me I should, according to your philosophy, go straight to heaven.'

'We are not here to discuss philosophy,' said Chinanda. 'You stupid old woman, what do you know about the suffering of the workers?'

Mrs de Frackas turned her attention to his clothes. 'Rather more than you do by the cut of your coat, young man. It may not be obvious but I spent several years working in a children's hospital in the slums of Calcutta and I think I know what misery means. Have you ever done a hard day's work in your life?'

Chinanda evaded the question. 'But what did you do about this misery?' he yelled, poking his face close to hers. 'You washed your conscience in the hospital and then went back and lived in luxury.'

'I had three square meals a day if that's what you mean by luxury. I certainly couldn't have afforded the sort of expensive car you drive around in,' riposted the old lady. 'And while we're on the subject of washing, I think it might help to quieten the children if you allowed me to bath them.'

155

The terrorists looked at the quads and tended to agree. The quads were not a pleasant sight.

'OK, we bring you water down and you can wash them here,' said Chinanda, who went up to the darkened kitchen and finally found a plastic bucket under the sink. He filled it with water and brought it down with a bar of soap. Mrs de Frackas looked into the bucket doubtfully.

'I said "Wash them." Not dye them.'

'Die them? What do you mean die them?'

'Take a look for yourself,' said Mrs de Frackas. The two terrorists did, and were appalled. The bucket was filled with dark blue water.

'Now they're trying to poison us,' yelled Baggish and headed up the stairs to register this fresh complaint against the Anti-Terrorist Squad.

Inspector Flint took the call. 'Poison you? By putting something in the water supply? I can assure you I know nothing about it.'

'Then how come it's blue?'

'I've no idea. Are you sure the water's blue?'

'I know fucking well it's blue,' shouted Baggish. 'We turn the tap and the water comes out blue. You think we're idiots or something.'

Flint hesitated but suppressed his true opinion in the interest of the hostages. 'Never mind what I think,' he said, 'all I'm saying is that we have done absolutely nothing to the water supply and—'

'Lying pig,' shouted Baggish. 'First you try trapping us by raping Gudrun and now you poison the water. We don't wait any longer. The water is clean in one hour and you let Gudrun go or we execute the old woman.'

He slammed the phone down, leaving Flint more mystified than ever. 'Raping Gudrun? The man's off his head. I wouldn't touch the bitch with a bargepole and how I can be in two places at the same time defeats me. And now he's saying the water's gone blue.'

'Could be they're on drugs,' said the sergeant. 'Gets them hallucinating sometimes, especially when they're under stress.'

'Stress? Don't talk to me about stress,' said Flint and turned his anger on a P.L.D. operator. 'And what the hell are you smirking about?'

'They're trying it out in the bath now, sir. Wilt's idea. Randy little sod.'

'If you're seriously suggesting that a couple copulating in a bath can turn the rest of the water in the house blue, think again,' snapped Flint.

He leant his head back against an antimacassar and shut his eyes. His mind was churning with opinions. Wilt was mad. Wilt was a terrorist. Wilt was a mad terrorist. Wilt was possessed. Wilt was a bloody enigma. Only the last was certain, that and the Inspector's fervent wish that Wilt was a thousand miles away and that he had never heard of the bastard. Finally he roused himself.

'All right, I want that helicopter back and this time no balls-ups. The house is floodlit and it's going to stay that way. All they have to do is land that telephone through the balcony window and considering what they've done here that should be child's play. Tell the pilot he can rip the roof off if he wants to but I want a line through to that flat and fast. That's the only way we're going to find out exactly what Wilt's playing at.'

'Will do,' said the Major, and began issuing fresh instructions.

'He's playing politics now, sir,' said the operator. 'Makes Marx sound like a right-winger. Want to hear?'

'I suppose I'd better,' said Flint miserably, and the loudspeaker was switched on. Through the crackle Wilt could be heard expounding violently.

'We must annihilate the capitalist system lock stock and barrel. There must be no hesitation in exterminating the last vestiges of the ruling class and instilling a proletarian consciousness into the minds of the workers. This can best be achieved by exposing the fascistic nature of pseudo-democracy through the praxis of terror against the police and the lumpen executives of international finance. Only by demonstrating the fundamental antithesis between . . .'

'Christ, he sounds like a bloody textbook,' said Flint with unintentional accuracy. 'We've got a pocket Mao in the attic. Right, get these tapes through to the Idiot Brigade. Perhaps they can tell us what a lumpen executive is.'

'Helicopter's on its way,' said the Major. 'The telephone's

fitted with a micro-television camera. If all goes well we'll soon see what's going on up there.'

'As if I wanted to,' said Flint and retreated to the safety of the downstairs toilet.

Five minutes later the helicopter swirled across the orchard at the bottom of the garden, poised for a moment over Number 9, and a field telephone swung through the balcony window into the flat. As the pilot lifted the machine away a trail of wire spun out behind it like the thread of a mechanical spider.

Flint emerged from the toilet to find that Chinanda was back on the phone.

'Wants to know why we haven't cleared the water, sir,' said the operator.

Inspector Flint sat down with a sigh and took the call. 'Now listen, Miguel,' he began, imitating the friendly approach of the Superintendent, 'you may not believe this—'

A stream of abuse indicated all too clearly that the terrorist didn't.

'All right, I accept all that,' said Flint when the epithets dried up. 'But what I'm saying is that we aren't in the attic. We haven't put anything in the water.'

'Then why are you supplying them with weapons by helicopter?'

'That wasn't a weapon. It happened to be a telephone so we can talk to them . . . Yes, I daresay it doesn't sound likely. I'm the first to agree . . . No, we haven't. If anyone has it's the . . .'

'People's Alternative Army,' prompted the sergeant.

'The People's Alternative Army,' repeated Flint. 'They must have put something in the water, Miguel . . . What? . . . You don't like being called Miguel . . . Well as a matter of fact I don't particularly like being called fuzzpig . . . Yes, I heard you. I heard you the first time. And if you'll get off the line I'll talk to the bastards up there.'

And Flint slammed down the phone. 'All right, now get me through to the attic. And make it snappy. Time's running out.'

It was to run out for a further quarter of an hour. The sudden reappearance of the helicopter just when the Wilt alternative had switched from sex to politics had thrown Wilt's tactics out

158

of joint. Having softened his victim up on the physical level he had begun confusing her still more by quoting the egregious Bilger at his most Marcusian. It hadn't been too difficult, and in any case Wilt had speculated on the injustice of human existence over many years. His dealings with Plasterers Four had taught him that he belonged to a relatively privileged society. Plasterers earned more than he did, and Printers were positively rich, but allowing for these discrepancies it was still true that he had been born into an affluent country with a favoured climate and sophisticated political institutions developed over the centuries. Above all an industrial society. The vast majority of mankind lived in abject poverty, were riddled with curable disease which went uncured, were subject to despotic governments and lived in terror and in danger of dying by starvation. To the extent that anyone tried to change this inequity, Wilt sympathized. Eva's Personal Assistance for Primitive People might be ineffectual but it had at least the merit of being personal and moving in the right direction. Terrorizing the innocent and murdering men, women and children was both ineffectual and barbaric. What difference was there between the terrorists and their victims? Only one of opinion. Chinanda and Gudrun Schautz came from wealthy families and Baggish, whose father had been a shopkeeper in Beirut, could hardly be called poor. None of these self-appointed executioners had been driven to murder by the desperation of poverty, and as far as Wilt could tell their fanaticism had its roots in no specific cause. They weren't trying to drive the British from Ulster, the Israelis from the Golan Heights or even the Turks from Cyprus. They were political poseurs whose enemy was life. In short they were murderers by personal choice, psychopaths who camouflaged their motives behind a screen of utopian theory. Power was their kick, the power to inflict pain and to terrify. Even their own readiness to die was a sort of power, some sick and infantile form of masochism and expiation of guilt, not for their filthy crimes, but for being alive at all. Beyond that there were doubt-less other motives concerned with parents or toilet training. Wilt didn't care. It was enough that they were carriers of the same political rabies that had driven Hitler to construct Auschwitz and kill himself in the bunker, or the Cambodians to murder one another by the million. As such they were beyond the pale of sympathy. Wilt had his children to protect and only his wits to help him.

And so, in a desperate attempt to keep Gudrun Schautz isolated and uncertain, he mouthed Marcusian dogma until the helicopter interrupted his recital. As the telephone encased in a wooden box swung through the window Wilt hurled himself to the floor in the kitchen.

'Back into the bathroom,' he yelled convinced that the thing was some sort of tear-gas bomb. But Gudrun Schautz was already there. Wilt crawled through to her.

'They know we're here,' she whispered.

'They know I'm here,' said Wilt, grateful to the police for seeming to provide proof that he was a wanted man. 'What would they want with you?'

'They locked me in the bathroom. Why would they do that if they didn't want me?'

'Why would they do it if they did?' asked Wilt. 'They'd have dragged you out straightaway.' He paused and looked hard at her in the light reflected from the ceiling. 'But how did they get on to me? I ask myself that question. Who told them?'

Gudrun Schautz looked back and asked herself a great many questions. 'Why do you look at me? I don't know what you are talking about.'

'No?' said Wilt, deciding the time was ripe to switch to full-scale mania. 'That's what you say now. You come to my house when everything is going so good with the plan and now suddenly the Israelis arrive and everything is kaput. No assassination of the Queen, no use for the nerve-gas, no annihilation of the entire pseudo-democratic parliamentary cadres in the House of Commons at one fell swoop, no . . .'

In the living-room the telephone interrupted this insane catalogue. Wilt listened to it with relief. So did Gudrun Schautz. The paranoia which was part of her make-up was beginning to assume new proportions in her mind with every shift in Wilt's position.

'I'll answer it,' she said but Wilt glared at her ferociously.

'Informer,' he snarled, 'you've done enough harm already. You will stay where you are. That's your only hope.'

And leaving her to work out this strange logic, Wilt crawled through the kitchen and opened the box.

160

'Listen you fascist pig swine,' he yelled before Flint could get a word in edgeways, 'don't think you're going to sweet-talk the People's Alternative Army into one of your lying dialogues. We demand—'

'Shut up, Wilt,' snapped the Inspector. Wilt shut up. So the sods knew. In particular, Flint knew. Which would have been good news if he hadn't had a bloody murderess breathing down his neck. 'So there's no use trying to bluff us. For your information, if you want to see your daughters alive again you had better stop trying to poison your little comrades on the ground floor.'

'Trying to what?' asked Wilt, stunned by this new accusation into using his normal voice.

'You heard me. You've been doctoring the water supply and they want it undoctored as of now.'

'Doctoring the . . .' Wilt began before remembering he couldn't talk openly in present company.

'The water supply,' said Flint. 'They've set a deadline for it to be cleared and it runs out in half an hour. And I do mean deadline.'

There was a moment's silence while Wilt tried to think. There must have been something in that bloody hold-all that was poisonous. Perhaps the terrorists carried their own supply of cyanide. He'd have to get the bag out but in the meantime he had to maintain his lunatic stand. He fell back on his earlier approach.

'We make no deals,' he shouted. 'If our demands aren't met by eight in the morning the hostage dies.'

There was the sound of laughter at the other end of the line. 'Pull the other one, Wilt,' said Flint. 'How are you going to kill her? Screw her to death perhaps?'

He paused to let this information sink in before continuing, 'We've got every little antic you've been up to on tape. It's going to sound great when we play it back in court.'

'Shit,' said Wilt, this time impersonally.

'Mrs Wilt particularly enjoyed it. Yes, you heard me right. Now then, are you going to clear that water or do you want your daughters to have to drink it?'

'All right, I agree. You have the aircraft waiting on the runway and I don't move from here until the car arrives. One

161

driver and no tricks or the woman dies with me. You understand?'

'No,' said Flint beginning to feel confused himself but Wilt had ended the conversation. He was sitting on the floor trying to think himself out of this new dilemma. He couldn't do anything about the water tank with the Schautz woman watching. He would have to continue his bluff. He went back into the kitchen and found her standing uncertainly by the bathroom door.

'So now you know,' he said.

Gudrun Schautz didn't. 'Why did you say you would kill me?' she asked.

'Why do you think?' said Wilt, plucking up sufficient courage to move towards her with something approximating to menace. 'Because you are an informer? Without you the plan . . .'

But Gudrun Schautz had heard enough. She retreated into the bathroom, slammed the door and bolted it. This little man was insane. The whole situation was insane. Nothing made any sort of sense, and contradiction piled on contradiction so that the outcome was an incomprehensible flux of impressions. She sat on the toilet and tried to think her way through the chaos. If this weird man with his talk of assassinating the Queen was wanted by the police, and everything seemed to point in that direction, however illogically, there was something to be said for seeming to be his hostage. The British police weren't supposed to be fools but they might free her without asking too many awkward questions. It was the only chance she had. And through the door she could hear Wilt muttering to himself alarmingly. He had started to wire the doorhandle again.

When he had finished Wilt climbed back into the attic space and was presently elbow-deep in the water tank. It was certainly a very murky colour and when he finally managed to drag the hold-all out his arm was blue. Wilt laid the bag on the floor and began to rummage through its contents. At the bottom he found a portable typewriter and a large ink pad with a rubber stamp. There was nothing to suggest poison, but the typewriter ribbon and the ink pad had certainly polluted the water. Wilt went back to the kitchen and turned on the tap. 'No wonder the buggers thought they were being doctored,' he muttered and, leaving the tap running, climbed back into the roof space. By

162

the time he had crawled round the back of the tank with the hold-all and hidden it under the fibreglass insulation the dawn was beginning to compete with the floodlights. He emerged, went through to the living-room, lay down on the sofa and wondered what to do next.

Chapter 18

And so Day Two of the siege of Willington Road began. The sun rose, the floodlights faded, Wilt nodded fitfully in a corner of the attic, Gudrun Schautz lay in the bathroom, Mrs de Frackas sat in the cellar, and the quads huddled together under a pile of sacks in which Eva had once stored 'organic' potatoes. Even the two terrorists snatched some sleep, while in the Communications Centre the Major, installed on a camp bed, snored and twitched in his sleep like a hound dreaming of the hunt. Elsewhere in Mrs de Frackas' house several Anti-Terrorist men had made themselves comfortable. The sergeant in charge of the listening devices was curled on a sofa and Inspector Flint had commandeered the main bedroom. But for all this human inactivity the electronic sensors relayed information to the tapes and via them to the computer and the Psycho-Warfare team, while the field telephone, like some audio-visual Trojan horse, monitored Wilt's breathing and scanned his movements through its TV camera eye.

Only Eva didn't sleep. She lay in a cell in the police station staring at the dim lightbulb in the ceiling and kept the duty sergeant in a state of uncertainty by demanding to see her solicitor. It was a request he didn't know how to refuse. Mrs Wilt was not a criminal and to the best of his knowledge there were no legal grounds for keeping her locked in a cell. Even genuine villains were allowed to see their solicitors, and after fruitlessly trying to contact Inspector Flint the sergeant gave in.

'You can use the telephone in here,' he told her, and discreetly left her in the office to make as many calls as she chose. If Flint didn't like it he could lump it. The duty sergeant wasn't laying his own head on the chopping-block for anyone.

Eva made a great many phone calls. Mavis Mottram was woken at four and was mollified to learn that the only reason Eva hadn't contacted her before was because she was being held illegally by the police.

'I never heard anything so scandalous in my life. You poor thing. Now don't worry we'll have you out of there in no time,' she said, and promptly woke Patrick to tell him to get in touch with the Chief Constable, the local M.P. and his friends at the B.B.C.

'I won't have any friends at the Beeb if I call them at half-past four.'

'Nonsense,' said Mavis, 'it will give them plenty of time to get it on the early-morning news.'

The Braintrees were woken too. This time Eva horrified them by describing how she had been assaulted by the police and asked them if they knew anyone who could help. Peter Braintree phoned the secretary of the League of Personal Liberties and, as an afterthought, every national newspaper with the story.

And Eva continued her calls. Mr Gosdyke, the Wilts' solicitor, was dragged from his bed to answer the phone and promised to come to the police station at once.

'Don't say anything to anyone,' he advised her, in the firm belief that Mrs Wilt must have committed some crime. Eva ignored his advice. She spoke to the Nyes, the Principal of the Tech. and as many people as she could think of, including Dr Scully. She had just finished when the B.B.C. called back and Eva gave a taped interview as the mother of the quadruplets held by the terrorists who was herself being held by the police for no good reason.

From that moment on a crescendo of protest gathered. The Home Secretary was woken by his Permanent Under-Secretary with the news that the B.B.C. was refusing his request not to broadcast the interview in the national interest on the grounds that the illegal detention of the hostages' mother was diametrically opposed to the national interest. From there the information reached the Police Commissioner, who was held responsible for the activities of the Anti-Terrorist Squad, and even the Ministry of Defence, whose Special Ground Services had assaulted Mrs Wilt in the first place.

Eva hit the radio news at seven and the headlines of every paper in time for the morning rush hour, and by half-past seven the Ipford police station was more obviously besieged by press men, TV cameras, photographers, Eva's friends and onlookers, than the house in Willington Road. Even Mr Gosdyke's

165

scepticism had evaporated in the face of the sergeant's confession that he did not know why Mrs Wilt was in custody.

'Don't ask me what she's supposed to have done,' said the sergeant. 'I was ordered to keep her in the cells by Inspector Flint. If you want any further information, ask him.'

'I intend to,' said Mr Gosdyke. 'Where is he?'

'At the siege. I can try and get him on the phone for you.'

And so it was that Flint, who had finally snatched some sleep with the happy thought that he had at long last got that little bastard Wilt where he wanted him, up to his eyes in a genuine crime, suddenly found that the tables had been turned on him.

'I didn't say arrest her. I said she was to be held in custody under the Terrorism Act.'

'Are you suggesting for one moment that my client is a terrorist suspect?' demanded Mr Gosdyke. 'Because if you are . . .'

Inspector Flint considered the law on slander and decided he wasn't. 'She was being kept in custody for her own safety,' he equivocated. Mr Gosdyke doubted it.

'Well, having seen the state she's in all I can say is that it's my considered opinion that she would have been safer outside the police station than in it. She has obviously been badly beaten, dragged through the mud, and, if I'm any judge of the matter, several hedges into the bargain, has suffered multiple abrasions to the hands and legs and is in a state of nervous exhaustion. Now are you going to allow her to leave or do I have to apply for . . .'

'No,' said Flint hastily, 'of course she can go, but I'm not taking any responsibility for her safety if she comes here.'

'I hardly need any assurances from you on that score,' said Mr Gosdyke, and escorted Eva out of the police station. She was greeted by a barrage of questions and cameras.

'Mrs Wilt, is it correct that the police beat you up?'

'Yes,' said Eva before Mr Gosdyke could interject that she was making no comments.

'Mrs Wilt, what do you intend to do now?'

'I'm going home,' said Eva, but Mr Gosdyke hustled her into the car.

'That's out of the question, my dear. You must have some friends you can stay with for the time being.'

166

From the crowd Mavis Mottram was trying to make herself heard. Eva ignored her. She had begun thinking about Henry and that awful German girl in bed together, and the last person she wanted to talk to now was Mavis. Besides, at the back of her mind she still blamed Mavis for insisting on going to that stupid seminar. If she had stayed at home none of this would have happened.

'I'm sure the Braintrees won't mind my going there,' she said, and presently she was sitting in their kitchen sipping coffee and telling Betty all about it.

'Are you sure, Eva?' said Betty. 'I mean, it doesn't sound at all like Henry?'

Eva nodded tearfully. 'It did. They have these loudspeaker things all round the house and they can hear everything that's going on inside.'

'I must say I can't understand.'

Nor could Eva. It wasn't simply that it was unlike Henry to be unfaithful; it wasn't Henry at all. Henry never even looked at other women. She had always known he didn't and there had been times when she had been almost irritated by his lack of interest. It somehow deprived her of the little jealousy she was entitled to as his wife, and there was also the suspicion that his lack of interest extended to her too. Now she felt doubly betrayed.

'You'd think he'd be far too worried about the children,' she went on. 'They're downstairs and there he is up in the flat with that creature . . .' Eva broke down and wept openly.

'What you need is a bath and then a good sleep,' said Betty, and Eva allowed herself to be led upstairs to the bathroom. But as she lay in the hot water, instinct and thought combined again. She was going home. She had to, and this time she would go in broad daylight. She got out of the bath, dried herself, and put on the maternity dress which was the only thing Betty Braintree had been able to find that would fit her, and went downstairs. She had made up her mind what to do.

In the temporary conference room which had once been Major-General de Frackas' private den, Inspector Flint, the Major and the members of the Psycho-Warfare team sat looking at a television set which had been placed incongruously in the middle of the Battle of Waterloo. The late Major-General's obsession with toy soldiers and their precise deployment on a large ping-pong table where they had been gathering dust since his death added a surrealist element to the extraordinary sights and sounds being relayed by the TV camera in the field telephone next door. The Wilt alternative had entered a new phase, one in which he had apparently gone clean off his rocker.

'Mad as a March hare,' said the Major as Wilt, horribly distorted by the fish-eye lens, loomed and dwarfed as he strode about the attic mouthing words that made no sense at all. Even Flint found it hard not to accept the verdict.

'What the hell does "Life is prejudicial to Infinity" mean?' he asked Dr Felden, the psychiatrist.

'I need to hear more before I express a definite opinion,' said the doctor.

'I'm damned if I do,' muttered the Major, 'it's like peering into a padded cell.'

On the screen Wilt could be seen shouting something about fighting for the religion of Allah and death to all unbelievers. He then made some extremely disturbing noises which suggested a village idiot having trouble with a fishbone, and disappeared into the kitchen. There was a moment's silence before he began chanting, 'The bells of hell go tingalingaling for you but not for me,' in a frightening falsetto. When he reappeared he was armed with a bread knife and yelling, 'There's a crocodile in the cupboard, mother and its eating up your coat. Bats and lizards braving blizzards keep the world afloat.' Finally he lay on the bed and giggled.

Flint leant across the sunken road and switched the set off. 'Much more of that and I'll go off my head too,' he muttered. 'All right, you've seen and heard the sod, and I want to know your opinion as to the best way of handling him.'

'Looked at from the standpoint of a coherent political ideology,' said Professor Maerlis, 'I must confess that I find it hard to express an opinion.'

'Good,' said the Major, who still harboured the suspicion that the professor shared the views of the terrorists.

'On the other hand the transcripts of the tapes made last night indicate definite evidence that Mr Wilt has a profound knowledge of terrorist theory and was apparently engaged in a conspiracy to assassinate the Queen. What I don't understand is where the Israelis come in.'

'That could easily be a symptom of paranoia,' said Dr Felden. 'A very typical example of persecution mania.'

'Never mind about the "could be",' said Flint, 'is the bugger mad or not?'

'Difficult to say. In the first place the subject may well be suffering the after-effects of the drugs he was given yesterday before entering the house. I have ascertained from the so-called medical officer who administered it that the concoction consisted of three parts Valium, two Sodium Amytal, a jigger of Bromide and what he chose to call a bouquet of Laudanum. He couldn't specify the actual quantities involved, but in my opinion it says something for Mr Wilt's constitution that he is still alive.'

'Says something for the canteen coffee that the bugger drank it without noticing,' said Flint. 'Anyway, do we get him on the blower and ask him what he has done with the Schautz woman or not?'

Dr Felden toyed with a lead Napoleon pensively. 'On the whole I am against the idea. If Fräulein Schautz is still alive I wouldn't want to be responsible for introducing the notion of murdering her to a man in Mr Wilt's condition.'

'That's a big help. So when those swine demand her release again I suppose I'll have to tell them she's being held by a lunatic.' And wishing to God the replacement for the Head of the Anti-Terrorist Squad would arrive before mass murder began next door, Flint went through to the Communications Centre.

'No go,' he told the sergeant. 'The Idiot Brigade reckon we're dealing with a homicidal maniac.'

It was more or less the reaction that Wilt wanted. He had spent a miserable night pondering his next move. So far he had played a number of roles—a revolutionary terrorist group, a grateful father, a chinless wonder, an erratic lover and a man who had intended to assassinate the Queen—and with each fresh fabrication he had seen Gudrun Schautz's sense of certainty waver. Stoned out of her mind by the drug of revolutionary dogma, she was incapable of adjusting to a world of absurd fantasy. And Wilt's world was absurd; it always had been and as far as he could tell it always would be. It was fantastic and absurd that Bilger had made the bloody film about the crocodile but it was true, and Wilt had spent his adult life surrounded by pimply youths who thought they were God's gift to women, and by lecturers who imagined that they could convert Plasterers and Motor Mechanics into sensitive human beings by forcing them to read *Finnegan's Wake* or instil them with a truly proletarian consciousness by handing out dollops of *Das Kapital*. And Wilt himself had been through the gamut of fantasy, those internal dreams of being a great writer which had been re-awakened by his first glimpse of Irmgard Mueller and, on a previous occasion, the cold-blooded murderer of Eva. And for eighteen years he had lived with a woman who had changed roles almost as frequently as she changed her clothes. With such a wealth of experience behind him Wilt could produce new fantasies at a moment's notice just so long as he wasn't called upon to give them greater credibility by doing anything more practical than gloss them with words. Words were his medium and had been through all the years at the Tech. With Gudrun Schautz locked in the bathroom he was free to use them to his heart's content and her discomfort. Provided those creatures down below didn't start doing anything violent.

But Baggish and Chinanda had their hands full with another form of bizarre behaviour. The quads had woken early to renew their assault on Eva's freezer and stock of bottled fruit, and Mrs de Frackas had given up the unequal battle to keep them moderately clean. She had spent an exceedingly uncomfortable night on the wooden chair and her rheumatism had given her hell. In the end she had been driven to drink, and since the only drink available was Wilt's patented homebrew the results had been remarkable.

From the first appalling mouthful the old lady wondered what the hell had hit her. It wasn't simply that the stuff tasted foul, so foul that she had immediately taken another shot to try to wash her mouth out, it was also extremely potent. Having choked down a second mouthful Mrs de Frackas looked at the bottle with downright disbelief. It was impossible to suppose that anyone had seriously distilled the stuff for human consumption, and for a moment or two she considered the awful possibility

170

that Wilt had, for some diabolical reason of his own, laid up a binful of undiluted paint stripper. It didn't seem likely somehow, but then again what she had just swallowed hadn't seemed likely either. It had seared its way down her gullet with all the virulence of a powerful toilet-cleaner going to work on a neglected U-bend. Mrs de Frackas examined the label and felt reassured. The muck proclaimed itself 'Lager' and while the title was in blatant disregard of the facts, whatever the bottle contained was meant to be drunk. The old lady took another mouthful and instantly forgot her rheumatism. It was impossible to concentrate on two ailments simultaneously.

By the time she had finished the bottle she had difficulty concentrating on anything. The world had suddenly become a delightful place and all it needed to make it even better was more of the same. She swayed back to the wine store and selected a second bottle and was in the process of unscrewing the top when the thing exploded. Doused with beer and holding the neck of the bottle Mrs de Frackas was about to try a third when she caught sight of several larger bottles in the bottom rack. She pulled one out and saw that it had once contained champagne. What it contained now she couldn't imagine but at least it seemed safer to open and less likely to fragment than the beer bottles. She took two bottles out into the cellar and tried to uncork them. It was easier said than done. Wilt had fastened the corks down with Sellotape and what looked like the remnants of a wire coathanger.

'Need some pliers,' she muttered as the quads gathered round with interest.

'That's daddy's best,' said Josephine. 'He wouldn't like it if you drank it.'

'No dear, I daresay he wouldn't,' said the old lady with a belch that suggested her stomach was of the same opinion.

'He calls it his four-star BB,' said Penelope. 'But mummy says it ought to be called peepee.'

'Does she?' said Mrs de Frackas with mounting disgust.

'That's because he has to get up in the night when he's drunk it.'

Mrs de Frackas relaxed. 'We wouldn't want to do anything that would upset your father,' she said, 'and anyway, champagne needs to be chilled.'

171

She went back to the bins, returned with two opened bottles that had proved less explosive than the others, and sat down again. The quads were gathered round the freezer but the old lady was too busy to care what they were doing. By the time she had finished the third bottle the Wilt quads were octuplets in her eyes and she was having difficulty focusing. In any case she had begun to understand what Eva had meant about peepee. Wilt's homebrew was making its presence felt. Mrs de Frackas got up, fell over and finally crawled up the steps to the door. The damned thing was locked.

'Let me out,' she shouted, and banged on the door. 'Let me out this inshtant.'

'What you want?' demanded Baggish.

'Never you mind what I want. Itsh what I need that matters and thatsh no concern of yours.'

'Then you stay where you are.'

'I shan't be reshponsible for what happens if I do,' said Mrs de Frackas.

'What you mean?'

'Young man, there are shome things better left unshaid and I don't intend dishcushing them with you.'

Through the door the two terrorists could be heard struggling with slurred English sentences. 'Things better left unshed' had them baffled, while 'not be reshponshible for what happens' sounded faintly ominous, and they had already been alarmed by several popping noises and the crunch of glass from the cellar.

'We want to know what happens if we don't let you out,' said Chinanda finally.

Mrs de Frackas was in no doubt. 'I shall almosht shertainly burst,' she yelled.

'You what?'

'Burst, burst, burst. Like a bomb,' screamed the old lady, now convinced she was in the terminal stage of diuresis. A muttered conversation took place in the kitchen.

'You come out with your hands up,' Chinanda ordered, and unlocked the door before backing away into the hall and aiming his automatic. But Mrs de Frackas was no longer in a condition to obey. She was trying to reach one of several doorknobs and missing. From the bottom of the steps the quads watched in fascination. They were used to Wilt's occasional bouts of booziness but they had never seen anyone paralytically drunk before.

'For Heaven's shake shomeone open the door,' Mrs de Frackas burbled.

'I will,' squealed Samantha and a rush of competing girls fought their way over the old lady for the privilege. By the time Penelope had won and the quads had cascaded over her into the kitchen the old lady had lost all interest in toilets. She lay across the threshold and, raising her head with difficulty, delivered her verdict on the quads.

'Do me a favour, shomeone, and shoot the little shits,' she gurgled before passing out. The terrorists didn't hear her. They knew now what she had meant about a bomb. Two devastating explosions came from the cellar and the air was filled with frozen peas and broad beans. In the freezer Wilt's BB had finally burst.

Chapter 19

Eva had been busy too. She had spent part of the morning on the phone to Mr Gosdyke and the rest arguing with Mr Symper, the local representative of the League of Personal Liberties. He was a very earnest and concerned young man, and in the normal course of events, would have been dismayed at the outrageous behaviour of the police in putting at risk the lives of a senior citizen and four impressionable children by refusing to meet the legitimate demands of the freedom fighters besieged in Number 9 Willington Road. Instead, Eva's treatment at the hands of the police had put Symper in the extremely uncomfortable position of having to look at the problem from her point of view.

'I do understand the case you're making, Mrs Wilt,' he said forced by her bruised appearance to subdue his bias in favour of radical foreigners, 'but you must admit you are free.'

'Not to enter my own house. I am not at liberty to do that. The police won't let me.'

'Now if you want us to take up your case against the police for infringing your liberty by holding you in custody, we'll . . .'

Eva didn't. 'I want to enter my own home.'

'I do sympathize with you, but you see our organization aims to protect the individual from the infringement of her personal liberty by the police and in your case . . .'

'They won't let me go home,' said Eva. 'If that isn't infringing my personal liberty I don't know what is.'

'Yes, well I do see that.'

'Then do something about it.'

'I don't really know what I can do about it,' said Mr Symper.

'You knew what to do when the police stopped a container truck of deep-frozen Bangladeshis outside Dover,' said Betty. You organized a protest rally and . . .'

'That was quite different,' said Mr Symper, bridling. 'The Customs officials had no right to insist that the refrigeration

174

unit be turned on. They were suffering from acute frostbite. And besides, they were in transit.'

'They shouldn't have labelled themselves cod fillets, and anyhow you argued that they were simply coming to join their families in Britain.'

'They were in transit to their families.'

'And so is Eva, or should be,' said Betty. 'If anyone has a right to join her family it's Eva.'

'I suppose we could apply for a court order,' said Mr Symper sighing for less domestic issues, 'that would be the best way.'

'It wouldn't,' said Eva, 'it would be slowest. I am going home now and you are coming with me.'

'I beg your pardon?' said Mr Symper, whose concern didn't extend to becoming a hostage himself.

'You heard me,' said Eva, and loomed over him with a ferocity that put in question his ardent feminism, but before he could make a plea for his own personal liberty he was being hustled out of the house. A crowd of reporters had gathered there.

'Mrs Wilt,' said a man from the *Snap*, 'our readers would like to hear how it feels as the mother of quads to know that your loved ones are being held hostage.'

Eva's eyes bulged in her head. 'Feel?' she asked. 'You want to know how I feel?'

'That's right,' said the man, licking his ballpen, 'human interest—'

He got no further. Eva's feelings had passed beyond the stage of words or human interest. Only actions could express them. Her hand came up, descended in a karate chop and as he fell her knee caught him in the stomach.

'That's how it feels,' said Eva as he rolled into a foetal position on the flowerbed. 'Tell your readers that.' And she marched the now thoroughly cowed Mr Symper to his car and pushed him in.

'I am going home to my children,' she told the other reporters. 'Mr Symper of the League of Personal Liberties is accompanying me and my solicitor is waiting for us.'

And without another word she got into the driver's seat. Ten minutes later, followed by a small convoy of press cars, they reached the road block in Farringdon Road to find Mr Gosdyke arguing ineffectually with the police sergeant.

175

'I'm afraid it's no use, Mrs Wilt. The police have orders to let no one through.'

Eva snorted. 'This is a free country,' she said, dragging Mr Symper out of the car with a grip that contradicted her statement. 'If anyone tries to stop me from going home we will take the matter to the courts, to the Ombudsman and to Parliament. Come along, Mr Gosdyke.'

'Now hold it, lady,' said the sergeant, 'my orders . . .'

'I've taken your number,' said Eva, 'and I shall sue you personally for denying me free access to my children.'

And pushing the unwilling Mr Symper before her she marched through the gap in the barbed wire, followed cautiously by Mr Gosdyke. Behind them a cheer went up from the crowd of reporters. For a moment the sergeant was too stunned to react and by the time he reached for his walkie-talkie the trio had turned the corner into Willington Road. They were stopped halfway down by two armed S.G.S. men.

'You've no right to be here,' one of them shouted. 'Don't you know there's a siege on?'

'Yes,' said Eva, 'which is why we're here. I'm Mrs Wilt, this is Mr Symper of the League of Personal Liberties and Mr Gosdyke is here to handle negotiations. Now kindly take us to . . .'

'I don't know anything about this,' said the soldier. 'All I know is that we've got orders to shoot . . .'

'Then shoot me,' said Eva defiantly, 'and see where that gets you.'

The S.G.S. man hesitated. Shooting mothers wasn't included in Queen's Rules and Regulations, and Mr Gosdyke looked too respectable to be a terrorist.

'All right, come this way,' he said, and escorted them into Mrs de Frackas' house to be greeted abusively by Inspector Flint.

'What the fuck's going on?' he yelled. 'I thought I gave orders for you to stay away.'

Eva pushed Mr Gosdyke forward. 'Tell him,' she said.

Mr Gosdyke cleared his throat and looked uncomfortably round the room. 'As Mrs Wilt's legal representative,' he said, 'I have come to inform you that she demands to join her family. Now to the best of my knowledge there is nothing in law to prevent her from entering her own home.'

176

Inspector Flint goggled at him. 'Nothing?' he spluttered.

'Nothing in law,' said Mr Gosdyke.

'Bugger the law,' shouted Flint. 'You think those sods in there give a tuppenny fuck for the law?'

Mr Gosdyke conceded the point.

'Right,' continued Flint, 'so there's a houseful of armed terrorists who'll blow the heads off her four blasted daughters if anyone so much as goes near the place. That's all. Can't you get that into her thick skull?'

'No,' said Mr Gosdyke bluntly.

The Inspector sagged into a chair and looked balefully at Eva. 'Mrs Wilt,' he said, 'tell me something. You don't by any chance happen to belong to some suicidal religious cult, do you? No? I just wondered. In that case let me explain the situation to you in simple four-letter words that even you will understand. Inside your house there are—'

'I know all that,' said Eva, 'I've heard it over and over again and I don't care. I demand the right to enter my own home.'

'I see. And I suppose you intend walking up to the front door and ringing the bell?'

'I don't,' said Eva, 'I intend to be dropped in.'

'Dropped in?' said Flint with a gleam of incredulous hope in his eyes, 'did you really say "dropped in"?'

'By helicopter,' explained Eva, 'the same way you dropped that telephone in to Henry last night.'

The Inspector held his head in his hands and tried to find words.

'And it's no use your saying you can't,' continued Eva, 'because I've seen it done on telly. I wear a harness and the helicopter . . .'

'Oh my God,' said Flint, closing his eyes to shut out this appalling vision. 'You can't be serious.'

'I can,' said Eva.

'Mrs Wilt, if, and I repeat if, you were to enter the house by the means you have described, will you be good enough to tell me how you think it would help your four daughters?'

'Never you mind.'

'But I do mind, I mind very much. In fact I'll go so far as to say that I mind what happens to your children rather more than you appear to and . . .'

'Then why aren't you doing something about it? And don't say you are, because you aren't. You're sitting in here with all this transistor stuff listening to them being tortured and you like it.'

'Like it? Like it?' yelled the Inspector.

'Yes, like it,' Eva yelled back. 'It gives you a feeling of importance and what's more you've got a dirty mind. You enjoyed listening to Henry in bed with that woman and don't say you didn't.'

Inspector Flint couldn't. Words failed him. The only ones that sprang to mind were obscene and almost certain to lead to an action for slander. Trust this bloody woman to bring her solicitor and the sod from the Personal Liberties mob with her. He rose from his chair and stumbled through to the toy-room, slamming the door behind him. Professor Maerlis, Dr Felden and the Major were sitting watching Wilt pass the time by idly examining his glans penis for signs of incipient gangrene on the television screen. Flint switched the unnerving image off.

'You're not going to believe this,' he mouthed, 'but that bloody Mrs Wilt is demanding that we use the helicopter to swing her through the attic window on the end of a rope so she can join her fucking family.'

'I hope you're not going to allow it,' said Dr Felden. 'After what she threatened to do to her husband last night I hardly think it's advisable.'

'Don't tempt me,' said Flint. 'If I thought I could sit here and watch her tear the little shit limb from limb . . .' He broke off to savour the thought.

'Damned plucky little woman,' said the Major. 'Blowed if I'd choose to swing into that house on the end of a rope. Well, not without a lot of covering fire anyhow. Still, there's something to be said for it.'

'What?' said Flint wondering how the hell anyone could call Mrs Wilt a little woman.

'Diversionary tactics, old man. Can't think of anything more likely to unnerve the buggers than the sight of that woman dangling from a helicopter. Know it would scare the pants off me.'

'I daresay. But since that doesn't happen to be the purpose of the exercise I'd like some more constructive suggestion.'

178

From the other room Eva could be heard shouting that she'd send a telegram to the Queen if she wasn't allowed to join her family.

'That's all we need,' said Flint. 'We've got the press baying for blood and there hasn't been a decent mass suicide for months. She'll hit the headlines.'

'Certainly hit that window with a hell of a bang,' said the Major practically. 'Then we could rush the sods and—'

'No! Definitely no,' shouted Flint and dashed into the Communications Centre. 'All right, Mrs Wilt, I am going to try to persuade the two terrorists holding your daughters to allow you to join them. If they refuse that's their business. I can't do more.'

He turned to the sergeant on the switchboard. 'Get the two wogs on the phone and let me know when they've finished their Fascist Pig Overture.'

Mr Symper felt called upon to protest. 'I really do think these racialist remarks are quite unnecessary,' he said. 'In fact they are illegal. To call foreigners wogs—'

'I'm not calling foreigners wogs. I'm calling two fucking murderers wogs and don't tell me I shouldn't call them murderers either,' said Flint as Mr Symper tried to interject. 'A murderer is a murderer is a murderer and I've had about as much as I can take.'

So, it seemed, had the two terrorists. There was no preliminary tirade of abuse. 'What do you want?' Chinanda asked.

Flint took the phone. 'I have a proposal to make,' he said. 'Mrs Wilt, the mother of the four children you are holding, has volunteered to come in to look after them. She is unarmed and is prepared to meet any conditions you may choose to make.'

'Say that again,' said Chinanda. The Inspector repeated the message.

'Any conditions?' said Chinanda incredulously.

'Any. You name them, she'll meet them,' said Flint looking at Eva, who nodded.

A muttered conference took place in the kitchen next door made practically inaudible by the squeals of the quads and the occasional moan from Mrs de Frackas. Presently the terrorist came back on the line.

'Here are our conditions. The woman must be naked first of all. You hear me, naked.'

'I hear what you say but I can't say I understand . . .'

'No clothes on. So we see she has no weapons. Right?'

'I'm not sure Mrs Wilt will agree . . .'

'I do,' said Eva adamantly.

'Mrs Wilt agrees,' said Flint with a sigh of disgust.

'Second. Her hands are tied above her head.'

Again Eva nodded.

'Third. Her legs are tied.'

'Her legs are tied?' said Flint. 'How the hell is she going to walk if her legs are tied?'

'Long rope. Half metre between ankles. No running.'

'I see. Yes, Mrs Wilt agrees. Anything else?'

'Yes,' said Chinanda. 'As soon as she comes in, out go the children.'

'I beg your pardon?' said Flint. 'Did I hear you say "Out go the children"? You mean you don't want them?'

'Want them!' yelled Chinanda. 'You think we want to live with four dirty, filthy, disgusting little animals who shit all over the floor and piss . . .'

'No,' said Flint, 'I take your point.'

'So you can take the fucking little fascist shit-machines too,' said Chinanda, and slammed the phone down.

Inspector Flint turned to Eva with a happy smile. 'Mrs Wilt, I didn't say it, but you heard what the man said.'

'And he'll live to regret it,' said Eva with blazing eyes. 'Now, where do I undress?'

'Not in here,' said Flint firmly. 'You can use the bedrooms upstairs. The sergeant here will tie your hands and legs.'

While Eva went up to undress the Inspector consulted the Psycho-Warfare Team. He found them at odds with one another. Professor Maerlis argued that by exchanging four co-terminously conceived siblings for one woman whom the world would scarcely miss, there was propaganda advantage to be gained from the swop. Dr Felden disagreed.

'It's evident that the terrorists are under considerable pressure from the girls,' he said. 'Now, by relieving them of that psychological burden we may well be giving them a morale boost.'

'Never mind about their morale,' said Flint. 'If the bitch goes in she'll be doing me a favour and after that the Major here can mount Operation Slaughterhouse for all I care.'

'Whacko,' said the Major.

Flint went back to the Communications Centre, averted his eyes from the monstrous revelations of Eva in the raw, and turned to Mr Gosdyke.

'Let's get one thing straight, Gosdyke,' he said. 'I want you to understand that I am totally opposed to your client's actions and am not prepared to take responsibility for what happens.'

Mr Gosdyke nodded. 'I quite understand, Inspector, and I would just as soon not be involved myself. Mrs Wilt, I appeal to you . . .'

Eva ignored him. With her hands tied above her head and with her ankles linked by a short length of rope, she was an awesome sight and not a woman with whom anyone would willingly argue.

'I am ready,' she said. 'Tell them I'm coming.'

She hobbled out of the door and down Mrs de Frackas' drive. In the bushes S.G.S. men blanched and thought wistfully of booby traps in South Armagh. Only the Major, surveying the scene from a bedroom window, gave Eva his blessing. 'Makes a chap proud to be British,' he told Dr Felden. 'By God that woman's got some guts.'

'I must say I find that remark in singularly bad taste,' said the doctor, who was studying Eva from a purely physiological point of view.

There was something of a misunderstanding next door. Chinanda, viewing Eva through the letter-box in the Wilt's front door, had just begun to have second thoughts when a waft of vomit hit him from the kitchen. He opened the door and aimed his automatic.

'Get the children,' he shouted to Baggish, 'I'm covering the woman.'

'You're what?' said Baggish, who had just glimpsed the expanse of flesh that was moving towards the house. But there was no need to fetch the children. As Eva reached the doormat they rushed towards her squealing with delight.

'Back,' yelled Baggish, 'back or I fire!'

It was too late. Eva swayed on the doorstep as the quads clutched at her.

'Oh mummy, you do look funny,' shrieked Samantha, and grabbed her mother's knees. Penelope clambered over the others and flung her arms round Eva's neck. For a moment they swayed uncertainly and then Eva took a step forward, tripped and with a crash fell heavily into the hall. The quads slithered before her across the polished parquet and the hatstand, seismically jolted from the wall, crashed forward against the door and slammed it. The two terrorists stood staring down at their new hostage while Mrs de Frackas raised a drunken head from the kitchen, took one look at the amazing sight and passed out again. Eva heaved herself to her knees. Her hands were still tied above her head but her concern was all for the quads.

'Now don't worry, darlings. Mummy's here,' she said. 'Everything is going to be all right.'

From the safety of the kitchen the two terrorists surveyed the extraordinary scene with dismay. They didn't share her optimism.

'Now what do we do?' asked Baggish. 'Throw the children out the door?'

Chinanda shook his head. He wasn't going within striking distance of this powerful woman. Even with her hands tied above her head there was something dangerous and frightening about Eva, and now she seemed to be edging towards him on bulging knees.

'Stay where you are,' he ordered, and raised his gun. Next to him the telephone rang. He reached for it angrily.

'What do you want now?' he asked Flint.

'I might ask you the same question,' said the Inspector. 'You've got the woman and you said you'd let the children go.'

'If you think I want this fucking woman you're crazy,' Chinanda yelled, 'and the fucking children won't leave her. So now we've got them all.'

What sounded like a chuckle came from Flint. 'Not my fault. We didn't ask for the children. You volunteered to . . .'

'And we didn't ask for this woman,' screamed Chinanda his voice rising hysterically. 'So now we do a deal. You . . .'

'Forget it, Miguel,' said Flint, beginning to enjoy himself.

182

'Deals are out and for your information you'd be doing me a favour shooting Mrs Wilt. In fact you go right ahead and shoot whoever you want, mate, because the moment you do I'm sending my men in and where they shoot you and Comrade Baggish you won't die in a hurry. You'll be . . .'

'Fascist murderer,' screamed Chinanda, and pulled the trigger of his automatic. Bullets spat holes across a chart on the kitchen wall which had until that moment announced the health-giving properties of any number of alternative herbs, most of them weeds. Eva regarded the damage balefully and the quads sent up a terrible wail.

Even Flint was horrified. 'Did you kill her?' he asked, suddenly conscious that his pension came before personal satisfaction.

Chinanda ignored the question. 'So now we deal. You send Gudrun down and have the jet ready in one hour only. From now on we don't play games.'

He slammed the phone down.

'Shit,' said Flint. 'All right, get me Wilt. I've got news for him.'

Chapter 20

But Wilt's tactics had changed again. Having run the gamut of roles from chinless wonder to village idiot by way of revolutionary fanatic, which to his mind was merely a more virulent form of the same species, it had slowly dawned on him he was approaching the destabilization of Gudrun Schautz from the wrong angle. The woman was an ideologue, and a German one at that. Behind her a terrible tradition stretched back into the mists of history, a cultural heritage of solemn, monstrously serious and ponderous *Dichter und Denker*, philosophers, artists, poets and thinkers obsessed with the meaning, significance and process of social and historical development. The word Weltanschauung sprang, or at least lumbered, to mind. Wilt had no idea what it meant and doubted if anyone else knew. Something to do with having a world view and about as charming as Lebensraum which should have meant Living-Room but actually signified the occupation of Europe and as much of Russia as Hitler had been able to lay his hands on. And after Weltanschauung and Lebensraum there came, even less comprehensibly, Weltschmerz or world pity which, considering Fräulein Schautz's propensity for putting bullets into unarmed opponents without a qualm, topped the bill for codswallop. And beyond these dread concepts there were the carriers of the virus, Hegel, Kant, Fichte, Schopenhauer, and Nietzsche who had gone clean off his nut from a combination of syphilis, superman and large ladies in helmets trumpeting into theatrical forests at Bayreuth. Wilt had once waded lugubriously through *Thus Spake Zarathustra* and had come out convinced that either Nietzsche hadn't known what the hell he was on about or, if he had, he had kept it very verbosely to himself. And Nietzsche was sprightly by comparison with Hegel and Schopenhauer, tossing off meaningless maxims with an abandon that was positively joyful. If you wanted the real hard stuff Hegel was your man, while Schopenhauer hit a nadir of gloom that made

184

King Lear sound like an hysterical optimist under the influence of laughing gas. In short, Gudrun Schautz's weak spot was happiness. He could blather on about the horrors of the world until he was blue in the face but she wouldn't bat an eyelid. What was needed to send her reeling was a dose of undiluted good cheer, and Wilt beneath his armour of domestic grumbling was at heart a cheerful man.

And so while Gudrun Schautz cowered in the bathroom and Eva stumbled across the threshold downstairs he bombarded his captive audience with good tidings. The world was a splendid place.

Gudrun Schautz disagreed. 'How can you say that when millions are starving?' she demanded.

'The fact that I can say it means that I'm not starving,' said Wilt, applying the logic he had learnt with Plasterers Two, 'and anyway now that we know they're starving means we can do something about it. Things would be much worse if we didn't know. We couldn't send them food for one thing.'

'And who is sending food?' she asked unwisely.

'To the best of my knowledge the wicked Americans,' said Wilt. 'I'm sure the Russians would if they could grow enough but they don't so they do the next best thing and send them Cubans and tanks to take their minds off their empty stomachs. In any case, not everyone is starving and you've only got to look around you to see what fun it is to be alive.'

Gudrun Schautz's view of the bathroom didn't include fun. It looked uncommonly like a prison cell. But she didn't say so.

'I mean, take me for example,' continued Wilt. 'I have a wonderful wife and four adorable daughters . . .'

A snort from the bathroom indicated that there were limits to the Schautz woman's credulity.

'Well, you may not think so,' said Wilt, 'but I do. And even if I didn't you've got to admit that the quads love life. They may be a trifle exuberant for some people's taste, but no one can say they're unhappy.'

'And Mrs Wilt is a wonderful wife?' said Gudrun Schautz with advanced scepticism.

'As a matter of fact I couldn't ask for a better,' said Wilt. 'You may not believe me but—'

'Believe you? I have heard what she calls you and you are always fighting.'

'Fighting?' said Wilt. 'Of course we have our little differences of opinion, but that is essential for a happy marriage. It's what we British call give and take. In Marxist terms I suppose you'd call it thesis, antithesis and synthesis. And the synthesis in our case is happiness.'

'Happiness,' snorted Gudrun Schautz. 'What is happiness?'

Wilt considered the question and the various ways he could answer it. On the whole it seemed wisest to steer clear of the metaphysical and stick to everyday things. 'In my case it happens to be walking to the Tech. on a frosty morning with the sun shining and the ducks waddling and knowing I don't have any committee meetings and teaching and going home by moonlight to a really good supper of beef stew and dumplings and then getting into bed with an interesting book.'

'Bourgeois pig. All you think about is your own comfort.'

'It's not all I think about,' said Wilt, 'but you asked for a definition of happiness and that happens to be mine. If you want me to go on I will.'

Gudrun Schautz didn't but Wilt went on all the same. He spoke of picnics by the river on hot summer days and finding a book he wanted in a secondhand shop and Eva's delight when the garlic she had planted actually managed to show signs of growing and his delight at her delight and decorating the Christmas tree with the quads and waking in the morning with them all over the bed tearing open presents and dancing round the room with toys they had wanted and would probably have forgotten about in a week and . . . Simple family pleasures and surprises which this woman would never know but which were the bedrock of Wilt's existence. And as he re-told them they took on a new significance for him and soothed present horrors with a balm of decency and Wilt felt himself to be what he truly was, a good man in a quiet and unobtrusive way married to a good woman in a noisy and ebullient way. If nobody else saw him like this he didn't care. It was what he was that mattered and what he was grew out of what he did, and for the life of him Wilt couldn't see that he had ever done anyone wrong. If anything he had done a modicum of good.

That wasn't the way Gudrun Schautz viewed things. Hungry,

cold and fearful, she heard Wilt tell of simple things with a growing sense of unreality. She had lived too long in a world of bestial actions taken to achieve the ideal society to be able to stand this catechism of domestic pleasures. And the only answers she could give him were to call him a fascist swine and secretly she knew she would be wasting her breath. In the end she stayed silent and Wilt was about to take pity on her and cut short a modified version of the family's holiday in France when the telephone rang.

'All right, Wilt,' said Flint, 'you can forget the travelogue. This is the crunch. Your missus is downstairs with the children and if the Schautz doesn't come down right now you're going to be responsible for a minor massacre.'

'I've heard that one before,' said Wilt. 'And for your information . . .'

'Oh no, you haven't. This time it's for real. And if you don't bring her down, by God, we will. Take a look out the window.' Wilt did. Men were climbing into the helicopter in the field.

'Right,' continued Flint, 'so they'll land on the roof and the first person they'll take out is you. Dead. The Schautz bitch we want alive. Now move.'

'I can't say I like your priorities,' said Wilt, but the Inspector had rung off. Wilt went through the kitchen and untied the bathroom door.

'You can come out now,' he said. 'Your friends downstairs seem to be winning. They want you to join them.'

There was no reply from the bathroom. Wilt tried the door and found it was locked.

'Now listen. You've got to come out. I'm serious. Messrs Baggish and Chinanda are downstairs with my wife and children and the police are prepared to meet their demands.'

Silence suggested that Gudrun Schautz wasn't. Wilt put his ear to the door and listened. Perhaps the wretched creature had escaped somehow or, worse still, committed suicide.

'Are you there?' he asked inanely. A faint whimper reassured him.

'Right. Now then, nobody is going to hurt you. There is absolutely no point in staying in there and . . .' A chair was jammed under the doorhandle on the other side.

'Shit,' said Wilt, and tried to calm himself. 'Please listen to

187

reason. If you don't come out and join them all hell is going to be let loose and someone is going to get hurt. You've got to believe me.'

But Gudrun Schautz had listened to too much unreason already to believe anything. She gibbered faintly in German.

'Yes, well that's a great help,' said Wilt, suddenly conscious that his alternative had gone into overkill. He went back to the living-room and called Flint.

'We've got a problem,' he said before the Inspector stopped him.

'You've got problems, Wilt. Don't include us.'

'Yes, well we've all got problems now,' said Wilt. 'She's in the bathroom and she's locked the door and the way things sound she isn't going to come out.'

'Still your problem,' said Flint. 'You got her in there and you get her out.'

'Now hold on. Can't you persuade those two goons . . .'

'No,' said Flint and ended the discussion. With a weary sigh Wilt went back to the bathroom but the sounds inside didn't suggest that Gudrun Schautz was any more amenable to rational persuasion than before, and after putting his case as forcibly as he could and swearing to God that there were no Israelis downstairs he was driven back to the telephone.

'All I want to know,' said Flint when he answered, 'is whether she's down with Bonnie and Clyde or not. I'm not interested in . . .'

'I'll open the attic door. I'll stand where the buggers can see I'm not armed and they can come up and get her. Now will you kindly put that suggestion to the sods?'

Flint considered the offer in silence for a moment and said he would call back.

'Thank you,' said Wilt and having pulled the bed away from the door lay on it listening to his heart beat. It seemed to be making up for lost time.

Two floors below Chinanda and Baggish were edgy too. Eva's arrival, far from quietening the quads, had aroused their curiosity to new levels of disgusting frankness.

'You've got ever so many wrinkles on your tummy, mummy,' said Samantha, putting into words what Baggish had already noticed with revulsion. 'How did you get them?'

'Well, before you were born, dear,' said Eva, who had crossed the Rubicon of modesty by hobbling naked into the house, 'mummy's tummy was much bigger. You see, you were inside it.'

The two terrorists shuddered at the thought. It was bad enough being stuck in a kitchen and hall with these revolting children without being regaled with the physiological intimacies of their pre-natal existence in this extraordinary woman.

'What were we doing inside you?' asked Penelope.

'Growing, dear.'

'What did we eat?'

'You didn't exactly eat.'

'You can't grow unless you eat. You're always telling Josephine she won't grow up big and strong unless she eats her muesli.'

'Don't like muesli,' said Josephine. 'It's got sultanas in it.'

'I know what we ate,' said Samantha with relish, 'blood.'

In the corner by the cellar stairs Mrs de Frackas, in the throes of a stupendous hangover, opened a veined eye.

'I shouldn't be at all surprised,' she mumbled. 'Nearest thing to human vampires I've ever met. Whoever called it baby-sitting? Some damned fool.'

'But we didn't have teeth,' continued Samantha.

'No, dear, you were tied to mummy by your umbilical cords. And what mummy ate went through the cord . . .'

'Things can't go through cords, mummy,' said Josephine. 'Cords are string.'

'Knives can go through string,' said Samantha.

Eva looked at her appreciatively. 'Yes, dear, so they can . . .'

The discussion was cut short by Baggish. 'Shut up and cover yourself,' he shouted throwing the Mexican rug from the living-room at Eva.

'I don't see how I can with my hands tied,' Eva began, but the telephone was ringing. Chinanda answered.

'No more talking. Either . . .' he said before stopping and listening. Behind him Baggish clutched his sub-machine gun and kept a wary eye on Eva.

'What are they saying?'

'That Gudrun won't come down,' said Chinanda. 'They want for us to go up.'

'No way. It's a trap. The police are up there. We know that.'

Chinanda took his hand from the phone. 'No one goes up and Gudrun comes down. Five minutes we give you or . . .'

'I'll go up,' Eva called out. 'The police aren't up there. My husband is. I'll bring them both down.'

The terrorists stared at her. 'Your husband?' they asked in unison. The quads joined in. 'You mean daddy's in the attic? Oh, mummy do bring him down. He's going to be ever so cross with Mrs de Frackas. She drank ever such a lot of daddy's peepee.'

'You can say that again,' moaned the old lady, but Eva ignored the extraordinary statement. She was looking fixedly at the terrorists and willing them to let her go up to the flat.

'I promise you I'll . . .'

'You're lying. You want to go up there to report to the police.'

'I want to go up there to save my children,' said Eva, 'and if you don't believe me tell Inspector Flint that Henry has got to come down now.'

The terrorists moved away down the kitchen and conferred.

'If we can free Gudrun and get rid of this woman and her filthy children it's good,' said Baggish. 'We have the man and the old woman.'

Chinanda disagreed. 'We keep the children. That way the woman does nothing wrong.'

He went back to the phone and repeated Eva's message. 'Five minutes we give you only. The man Wilt comes down . . .'

'Naked,' said Eva, determined to see that Henry shared her discomfort.

'He comes down naked,' Chinanda repeated, 'and with his hands tied . . .'

'He can't tie his own hands,' said Flint practically.

'Gudrun can tie them for him,' answered Chinanda. 'Those are our conditions.'

He put the phone down and sat looking wearily at Eva. The English were strange people. With women like this, why had they ever given up their Empire? He was roused from his reverie. Mrs de Frackas was getting woozily to her feet.

'Sit down,' he shouted at her but the old lady ignored him. She wobbled across to the sink.

190

'Why don't I shoot her?' said Baggish. 'That way they'll know we mean what we say.'

Mrs de Frackas squinted at him with bloodshot eyes. 'Young man,' she said, 'with a head like mine you'd be doing me a favour. Just don't miss.' And to emphasize the point she turned her back on him and stuck her bun under the cold tap.

Chapter 21

In the Communications Centre there was confusion too. Flint was happily relaying the message to Wilt and enjoying his protest that it was bad enough risking death by gunshot but he didn't see why he had to go naked and risk double pneumonia into the bargain and anyway how the hell he was going to tie his own hands together he hadn't the faintest idea, when he was stopped by the new Head of the Anti-Terrorist Squad.

'Hold everything,' the Superintendent told Flint. 'The Idiot Brigade have just come up with a psycho-political profile of Wilt and it looks bad.'

'It's going to look a damned sight worse if the bastard doesn't get down out of that flat in the next three minutes,' said Flint, 'and anyway what the hell is a psycho-political profile?'

'Never mind that now. Just go into a holding pattern with the terrorists on the ground floor.'

Leaving Flint feeling like a flight controller trying to deal with two demented pilots on a collision course, he hurried through to the conference room.

'Right,' he said, 'I've ordered all armed personnel to fall back to lessen the tension. Now do we allow the swop to go ahead or not?'

Dr Felden was in no doubt. 'No,' he said. 'From the data we have accumulated there is no doubt in my mind that Wilt is a latent psychopath with extremely dangerous homicidal tendencies and to let him loose . . .'

'I cannot agree,' said Professor Maerlis. 'The transcripts of the conversations he has been having with the Schautz woman indicate a degree of ideological commitment to post-Marcusian anarchism of the highest possible order. I would go further . . .'

'We haven't time, Professor. In fact we've got precisely two minutes and all I want to know is whether to make the swop.'

'My advice is definitely negative,' said the psychiatrist. 'If we add the subject Wilt together with Gudrun Schautz to the two terrorists holding the children the effect will be explosive.'

'That's a great help,' said the Superintendent. 'We're sitting on a keg of dynamite and . . . yes, Major?'

'I suppose if we got all four of them together on the ground floor we could kill two birds with one stone,' said the Major.

The Superintendent looked at him keenly. He had never understood why the S.G.S. had been called in from the beginning and the Major's lack of obvious logic had him baffled.

'If by that you mean we could slaughter everyone in the house I can't see any reason for going ahead with the exchange. We can do that already. The purpose of the exercise is not to kill anyone at all. I want to know how to avoid a bloodbath, not achieve one.'

But events in the house next door had already moved ahead of him. Far from getting the terrorists into a holding pattern, Flint's message that there was a slight technical hitch had met with an immediate reply that if Wilt didn't come down in exactly one minute he would be the father of triplets. But it had been Eva who had forced Wilt to act.

'Henry Wilt,' she yelled up the stairs, 'if you don't come down this minute I'll . . .'

Flint, with his ear glued to the phone heard Wilt's tremulous 'Yes, dear, I'm coming.' He switched on the monitoring device in the field telephone and could hear Wilt stumbling about undressing and presently his faint steps on the staircase. They were followed a moment later by the heavier tread of Eva coming up. Flint went through to the conference room and announced this latest development.

'I thought I told you . . .' began the Superintendent before sitting down heavily. 'So now we're really into a different ballgame.'

The quads had reached much the same conclusion, though they didn't put it like that. As Wilt moved cautiously across the hall into the kitchen they squealed with delight.

'Daddy's got a wigwag, Mummy's got a cunt. Mummy wee-wees down her legs and Daddy out in front,' they chanted to the amazement of the terrorists and the disgust of Mrs de Frackas.

'How utterly revolting,' she said, combining criticism of their language with her verdict on Wilt. She had never liked him with

193

his clothes on: without them she detested him. Not only was this wretch responsible for the lethal concoction that had made her head behave like a sensient ping-pong ball in a mixing bowl, and was now, by the flaming feel of things, busily at work cauterizing her waterworks but he was presenting a full frontal view of that diabolical organ which had once helped to thrust four of the most loathsome little girls she had ever met onto an already suffering world. And all this with a blatant disregard for those social niceties to which she was accustomed. Mrs de Frackas threw caution to the winds.

'If you think for one moment I intend to remain in a house with a naked man you're much mistaken,' she said and headed for the kitchen door.

'Stay where you are,' shouted Baggish, but Mrs de Frackas had lost what little fear she had ever possessed. She kept on going.

'One more move and I fire,' yelled Baggish. Mrs de Frackas snorted derisively and moved. So did Wilt. As the gun came up he hurled himself and the quads who were clutching him out of the line of fire. It was also out of the kitchen. The cellar door stood open. Wilt and his brood shot through it, cascaded down the steps, slid across the pea-strewn floor and ended up in the coal-heap. Above them a shot rang out, a thud, and the cellar door slammed to as Mrs de Frackas crashed against it and slumped to the ground.

Wilt waited no longer. He had no wish to hear any more shots. He scrambled up the pile of coal and heaved with his shoulders against the iron lid of the chute. Beneath his feet the coal slithered but the cover was moving and his head and shoulders were in the open air. The cover slid forward and Wilt crawled out before dragging each quad up and dropping the lid back in place. For a moment he hesitated. To his right were the kitchen windows, to his left the door, but beyond that were the dustbins and more usefully Eva's Organic Compost Collector. For the first time Wilt regarded the bin with gratitude. No matter what it contained it had space for them all and was, thanks to the insistence of the Health Authorities, constructed of alternative wood or concrete. Wilt hesitated long enough to scoop the quads up under his arms and then dashed for the thing and dropped them in before hurling himself on top of them.

'Oh, daddy, this is fun,' squawked Josephine, raising a face that was largely covered with rotten tomato.

'Shut up,' snarled Wilt and shoved her down into the mess. Then, conscious that anyone opening the kitchen door might see them, he burrowed down into the stinking remains of cabbages, fish ends and the household garbage until it was almost impossible to tell where Wilt and the children began and the compost ended.

'It's ever so warm,' squeaked the indefatigable Josephine from beneath a seasoning of decomposing courgettes.

'It will be a sight warmer if you don't keep your trap shut,' said Wilt wishing to hell he had. His mouth was half-filled with eggshell and something that suggested it had once seen the inside of a vacuum cleaner and should have stayed there. Wilt spat the mixture out and as he did so there came the sound of rapid fire from somewhere within the house. The terrorists were shooting at random into the darkness of the cellar. Wilt stopped spitting and wondered what the hell was going to happen to Eva now.

He had no need to worry. In the attic Eva was busy. She had already used the broken glass of the balcony window to cut the ropes on her hands and had untied her legs. Then she had gone through to the kitchen. As Wilt had passed her on the stairs he had whispered something about the bitch being in the bathroom. Eva had said nothing. She was reserving her comments on his behaviour with the bitch until the children were safe and the way to ensure that was to take Gudrun Schautz downstairs and do what the terrorists wanted. But now as she tried the bathroom door she heard the shot that had felled Mrs de Frackas. It was the signal for all the pent-up fury inside her to let itself loose. If any of the children had been murdered, the vile creature she had invited into her house would die too. And if Eva had to die she would take as many of the terrorists as she could with her. Standing in front of the bathroom door she raised a muscular leg. The next moment a further volley of shots came from below and the sole of Eva's foot slammed forward. The door tore from its hinges and the lock splintered. Eva kicked again; the door fell back into the bath and Eva Wilt stepped over it. In the corner by the washbasin crouched a woman as naked as Eva herself. They had nothing else in common. Gudrun Schautz's body bore no marks of birth upon it. It was as smooth and synthetically attractive as the centre-page of a girlie magazine and her face mocked its appeal. From a mask of terror and madness her eyes stared blankly, her cheeks were the colour of putty, and her mouth uttered the meaningless sounds of a terrified animal.

But Eva was beyond pity. She moved forward, ponderously implacable, and then with surprising swiftness her hands struck out and clenched in the woman's hair. For a moment Gudrun Schautz struggled before Eva's knee came up. Gasping for breath and doubled over, Gudrun was dragged from the bath-room and thrown to the kitchen floor. Eva pinned her down with a knee between her shoulder blades and twisting her arms behind her tied her wrists with the electric cord before gagging her with a cloth from the sink. Finally she bound her legs together with a strip of towel.

All this Eva did with as little compunction as she would have trussed a chicken for Sunday lunch. A plan had matured in her mind, a plan that seemed almost to have been waiting for this moment, a plan born of desperation and murder. She turned and foraged in the cupboard under the sink and found what she was looking for, the rope fire escape she had had installed when the flat was first built. It was designed to hang from a hook over the balcony window to save lives in an emergency, but she had a different purpose for it now. And as more shots echoed from below she went swiftly to work. She cut the rope in two and fetched an upright chair which she placed in the middle of the bedroom facing the door. Then she dragged the bed over and wedged it on top of the chair before going back to the kitchen and pulling her captive by the ankles across the room onto the balcony. A minute later she was back with the two lengths of rope and had tied them to the legs of the chair, slid them over the hook and, leaving one slack, threaded the other under the woman's arms, wound it round her body and knotted it. The second she coiled neatly on the floor by the chair and, with unconscious expertise, looped the other end into a noose and slipped it over the terrorist's head and around her throat.

Then Gudrun Schautz, who had put the fear of death into so many other innocent people, came to know its terror herself.

196

For a moment she squirmed on the balcony, but Eva was already back in the room and dragging on the rope round her chest. Gudrun Schautz rose sagging to her feet as Eva hauled. Then she was off the ground and level with the railing. Eva tied the rope to the bed and went back to the balcony and hoisted her over the railing. Below lay the patio and oblivion. Finally Eva removed the gag and returned to the chair. But before sitting down she opened the door to the stairs and loosened the rope from the bed. Grasping it in both hands, she played it out until it had run over the balcony rail and seemed taut. Still grasping it, she pushed the bed off the chair and sat down. Then she let go. For a second it felt as if the chair would lift under the strain but her weight held it down. The moment she was shot or rose from the chair it would hurtle away across the room and the murderess now dangling on the makeshift scaffold would drop to her death by hanging. In her own frighteningly domestic way Eva Wilt had re-established the terrible scales of Justice.

That was hardly the way it looked to the viewers in the Conference Room next door. On the TV screen Eva took on the dimensions of some archetypal Earth Mother and her actions had a symbolic quality surpassing mere reality. Even Dr Felden, whose experience of homicidal maniacs was extensive, was appalled, while Professor Maerlis, witnessing for the first time the awful preparations of a naked hangwoman, was heard to mutter something about a great beast slouching towards Bedlam. But it was the representative of the League of Personal Liberties who reacted most violently. Mr Symper could not believe his eyes.

'Dear God,' he squawked, 'she's going to hang the poor girl. She's out of her mind. Someone must stop her.'

'Can't see why, old boy,' said the Major. 'Always been in favour of capital punishment myself.'

'But it's illegal,' shrieked Mr Symper, and appealed to Mr Gosdyke, but the solicitor had shut his eyes and was considering a plea of diminished responsibility. On the whole he thought it less likely to convince a jury than justified homicide. Self-defence was clearly out. In the view of the wide-angle lens in the field telephone Eva bulked gigantic while Gudrun Schautz had the tiny proportions of one of Major-General de Frackas' toy soldiers. Professor Maerlis as usual took refuge in logic.

'An interesting ideological situation,' he said. 'I cannot think of a clearer example of social polarization. On the one hand we have Mrs Wilt and on the other . . .'

'A headless Kraut by the look of things,' said the Major enthusiastically as Eva, having hauled Gudrun Schautz into the air, shoved her over the balcony railing. 'I don't know what the proper drop for a hanging is but I should have thought forty feet was a bit excessive.'

'Excessive?' squeaked Mr Symper. 'It's positively monstrous. And what's more I take exception to your use of the word "kraut". I shall protest most vehemently to the authorities.'

'Odd bod,' said the Major as the secretary of the League of Personal Liberties rushed from the room. 'Anyone would think Mrs Wilt was the terrorist instead of a devoted mother.'

It was more or less the attitude adopted by Inspector Flint. 'Listen, mate,' he told the distraught Symper, 'you can lead as many protest marches as you fucking well like but don't come yelling at me that Mrs Bloody Wilt is a murderess. You brought her here . . .'

'I didn't know she was going to hang people. I refuse to be party to a private execution.'

'No, well you won't be that. You're an accessory. The bastards on the ground floor have bumped off Wilt and the children by the sound of things. How's that for loss of personal liberties?'

'But they wouldn't have if you had let them go. They . . .'

Flint had heard enough. Much as he had disliked Wilt the thought that this hysterical do-gooder was blaming the police for refusing to give way to the demands of a group of blood-thirsty foreigners was too much for him. He rose from his chair and grabbed Mr Symper by the lapels. 'All right, if that's the way you feel about it I'm sending you next door to persuade the Widow Wilt to come downstairs and let herself be shot by . . .'

'I won't go,' gibbered Mr Symper. 'You've no right . . .'

Flint tightened his grip and was frogmarching him backwards down the hall when Mr Gosdyke interrupted.

'Inspector, something has got to be done immediately. Mrs Wilt is taking the law into her own hands!'

'Good for her,' said Flint. 'This little shit has just volunteered to act as an emissary to our friendly neighbourhood freedom fighters . . .'

'I have done nothing of the sort,' squeaked Mr Symper. 'Mr Gosdyke, I appeal to you to . . .'

The solicitor ignored him. 'Inspector Flint, if you are prepared to give an undertaking that my client will not be held responsible, questioned, taken into custody, charged or placed on remand or in any way proceeded against for what she is evidently about to do . . .'

Flint released the egregious Mr Symper. Years of courtroom procedure told him when he was beaten. He followed Mr Gosdyke into the Conference Room and studied Eva Wilt's astonishing posterior with amazement. Gosdyke's remark about taking the law into her own hands seemed totally inappropriate. She was flattening the damned thing. Flint looked to Dr Felden.

'Mrs Wilt is obviously in an extremely disturbed mental state, Inspector. We must try to reassure her. I suggest you use the telephone. . . .'

'No,' said Professor Maerlis. 'Mrs Wilt may appear from this angle to have the proportions of an attenuated gorilla, but even so I doubt if she could reach the telephone without getting off the chair.'

'And what's so wrong with that?' demanded the Major aggressively. 'The Schautz bitch has it coming to her.'

'Perhaps, but we don't want to make a martyr of her. She already has a very considerable political charisma . . .'

'Bugger her charisma,' said Flint, 'she's had the rest of the Wilt family martyred and we can always claim that her death was accidental.'

The Professor looked at him sceptically. 'You could try, I suppose, but I think you'd have some difficulty persuading the media that a woman who has been suspended from a balcony on the end of two ropes, one of which had been expertly knotted round her neck, and who was subsequently hanged and/or decapitated, died in any meaningfully accidental manner. Of course its up to you but . . .'

'All right, then what the hell do you suggest?'

'Turn a blind eye, old boy,' said the Major. 'After all Mrs Wilt is only human . . .'

'Only?' muttered Dr Felden. 'A clearer example of anthromorphism . . .'

'And she's got to answer the call of nature sometime.'

'Call of nature?' shouted Flint. 'She's done that already. She's squatting there like a ruddy performing elephant . . .'

'Pee, old boy, pee,' continued the Major. 'She's got to get up to have a pee sooner or later.'

'Pray later than sooner,' said the psychiatrist. 'The thought of that ghastly shape getting off that chair would be too much to bear.'

'Anyway she's probably got a bladder like a barrage balloon,' said Flint. 'Mind you, she can't be any too warm and there's nothing like cold for making one hit the piss-pot.'

'In which case it's curtains for La Schautz,' said the Major. 'Lets us off the hook, what?'

'I can think of happier ways of putting it,' said the Professor, 'and it would still leave us with the problem of Fräulein Schautz's evident martyrdom.'

Flint left them arguing and went out to look for the Superintendent. As he passed through the Communication Centre he was stopped by the sergeant. A series of squeaks and squelches was coming from one of the listening devices.

'It's the boom aimed at the kitchen window,' the sergeant explained.

'Kitchen window?' said Flint incredulously. 'Sounds more like a squad of mice tap-dancing in a septic tank. What the hell are those squeaks?'

'Children,' said the sergeant. 'Hardly likely, I know, but I've yet to hear one mouse tell another to shut its fucking trap. And it's not coming from inside the house. The two wogs have been complaining that they haven't anyone left to shoot. If you want my opinion . . .'

But Flint was already clambering across the rubble of the conservatory in search of the Superintendent. He found him lying in the grass beside the summerhouse at the bottom of the Wilts' garden, studying Gudrun Schautz's anatomy through a pair of binoculars.

'Extraordinary lengths these lunatics will go to gain some publicity,' he said by way of explanation. 'It's a good thing we've kept the TV cameras out of range.'

200

'She's not up there out of choice,' said Flint. 'It's Mrs Wilt's doing and we've got a chance to take the two swine on the ground floor. They're out of hostages for the time being.'

'Are they really?' said the Superintendent, and transferred his observation to the kitchen windows with some reluctance. A moment later he was refocusing his binoculars on the compost bin.

'Good God,' he muttered, 'I've heard of rapid fermentation but . . . Here, you take a look at that bin by the back door.'

Flint took the binoculars and looked. In close-up he could see what the Superintendent meant by rapid fermentation. The compost was alive. It moved, it heaved, several bean haulms rose and fell, while a beetroot suddenly emerged from the sludge and promptly disappeared again. Finally, and most disconcertingly of all, something that resembled a Hallowe'en pumpkin with matted hair peered over the side of the bin.

Flint closed his eyes, opened them again and found himself looking through a mask of decaying vegetable matter at a very familiar face.

Chapter 22

Five minutes later Wilt was hauled unceremoniously from the compost heap while a dozen armed policemen aimed guns at the kitchen door and windows.

'Bang, bang, you're dead,' squealed Josephine as she was lifted from the mess. A constable bundled her through the hedge and went back for Penelope. Inside the house the terrorists made no move. They were being kept occupied on the phone by Flint.

'You can forget any deals,' he was saying as the Wilt family were led through the conservatory. 'Either you come out with your hands up and no guns or we're coming in firing, and after the first ten bullets you won't know what hit you . . . Christ, what's that revolting smell?'

'It says it's called Samantha,' said the constable who was carrying the foetid child.

'Well take it away and disinfect the beastly thing,' said Flint, groping for a handkerchief.

'I don't want to be disinfected,' bawled Samantha. Flint turned a weary eye on the group and for a moment had the nightmarish feeling that he was looking at something in an advanced state of decomposition. But the vision faded. He could see now that it was simply Wilt clotted with compost.

'Well, look what the cat dragged in. If it isn't Compost Casanova himself, our beanstalk hero of the hour. I've seen some sickening sights in my time but . . .'

'Charming,' said Wilt. 'Considering what I've just been through I can do without cracks about nostalgie de la boue. And what about Eva? She's still in there and if you start shooting . . .'

'Shut up, Wilt,' said Flint, lumbering to his feet. 'For your information, if it weren't for Mrs Wilt's latest enthusiasm for hanging people we'd have been into that house an hour ago.'

'Her enthusiasm for *what*?'

'Someone give him a blanket,' said Flint, 'I've seen enough of this human vegetable to last me a lifetime.' He went into the Conference Room followed by Wilt wrapped rather meagrely in one of Mrs de Frackas' shawls.

'Gentlemen, I'd like you all to meet Mr Henry Wilt,' he told the dumbfounded Psycho-Warfare Team, 'or should I say Comrade Wilt?'

Wilt didn't hear the crack. He was staring at the television screen. 'That's Eva,' he said numbly.

'Yes, well, it takes one to know one, I suppose,' said Flint, 'and on the end of all those ropes is your playmate, Gudrun Schautz. The moment your missus gets up from that chair you're going to find yourself married to the first British female executioner. Now that's fine with me. I'm all in favour of capital punishment and women's lib. Unfortunately these gentlemen don't share my lack of prejudice and home hanging is against the law, so if you don't want to see Mrs Wilt on a charge of justifiable homicide you'd better come up with something quick.' But Wilt sat staring in dismay at the screen. His own alternative terrorism had been tame by comparison with Eva's. She was sitting there calmly waiting to be murdered and had devised a hideous deterrent.

'Can't you call her on the telephone?' he asked finally.

'Use your loaf. The moment she gets off . . .'

'Quite,' said Wilt hastily. 'And I don't suppose there's any way of putting a net or something under Miss Schautz. I mean . . .'

Flint laughed nastily. 'Oh, it's Miss Schautz now, is it? Such modesty. Considering that only a few hours ago you were pork-swording the bitch I must say I find . . .'

'Under duress,' said Wilt. 'You don't think I make a habit of leaping into bed with killers, do you?'

'Wilt,' said Flint, 'what you do in your spare time is no concern of mine. Or wouldn't be if you kept within the limits of the law. Instead of which you fill your house with terrorists and give them lectures in the theory of mass murder.'

'But that was—'

'Don't argue. We've got every word you said on tape. We've built up a psycho . . .'

'Profile,' prompted Dr Felden, studying Wilt in preference to watching Eva on the screen.

'Thank you, doctor. A psycho-profile of you . . .'

'Psycho-political profile,' said Professor Maerlis. 'I would like to hear Mr Wilt explain where he gained such an extensive knowledge of the theory of terrorism.'

Wilt scraped a carrot-peeling from his ear and sighed. It was always the same. No one ever understood him: no one ever would. He was a creature of infinite incomprehensibility and the world was filled with idiots, himself included. And all the time Eva was in danger of being killed and killing. He got wearily to his feet.

'All right, if that's the way you want it I'll go back into the house and put it to those maniacs that . . .'

'Like hell you will,' said Flint. 'You'll stay exactly where you are and come up with a solution to the mess you've got us all into.'

Wilt sat down again. There was no way he could think of to end the stalemate. Happenstance reigned supreme and only chaos could be counted on to determine man's fate.

As if to confirm this opinion there came the sound of a dull rumble from the house nextdoor. It was followed by a violent explosion and the crash of breaking glass.

'My God, the swine have blown themselves up kamikaze-style,' shouted Flint as several toy soldiers toppled on the ping-pong table. He turned and hurried into the Communications Centre with the rest of the Psycho-Warfare Team. Only Wilt remained behind staring fixedly at the television screen. For a moment Eva had seemed to lift from the chair, but she had settled back again and was sitting there as stolidly as ever. From the other room the sergeant could be heard shouting his version of the disaster to Flint.

'I don't know what happened. One moment they were arguing about giving themselves up and claiming we were using poison gas and the next minute the balloon had gone up. I shouldn't think they knew what hit them.'

But Wilt did. With a cheerful smile he stood up and went into the conservatory.

'If you'll just follow me,' he told Flint and the others, 'I can explain everything.'

204

'Hold it there, Wilt,' said Flint. 'Let's get something straight. Are you by any chance suggesting that you're responsible for that explosion?'

'Only in passing,' said Wilt with the sublime confidence of a man who knew he was telling nothing but the truth, 'only in passing. I don't know if you're at all acquainted with the workings of the bio-loo but—'

'Oh shit,' said Flint.

'Precisely, Inspector. Now shit is converted anerobically in the bio-loo or, more properly speaking, the alternative toilet, into methane, and methane is a gas which ignites with the greatest of ease in the presence of air. And Eva has been into self-sufficiency in what you may well call a big way. She had dreams of cooking by perpetual motion, or rather by perpetual motions. So the cooker is hooked to the bio-loo and what goes in one end has got to come out the other and vice versa. Take a boiled egg for instance . . .'

Flint looked incredulously at him. 'Boiled eggs?' he shouted. 'Are you seriously telling me that boiled eggs . . . oh no. No, definitely no. We've been through the pork-pie routine before. You're not fooling me this time. I'm going to get to the bottom of this.'

'Anatomically speaking . . .' began Wilt, but Flint was already floundering through the conservatory into the garden. One glance over the fence was enough to convince him that Wilt was right. The few remaining windows on the ground floor of the house were spattered with blobs of stained yellow paper and something else. But it was the stench that hit him which was so convincing. The Inspector groped for his handkerchief. Two extraordinary figures had lurched through the shattered patio windows. As terrorists they were unrecognizable. Chinanda and Baggish had taken the full force of the bio-loo and were perfect examples of the worth of their own ideology.

'Shits in shits' clothing,' murmured Professor Maerlis, gazing in awe at the human excreta that stumbled about the lawn.

'Hold it there,' shouted the Head of the Anti-Terrorist Squad as his men aimed revolvers at them, 'we've got you covered.'

'Rather an unnecessary injunction if you ask me,' said Dr Felden. 'I've heard of bullshit baffling brains but I've never realized the destabilizing potential of untreated sewage before.'

But the two terrorists were past caring about the destruction of pseudo-democratic fascism. Their concern was purely personal. They rolled on the ground in a frantic attempt to rid themselves of the filth while above them Gudrun Schautz looked down with an idiot smile.

As Baggish and Chinanda were dragged to their feet by reluctant policemen Wilt entered the house. He passed through the devastated kitchen and stepped over old Mrs de Frackas and climbed the stairs. On the landing he hesitated.

'Eva,' he called, 'it's me, Henry. It's all right. The children are safe. The terrorists are under arrest. Now don't get up from that chair. I'm coming up.'

'I warn you if this is some sort of trick I won't be responsible for what happens,' shouted Eva.

Wilt smiled to himself happily. That was the old Eva talking in defiance of all logic. He went up to the attic and stood in the doorway looking at her with open admiration. There was nothing silly about Eva now. Sitting naked and unashamed she possessed a strength he would never have.

'Darling,' he began incautiously before stopping. Eva was studying him with frank disgust.

'Don't you "darling" me, Henry Wilt,' she said. 'And how did you get in that filthy state?'

Wilt looked down at his torso. Now that he came to examine it he was in a filthy state. A piece of celery poked rather ambiguously from Mrs de Frackas' shawl.

'Well, as a matter of fact, I was in the compost heap with the children . . .'

'With the children?' shouted Eva furiously. 'In the compost heap?'

And before Wilt could explain she had risen from the chair. As it shot across the room Wilt hurled himself at the rope, clung to it, was slammed against the opposite wall and finally managed to wedge himself behind a wardrobe.

'For Christ's sake, help me pull her up,' he yelled, 'you can't let the bitch hang.'

Eva put her hands on her hips. 'That's your problem. I'm not doing anything to her. You're holding the rope.'

'Only just. And I suppose you're going to tell me that if I really love you I'll let go. Well, let me tell you . . .'

'Don't bother,' shouted Eva. 'I heard you in bed with her. I know what you got up to.'

'Up to?' yelled Wilt. 'The only way I got anything up was by pretending she was you. I know it seems unlikely . . .'

'Henry Wilt, if you think I'm going to stand here and let you insult me . . .'

'I'm not insulting you. I'm paying you the biggest bloody compliment you've ever received. Without you I don't know what I would have done. And now for goodness sake—'

'I know what you did without me,' shouted Eva, 'you made love to that horrible woman . . .'

'Love?' yelled Wilt. 'That wasn't love. That was war. The bitch battened onto me like a sex-starved barnacle and . . .' But it was too late to explain. The wardrobe was shifting and the next moment Wilt, still gripping the rope, rose slowly into the air and moved towards the hook. Behind him came the chair and presently he was crouched up against the ceiling with his head twisted at a curious angle. Eva looked up at him uncertainly. For a second she hesitated, but she couldn't let him stay there and it was wrong to hang the German girl now that the quads were safe.

Eva grabbed Wilt's legs and began to pull. Outside the police had reached Gudrun Schautz and were cutting her down. As the rope broke Wilt fell from his perch and mingled with portions of the chair.

'Oh my poor darling,' said Eva, her voice suddenly taking on a new and, to Wilt, thoroughly alarming solicitude. It was typical of the bloody woman to practically turn him into a cripple and then be conscience-stricken. As she took him in her arms Wilt groaned and decided the time had come to put the boot in diplomatically. He passed out.

On the patio below Gudrun Schautz was unconscious too. Before she could be more than partially strangled she had been lifted down and now the Head of the Anti-Terrorist Squad was giving her the kiss of life rather more passionately than was called for. Flint dragged himself away from this unnatural relationship and cautiously entered the house. A hole in the kitchen floor testified to the destructive force of a ruptured bio-loo. 'Out of their tiny minds,' he muttered behind his handker-

207

chief and slithered through into the hall before climbing the stairs to the attic. The scene that greeted him there confirmed his opinion. The Wilts were clasped in one another's arms. Flint shuddered. He would never understand what these two diabolical people saw in one another. Come to think of it, he didn't want to know. There were some mysteries better left unprobed. He turned back towards his more orderly world where there were no such awful ambiguities and was greeted on the landing by the quads. They were dressed in some clothes they had found in Mrs de Frackas' chest of drawers and wearing hats that had been fashionable before the First World War. As they tried to rush past him Flint stopped them.

'I don't think your mummy and daddy want to be disturbed,' he said, firmly holding to the view that nice children should be spared the sight of their naked parents presumably making love. But the Wilt quads had never been nice.

'What are they doing?' asked Samantha.

Flint swallowed. 'They're . . . er . . . engaged.'

'You mean they're not married?' asked Samantha gleefully adjusting her boa.

'I didn't say that . . .' began Flint.

'Then we're bastards,' squealed Josephine. 'Michael's daddy says if mummies and daddies aren't married their babies are called bastards.'

Flint stared down at the hideously precocious child. 'You can say that again,' he muttered, and went on downstairs. Above him the quads could be heard chanting something about daddies having wigwags and mummies having . . . Flint hurried out of earshot and found the stench in the kitchen a positive relief. Two ambulance men were carrying Mrs de Frackas out on a stretcher. Amazingly she was still alive.

'Bullet lodged in her stays,' said one of the ambulance men. 'Tough old bird. Don't make them like this any more.'

Mrs de Frackas opened a beady eye. 'Are the children still alive?' she asked faintly.

Flint nodded. 'It's all right. They're quite safe. You needn't worry about them.'

'Them?' moaned Mrs de Frackas. 'You can't seriously suppose I'm worried about them. It's the thought that I'll have to live next door to the little savages that . . .'

But the effort to express her horror was too much for her and she sank back on the pillow. Flint followed her out to the ambulance.

'Take me off the drip,' she pleaded as they loaded her inside.

'Can't do that, mum,' said the ambulance man, 'it's against union rules.'

He shut the doors and turned to Flint. 'Suffering from shock, poor old dear. They get like that sometimes. Don't know what they're saying.'

But Flint knew better, and as the ambulance drove away his heart went out to the courageous old lady. He was thinking of asking for a transfer himself.

Chapter 23

It was the end of term at the Tech. Wilt walked across the common with the frost on the grass, ducks waddling by the river and the sun shining out of a cloudless sky. He had no committee meetings to attend and no teaching to do. About the only cloud on the horizon was the possibility that the Principal might congratulate the Wilt family on their remarkable escape from danger. To avert it Wilt had already intimated to the Vice-Principal that such rank hypocrisy would be in the worst of taste. If the Principal were to express his true feelings he would have to admit that he wished to hell the terrorists had carried out their promises.

Dr Mayfield was certainly of this opinion. The Special Branch had been going through the students in Advanced English For Foreigners with a fine-tooth comb and the Anti-Terrorist Squad had detained two Iraquis for questioning. Even the curriculum had been under scrutiny and Professor Maerlis, ably assisted by Dr Board, had submitted a report condemning the seminars on Contemporary Theories of Revolution and Social Change as positively subversive and inciting to violence. And Dr Board had helped to exonerate Wilt.

'Considering the political lunatics he has to cope with in his department it's a wonder Wilt isn't a raving fascist. Take Bilger for example . . .' he had told the Special Branch officer in charge of enquiries. The officer had taken Bilger. He had also screened the film and had viewed it with incredulity.

'If this is the sort of filth you encourage your lecturers to produce it's no bloody wonder the country is in the mess it is,' he told the Principal, who had promptly tried to shift the blame to Wilt.

'I always considered the thing a disgrace,' said Wilt, 'and if you'll check the minutes of the Education Committee meeting you'll see I wanted to make the issue public. I think parents have a right to know when their children are being politically indoctrinated.'

210

And the minutes had proved him right. From that moment Wilt was given a clean ticket. Officially.

But on the domestic front suspicion still lurked. Eva had taken to waking him in the small hours to demand proof that he loved her.

'Of course I do, damn it,' grunted Wilt. 'How many times do I have to tell you?'

'Actions speak louder than words,' retorted Eva snuggling up to him.

'Oh all right,' said Wilt. And the exercise had done him good. It was a leaner, healthier Wilt who walked briskly to the Tech., and the knowledge that he would never have to take this path again buoyed his spirits. They were moving from Willington Road. The removal van had already arrived when he left and this afternoon the home he returned to would be 45 Oakhurst Avenue. The choice of the new house had been Eva's. It was several steps down the social ladder from Willington Road, but the big house there had bad vibes for her. Wilt deplored the word but agreed. He had always disliked the pretensions of the neighbourhood and Oakhurst Avenue was nicely anonymous.

'At least we'll be away from haute academe and the relicts of Imperial arrogance,' he told Peter Braintree as they sat in The Pig In The Poke after the Principal's pep talk. There had been no mention of Wilt's ordeal and they were celebrating. 'And there's a quiet little pub round the corner so I won't have to brew my own gutrot.'

'Thank heavens for that. But won't Eva pine for the compost heap and all that?'

Wilt drank his beer cheerfully. 'The educative effects of exploding septic tanks have to be seen to be believed,' he said. 'To say that ours revealed the fundamental flaws in the Alternative Society might be going too far but it certainly blew Eva's mind. I've noticed she's taken to medicated toilet paper and it wouldn't surprise me to learn she's making tea with distilled water.'

'But she'll have to find something to occupy her energy.'

Wilt nodded. 'She has. The quads. She's determined to see they don't grow up in the image of Gudrun Schautz. A losing battle, to my way of thinking, but at least I've managed to prise

211

her away from sending them to the Convent. It's remarkable how much better their language has become of late. All in all I have an idea that life is going to be more peaceful from now on.'

But as with so many of Wilt's predictions this one was premature. When, having spent an hour tidying his office, he sauntered contentedly up Oakhurst Avenue it was to find the new house unlit and empty. There was no sign of Eva, the quads or the furniture van. He waited about for an hour and then phoned from a call-box. Eva exploded at the other end.

'Don't blame me,' she shouted, 'the removal men have had to unload the van.'

'Unload the van? What on earth for?'

'Because Josephine hid in the wardrobe and they put that in first, that's why.'

'But they don't have to unload because of that,' said Wilt. 'She wouldn't suffocate and it would teach her a lesson.'

'And what about Mrs de Frackas' cat and the Balls' poodle and Jennifer Willis' four pet rabbits . . .'

'The what?' said Wilt.

'She was playing hostages,' shouted Eva, 'and . . .'

But the coin in the phone box ran out. Wilt didn't bother to put another in. He strolled out along the street wondering what it was about his marriage with Eva that turned everyday events into minor catastrophes. He couldn't bring himself to think what sort of time Josephine was having in the wardrobe. Talk about trauma . . . Oh well, there was nothing like experience. As he passed along Oakhurst Avenue towards the pub Wilt suddenly felt pity for his new neighbours. They still had no idea what was going to hit them.